Beautiful LIAR

USA *Today* and International Bestselling Author

Lauren Rowe

Books by Lauren Rowe

The Reed Rivers Trilogy (to be read in order)
Bad Liar
Beautiful Liar
Beloved Liar

The Club Trilogy (to be read in order)
The Club: Obsession
The Club: Reclamation
The Club: Redemption
The Club: Culmination (A Full-Length Epilogue Book)

The Josh and Kat Trilogy (to be read in order)
Infatuation
Revelation
Consummation

The Morgan Brothers (a series of related standalones):
Hero
Captain
Ball Peen Hammer
Mister Bodyguard
ROCKSTAR

The Misadventures Series (a series of unrelated standalones):
Misadventures on the Night Shift
Misadventures of a College Girl
Misadventures on the Rebound

Standalone Psychological Thriller/Dark Comedy
Countdown to Killing Kurtis

Music Playlist for *Beautiful Liar*

"A-YO"—Lady Gaga
"Cringe"—Matt Maeson
"Broken"--LovelyTheBand
"Girl is on My Mind"—The Black Keys
"She's Like Heroin to Me"—The Gun Club
"Obsession"—Animotion
"Waterfalls"—TLC
"Sweet but Psycho"—Ava Max
"My Addiction"—Adam French

Chapter 1
Georgina

T he iron gate in front of Reed's house comes into view in the car's headlights, and I smile to myself. *I can't believe this is my life.* I'm sitting next to Reed in the backseat of the black sedan that's driving us to Reed's house from the Red Card Riot show, and I'm losing my freaking mind. A mere nine days ago, I stood on the other side of that same iron gate, shrieking at Reed to let me out or I'd sue him for negligence and false imprisonment. And now, here I am, wanting nothing more than to get my horny ass back *inside* that damned gate, so Reed can take me to heaven again, the same way he did in that janitorial closet earlier tonight.

"Ah, the scene of the crime," Reed says playfully as the car approaches his house. He squeezes my hand, releasing an unexpected ripple of butterflies into my belly. "Are you, by any chance, feeling the sudden urge to double-flip me off—or perhaps sue me for 'negligence and false imprisonment'?"

I bat my eyelashes at him. "Now, why would I want to do that, when we buried the hatchet so deliciously earlier tonight?"

Reed leans forward and grazes his soft lips against my cheek. "And, oh, how amazing it felt to bury my hatchet inside you, Georgina Ricci. So damned good, I can't wait to bury it again and again, all week long—and even more *deliciously.*"

My clit pulses at Reed's words and then throbs with yearning when Reed skims his lips across the length of my jawline. I turn my head, intending to crush my hungry lips

1

against his, but it's not meant to be. The car has stopped, signaling we've arrived at our destination.

"Is there a code?" the driver says, referring to the gate, and Reed shoots me a heated smolder that says, *Hold that thought.*

"We'll just get out here," Reed tosses out.

After we pile out of the sedan together, Reed heads to the trunk to retrieve my suitcase—the one I packed thinking I'd be spending an exciting week on the road with rock royalty—while I head to the gate and stare slack-jawed through its metal slats at Reed's breathtaking house. After a moment, Reed appears at my side, wheeling my suitcase behind him. He unlocks a pedestrian gate and politely gestures for me to pass through first, which I do.

"Are you cold?" Reed asks as I walk by. "You're shaking."

I rub my upper arms. "Just excited. Also, nervous."

"Nervous?" He closes the gate behind us. "There's nothing to be nervous about, Georgie girl. I come in peace. For the next week, my home is yours."

Butterflies. They're not rippling inside me any longer. They're flapping up a damned storm.

"Thank you."

Inside the darkened house, Reed parks my suitcase and flips a switch, and I gasp at the magnificence illuminated before me. Reed's massive living room is fit for a modern-day king. Its ceilings aren't high—they're towering. Floor-to-ceiling windows announce the owner of this manor is literally, and figuratively, on top of the world. Dark wood and ironwork declare a masculine, powerful man resides in this castle. But colorful tiling and unexpected pops of decorative color—sapphire blues, ruby reds, royal purples—make it clear the powerful owner of this manor is a cultured gentleman who isn't afraid to take risks.

Reed motions to my bag at the front door. "Would you like me to bring your suitcase to my bedroom, or would you prefer to sleep in a guest room this week?"

Anticipation flickers across Reed's chiseled face. A flash of vulnerability, I'd even say—like he's momentarily possessed by the spirit of a teenager asking his crush to prom. But as fast as that vulnerability appears on Reed's handsome face, it vanishes again, supplanted by his usual confidence.

But there's no going back. I've caught a glimpse of what lies beneath Reed's usual swagger, however fleetingly—as if I'd gazed out the window of a speeding train and caught the briefest glimpse of a sparkling, silver lake through a thick blanket of pine trees—and, just this fast, I'm instantly hooked and want to see it again.

"I think I'd prefer to sleep in a guest room this week," I say. But I'm lying through my teeth. If I were telling the truth, I'd admit I want nothing more than to sleep next to Reed in his bed this week. But, unfortunately, my gut is telling me, rather forcefully, that carving out a safe space for me to take an occasional time out from Reed, and my thumping lust for him, will go a long way toward keeping me on-track to fulfill my higher purpose. I'm not only here to fulfill my carnal desires, after all. More importantly, I've got a job to do.

"Whatever makes you comfortable," Reed replies smoothly. But he can't hide the flash of disappointment that flickers across his face as he says it. This time, he's not a teenager asking his crush to prom. He's the boy who's just gotten flatly turned down.

I brush my fingertips against Reed's forearm. "Will you give me a tour?"

He clears his throat. "Of course." He turns and gestures to the expansive space. "This is my living room—the place you're going to party like a rock star this Saturday night."

"It's gorgeous."

"This room is the main reason I bought the house. I wanted a place where I could throw epic parties. And when I walked in here, I said to myself, *Bingo*."

"Why so many parties?"

3

"It's a big part of my business plan. Whenever one of my A-list artists kicks off a tour in LA, I throw their after-party here to celebrate and generate buzz for the tour. I also throw parties to celebrate award nominations and wins. Also, to celebrate whenever one of my artists' albums goes gold or platinum or diamond—which, thankfully, happens a lot these days. Plus, on top of all that, I allow certain charities to throw their annual fundraising galas here."

I look around the impressive space. "Do you ever throw parties here just for fun?"

"Sure. I've hosted bachelor parties and birthday parties. I even had a wedding here—for my best friend, Henn. You met him at the bar."

I nod. "That was sweet of you to let him have his wedding here. You're a good friend."

Reed shrugs. "Henn is a brother to me, and his wife, Hannah, is the best. It was my pleasure to do it for them."

Aw, damn. My heart just skipped a beat. "So, uh, what are some of the charities you've let use the place?"

Reed talks passionately for a bit about his favorite charities—one his sister is heavily involved with that helps kids with cancer, and another devoted to saving the planet. And as he speaks, I have the urge to do two things: one, jump his bones, just because he's yummy as hell, especially when he talks about making the world a better place. And, two, I'm dying to pull out my phone and record him speaking, or at least take furious notes, so I can quote him precisely when I eventually sit down to write my article. But I refrain, figuring Reed might clam up if he sees me pulling out my phone.

"And, of course," Reed says, "CeeCee's favorite charities always have an open invitation to throw their fundraisers here. When it comes to the indomitable CeeCee, my answer is almost always yes."

I shoot Reed a snarky side-eye. "Yeah, unless what CeeCee wants is an in-depth interview for *Dig a Little Deeper*."

Reed chuckles. "I said my answer is *almost* always yes. CeeCee knows she can have anything she wants from me, except *that*."

"Why is that, again?"

"Because the inner workings of my mind and life aren't anybody's fucking business."

I make a face that says, *Well, alrighty then.* And Reed smirks in reply before returning his attention to his expansive living room.

"It might seem like this house is too big for a bachelor to live here alone," he says. "But I've never once regretted buying this place."

Excitement about Saturday night's party ripples inside me. "I can't wait to see your house in action. Thank you so much for throwing the party, and for letting me invite Alessandra."

"No need to thank me. Like I said, I'm throwing the party for business reasons—because I've determined it will help you and the other writer assigned to the special issue bond with my musicians in a way that will elevate the end product."

I flash Reed a snarky look. "Sure, Reed. You not wanting me to party with C-Bomb this week didn't inspire your decision at all."

"Not at all." He matches my snarky expression. "Come on, Intrepid Reporter. There's a lot more to see." He takes two steps and tosses over his shoulder, "And, yes, you can take notes on your phone. But, please, don't record me speaking, unless I've expressly consented."

I stop walking, surprised he's read my mind so accurately, and Reed stops walking, too.

"Georgie, you've got the most expressive face I've ever seen, and I can already read it like a book." He crooks his finger. "Now, come, come, little kitty. I'll show you the whole house, anything you want to see. Just as long as the last stop is my bedroom upstairs."

Chapter 2
Georgina

R eed leads me through several rooms on the ground floor of his impressive home, while I "ooh" and "aah" and take furious notes on my phone. He shows me a game room. A wine room. A home theater. We walk down a hallway and turn a corner and, suddenly, I'm standing in the most spectacular kitchen imaginable—a beautiful, sleek space that instantly makes me wish my mother were alive to see it.

"Do you cook?" I ask, running my palm over a sleek countertop.

"I cook breakfast pretty well. But, mostly, it's my housekeeper, Amalia, who cooks in here. Caterers, too."

"When is Amalia at the house, typically?"

"She stays overnight Monday through Thursday every week, unless I've told her to take off at five during any given week. Some weeks, I want complete privacy when I get home from work."

I open my mouth to suggest perhaps this coming week should be one of those weeks of extra privacy, but the clever man beats me to the punch.

"Yes, Georgina. Of course, I've already told Amalia to take off at five every day this week. I had no choice, once I found out you're a screamer. My house is big, but it's not big enough to contain Georgina Ricci's screams of ecstasy."

I swat his shoulder. "I've never screamed like that with anyone but you."

"Well, that's a given." He gestures for me to follow him. "The quicker we get through this tour, the quicker I'll get to hear you scream again."

He leads me through a set of French doors and around a corner, and, suddenly, we're standing on a serene patio, complete with water features, twinkling lights, and manicured bushes and flowers.

"Am I dead?" I ask, looking around the peaceful space. "Is this heaven?"

Reed chuckles. "That's what Henn's wife, Hannah, said when she first saw this patio. That's why I offered to host their wedding here—because Hannah loved it so much."

"I can't believe you let them have their wedding here. That was so generous."

Reed shrugs it off. "All I did was open my house and wallet, and Hannah and her wedding consultant did the rest."

"Wait, you *paid* for the wedding? I thought you meant you let them *use* your house for it—which, right there, would have been an incredibly generous thing to do."

Reed pulls a face like that's a ridiculous notion. "What kind of person says to his best friend, 'Sure, you can *use* my house to marry the love of your life,' but then doesn't foot the bill?"

"Um, plenty of people say that. And I'm sure it's very much appreciated."

Reed waves at the air. "Go big or go home, baby. It's one of my favorite mantras." He points to my phone playfully. "Write that down, Intrepid Reporter. 'Reed lives by the mantra, Go big or go home.'"

I roll my eyes. "I think I can remember you're a big fan of 'going big' without writing it down." I motion to our surroundings. "All I'll have to do is look around me this week to remember that fact."

"Suit yourself. I wouldn't deign to tell a professional how to do her job." He flashes me a charming smile. "Ready to move on?"

"Lead on."

I follow Reed down a pathway, past a basketball court, and then past a beach-volleyball court, and a moment later, we're standing next to an elegant black-bottom swimming pool overlooking the twinkling lights of Los Angeles.

"This is spectacular," I say. "I love swimming—being weightless. If I lived here, I'd swim laps every day of my life. Or maybe, just come out here to float."

"Feel free to use the pool any time you like. It's heated."

"Thank you. I'll definitely take you up on that. Although, given that I didn't pack a swimsuit, I think I'll wait until after Amalia leaves each day. I wouldn't want to give the poor woman an unexpected view of my ass."

Reed arches his brow, his dirty thoughts etched all over his face. "As you wish. Full disclosure, though..." He gestures above us, to a second-story wall of windows. "That's my bedroom right there. If I hear a splash, I'm gonna head straight to my window, hoping to see an unexpected view of your ass."

"As you wish. As long as you join me after I've gotten my workout in."

"No need to swim as your work out. I work out every morning, first thing. I was assuming my shadow would join me."

"Oh, I love morning workouts. I taught some morning classes at the gym at UCLA."

"You *taught* classes?"

I nod. "Spin and Pilates."

He gestures to my body. "Well, that answers that question. Well, hell. If you like spin, you should try out my Peloton this week."

"Oh! I've always wanted to try one." I frown. "Except... shoot. I didn't pack my cycling shoes, any more than a swimsuit... probably because I *thought* I'd be on the road this week with one of my favorite bands."

Reed pulls out his phone, ignoring my snarky tone. "What's your shoe size, Ricci?"

"Oh. No. I didn't mean for you to—"

"I insist."

"I can't let you buy me cycling shoes, Reed."

"Tell me your damned shoe size, or I'll sic Amalia on you. And trust me, you don't want a determined Amalia on your ass."

Reluctantly, I tell Reed what he wants to know, and he places the order.

"Thank you. You're making me feel right at home."

"My home is yours." He drinks me in for a long beat, brazenly undressing me with his eyes. "How about we cut this tour short, and head straight to the last stop?"

"Nope," I say. "I want the full tour. Plus, don't pop a stiffy yet, dude. You're not getting into my pants again until you've fulfilled your end of our bargain."

He looks at me blankly.

"Alessandra's demo? You're required to listen to the first minute of all three songs."

"Aren't you forgetting a little something? Before I'm required to listen to a single song on that demo, you're required to give me two lap dances and a striptease."

I scoff. "I've already paid my debts to you, and then some. Letting you eat me out at the stadium was the equivalent of *five* stripteases. And the way you fucked me in that closet was the equivalent of *ten* lap dances. Plus, regardless, all bets were off the minute that PA walked in on us, and saw my tits and wahoo hanging out, and you camped between my legs with shiny lips. That was the most humiliating thing that's ever happened to me, Reed. I get a free pass for that."

Reed chuckles. "Fair enough. All right. I hereby release you from your debts, on one condition: I'll listen to the demo in bed—while lying next to you."

I raise my index finger. "If we're *on top* of the bed, yes. Not *in* it. And if we're fully clothed."

He chuckles. "On top of the bed, but in our pajamas."

I pause. "Agreed."

He winks. "Tricked ya. I sleep in the nude."

I giggle. "You've got to wear sweatpants, at least, or we'll get too distracted and never make it through the entire demo."

"I'll wear briefs. That's my final offer."

I roll my eyes. "Fine, but I'm wearing my actual pajamas."

He grins. "Always such a fierce negotiator. All right. Our contract is hereby amended. Sign here." He puts out his palm and I mime signing my name across it. And then, with a charming, seductive smile, he slides his hand in mine and leads me away from his swimming pool to continue the tour.

***

"And here I thought only guys with small dicks had a thing for sports cars," I say. "I couldn't have been more wrong."

We're standing in Reed's expansive garage, which is filled with not one, not two, not three, but *six* gleaming sports cars. As we've walked down the line of them, Reed has waxed poetic about all of them—although none more so than his Bugatti, parked at the far end. His pride and joy.

After Reed has finished telling me about his car collection, we come upon an elaborate shelving unit on the far end of the garage that's filled to bursting with outdoor-adventure and sporting equipment. I ask him a few questions about all of it, just to be thorough, and he talks enthusiastically about his love of fitness. I gesture to a surfboard, and he tells me a few stories. I gesture to a set of golf clubs and ask if he's a big golfer, expecting him to nonchalantly dazzle me with his prowess on the links. But to my surprise, Reed says he hates golf. "I'd actually rather get a root canal than spend a day golfing."

"Then why do you have a fancy set of clubs? Just in case you wake up one day with the nagging impulse to torture yourself?"

Surprisingly, the question elicits a contemplative expression from Reed. A deep furrow in his brow, followed by a deep exhale. "Okay, Intrepid Reporter," he says. "I'm going to throw you a bone, kid. I promised CeeCee I'd let you unpeel *one* layer of my onion during this interview. So, let's unpeel it now, and get it out of the way—like ripping off a Band-Aid. That way, we can relax the rest of the week with no stress."

"Sounds great," I say, even though I'm thinking, *Oh, honey, if you think I'm stopping at one layer unpeeled, then you don't know me at all.*

For a moment, Reed runs his fingertips over the gleaming head of a golf club, looking lost in thought. Finally, he says, "When I was growing up, my father was obsessed with golf. So, of course, since I idolized my father, I wanted to be obsessed with golf, too."

Holy crap. I didn't see that coming at all. I can't believe Reed is talking about his father, without any coaxing.

Reed says, "My father used to golf every weekend. And, of course, during the week, he was busy with work and his mistresses. Although I didn't know about that second thing until much later. All I knew was, if I wanted to spend time with my father, which I did, then I had to pick up golf and tag along with him on the weekends."

My pulse is thumping in my ears. My fingers feel like they're physically itching with the urge to take notes. But I stand still, holding my breath, afraid to do or say anything that might break this unexpected spell. I don't know what's prompted Reed to give me this scoop, and I don't want to do anything to make him change his mind.

"Finally, around age twelve, about a year before my father got arrested, I could finally hit from the back tees, where he teed off. And, man, he was so proud of that. In the clubhouse, my father would tell anyone who'd listen, 'My boy, Reed, is only twelve, and he's already hitting off the back tees!'" Reed looks wistful for a beat, before his face darkens. "And then, out of nowhere, the FBI raided our house at dawn one morning and dragged him away. Suddenly, his face was all over the news. The press was saying he was some kind of monster. But since I knew he was innocent, I kept playing golf every weekend by myself, so I'd continue making progress, and continue making him proud once the trial was over and he came home."

Oh, Reed. The look on his face is making my heart squeeze.

With a deep sigh, he frowns at his golf clubs like they're flipping him off. "Obviously, nothing worked out the way twelve-year-old Reed thought it would. The jury convicted my father on all counts. He got sentenced to one hundred sixty-seven years in federal prison. And, for the first time, I devoured all the articles about him. I learned about the mountain of evidence against him. And I realized the jury had gotten it right. My father had done all of it. He'd lied and cheated and stolen, over and over again, while pretending to be a pillar of the community." He sighs. "And, all of a sudden, I felt ashamed to be me. Ashamed of my name. I worried people would think I'm just like him. A liar and a thief." His dark eyes find mine. "And I sure as fuck didn't want to play fucking golf anymore."

My stomach clenches at the hardness in his eyes. "I'm so sorry for everything you've been through in your childhood, Reed."

"Everybody's got shit from their childhood. Terrence Rivers just happens to be mine." His Adam's apple bobs. He manages a thin smile. "All right, Intrepid Reporter. My onion has now officially been peeled, in accordance with my promise to CeeCee. How about I show you some memorabilia in my home office now?" He gestures to a side door. "From there, I'll show you the gym upstairs, your room... and, finally, mine."

Chapter 3
Reed

"This is so cool!" Georgie says, shoving her nose into a framed gold record on the wall. For the past ten minutes, I've been showing her various items of memorabilia in my home office, figuring it'll go into her article. And, as expected, she's been geeking out over all of it.

"That one was for RCR's debut," I explain, chuckling at Georgina's enthusiasm. "It was my first gold record, so I keep it here, rather than with the others at the office. When I got that first one, I didn't even have a full-time staff yet. River Records was just me, hustling my ass off. So I feel like it belongs here."

"You must be so damned proud of everything you've accomplished. Hell, *I'm* so damned proud of you."

I try not to smirk like an asshole at how adorable she is right now. So fresh-faced and excited. But, truly, in this moment, Georgie being "proud" of me is like a cute little house kitten congratulating the king of the jungle on a kill.

"Have I said something that amuses you?" she asks, resting her hand on her hip.

I pause. Shit. Apparently, this girl can read me like a book. "Only in the sense that I find your enthusiasm and adorableness slightly amusing."

"See, the thing is, though, when you look at me like I'm a silly little girl when I'm simply talking, it comes off as condescending—like you think I'm stupid or you're somehow better than me. I mean, yes, I realize you're wildly successful.

But that doesn't make you an inherently better or smarter person than me."

Oh, for the love of fuck. "Georgie, I don't think you're silly or stupid whatsoever. On the contrary, I think you're wickedly smart. And I don't think I'm better than you, or anyone else. I mean, yes, of course, I think I'm better than ninety-nine percent of the world's population in terms of my business acumen, at least in my industry. And, yes, I *know* I'm better in bed than any man you'll ever sleep with in your entire life. But, other than those two areas, I'm fully aware I'm just a humble, ordinary guy making his way through life, as best he can."

She rolls her eyes. "There are many adjectives to describe you, Reed Rivers. But humble and ordinary aren't two of them."

I cross my arms over my chest, beaming a huge smile at her. "You know, Georgie, when you roll your eyes at me like that, when I'm simply trying to have a conversation with you, it comes off condescending. Like you think I'm silly and stupid and you're better than me."

"Good. I'm glad you've understood my body language to a tee."

I chuckle.

"But, don't worry, I only think I'm better than you when it comes to a few distinct things: brains, beauty, and emotional intelligence. Other than those three areas, I'm fully aware I'm just a girl—a silly, adorable girl, who's play-acting confidence in her mommy's heels and doing the best she can to make her way through life."

I shake my head. "You're never going to forget that 'mommy's heels' comment, are you?"

"Never. Brace yourself. You're going to hear it a lot this week."

"Lovely." I perch an ass cheek on the edge of my desk. "Look, if I come off as condescending or arrogant at times, it's only because... *I am*."

14

She chuckles. "Well, points for honesty."

"I couldn't do what I do for a living, and have the success I've had, without sincerely believing I'm the best. But that doesn't mean I think I'm an inherently more valuable *human* than anyone else. In a lot of ways, I still feel like that same college kid who couldn't afford to fix the slipping transmission and busted window on his shitty-ass Honda."

"Well, that explains your six fancy sports cars."

"Seven, actually. My beloved Ferrari is in the shop."

"Oh, no. So sorry to hear that. Whatever will you do until your *seventh* sports car is returned safely to you?"

"Barely survive? Cry into my pillow every night? It'll be tough, but I'll soldier on."

"I'm sure the Bugatti will help get you through."

"Barely."

"So, what's wrong with your beloved Ferrari?"

"The front right fender got bashed in a couple weeks ago. It broke my damned heart."

"What happened?"

"It was the craziest thing. I was driving on Mulholland, taking a curve a bit too fast, when a tree jumped out into the middle of the road, right in front of me. Too quick to swerve."

I'm thinking she'll return my joking demeanor, but she looks concerned. "Were you hurt?"

I shift slightly on the edge of my desk. "No. But I can't say the same for the front right fender of my Ferrari. It was smashed up pretty badly."

Without warning, Georgina beelines to me at the edge of my desk, nudges her way between my thighs, and kisses me. I don't know what's prompted this sudden, urgent display of affection from her, but I don't question it. Without hesitation, I wrap my arms around her back and return her kiss with passion, every cell in my body exploding with desire for her.

Finally, when we break free from our passionate kiss, Georgie nuzzles her nose along my jawline and whispers,

"I'm so glad you weren't hurt in that crash. The world would really miss having Reed Rivers in it."

Goosebumps erupt on my arms and neck. *Where did this come from?* "Hey, are you okay? I'm fine. Really."

She nods. "It just scares me to think everything can change in the blink of an eye. That someone as young and fit as you could have been gone, just like that." She snaps her fingers. "Sorry. Was that too dark?"

I smile sympathetically. I'm sure Georgina's thought a lot about mortality these last few years, with her father fighting for his life. Far more than most people her age would think about it. "No, it's a good reminder. I was cocky driving around that corner. Going way too fast. It was a good wake-up call for me that I'm not actually invincible."

She nods her approval and then resumes looking around the room. She looks at a framed magazine article—a *Forbes* "30 Under 30" piece featuring me. She runs her fingertips across the spines of the books on my shelf. Self-help, motivational, business, and fitness titles, mostly. And then she notices a small framed photo on my desk.

"Is this you?" she asks, picking up the frame.

It's my favorite photo from when I was a kid. The one shot from my childhood where my smile, and my mother's, too, seemed genuine and not put on for the camera. It's also the one shot I've got that includes both my mother and Amalia. Also, a shot from my one and only childhood birthday party—the one time in my life when my mother, still grieving Oliver, somehow pulled her shit together enough to do that thing all the other kindergartners' mothers had done that year for my classmates: she threw me a big birthday party with balloons and a cake and paper plates bearing images of my favorite cartoon. It never happened again. But, to this day, I remember how much fun I had at that once-in-a-lifetime party. How much fun Mom had, too. Truly, I felt like I'd died and gone to heaven that unique, carefree day with my mother and Amalia and the kids from school—the mysterious place my mother had always told me my big brother Oliver had gone to live.

"Yeah, that's me with my mother and Amalia. That shot was taken on my fifth birthday."

"Amalia, as in, your housekeeper, Amalia?" Georgina says in surprise. "I didn't realize you've known Amalia your entire life."

I gaze at the photo in Georgina's hand. "Amalia was already working for my family when I was born. She only stopped when my father went to prison, when I was thirteen."

For a split-second, the chaos of that time flickers through my mind. I remember the shock of it all. The early morning raid by the FBI that took my father away from me forever. The shock I felt at being ripped away from Amalia and sent to live with some distant relative I'd never met before, since Mom was already living in a facility by then, thanks to the stress of the custody battle a few years earlier.

"And when did Amalia come back into your life?" Georgina asks, still looking at the photo.

I clear my throat. "About ten years later. The minute I could afford to pay Amalia a salary, she was my first 'purchase.' Long before my first sports car. I think I hired Amalia right after I'd turned twenty-four?"

"Aw, that's so sweet, Reed. That makes my heart go pitter-pat." She returns the photo to its spot on my desk, her face aglow. "What a lucky little boy you were to have not *one*, but *two*, mothers growing up."

I try to return Georgina's easy smile, but I can't. The little boy in that photo wasn't lucky. Far from it. And he didn't have *two* mothers. He barely had one. But only because two halves make a whole. In truth, my mother has never been fully functional. Not like other kids' mothers. And nothing like the kickass, nurturing mothers I've observed as an adult, like Henn's mother and my sister's mother-in-law. Hence, the reason my father hired Amalia in the first place: to help my woefully ill-equipped mother with Oliver when he was born. And, as much as I love and appreciate Amalia, and can't imagine life without her, I can't honestly say she's a "whole" mother to me, either, simply because she's my employee. In reality, I pay her to mother me. I pay her to love me. I'm literally the woman's job. What would it be like to have a mother like Amalia who's not on my payroll? I can't even imagine it.

"You and your mother aren't close?" Georgina asks tentatively, apparently reacting to something she's seeing on my face.

Shit. Is this woman a mind reader? "No, we're close," I say. It's a knee-jerk reaction. I don't talk about my mother. She's an aspect of my life I don't share with anyone, other than the staff at her facility. But Georgina's looking at me like she's unconvinced. Like she saw *something* on my face that doesn't jibe with my words. My cheeks flush. "It's just that my mother lives on the East Coast, so I don't get to see her as much as I'd like."

"Oh," Georgina says. "That's too bad."

"Yeah, I visit her whenever I get to New York on business, though. Which I do about once or twice a month."

Georgina looks thrilled by that response. "Oh, I'm so glad you're able to visit your mother so much, Reed. Both for your benefit, and hers. What do you do with your mom when you visit her?"

Fucking hell. Seriously? How did our conversation about my music memorabilia and the *Forbes* "30 Under 30" list wind up *here*—with talking about my mother? And, more importantly, how do I steer it back to the stuff I actually want her to write about?

"Um... well. My mother and I do all sorts of things when I visit her. We play Scrabble. We watch *Jeopardy* and eat chicken pot pies. We do yoga."

"Yoga? You do *yoga* with your mom? Oh my gosh, Reed. *Swoon*."

I bite my lower lip. She's swooning over *that*? I can't help returning her beaming smile. Actually, she looks so damned cute right now, so over-the-top adorable, I'm momentarily forgetting to be annoyed by this topic. "Yeah. We do yoga. Play ping pong and gin rummy. My mom loves to paint, so she's always got her latest masterpiece to show me, too. Whatever Mom wants to do, I'm always there for it."

Georgina puts her hand on her heart and sighs like a Disney princess looking into a wishing well. "That's the sweetest thing I've ever heard in my life. I love that you're so close to your mother. It makes my heart hurt, it's so sweet." Georgina flashes me another beaming smile that makes my heart physically palpitate before she says, "My father always told me, 'If you want to know the measure of a man, look no further than the way he treats his mother.'"

I nod vaguely, not sure how to respond to that. If you ask me, the measure of a man is the empire he's built from dirt, with nothing but his blood, sweat, and tears. But okay. Tomato. Tomahto.

"You grew up in LA, right?" Georgina asks.

"Correct."

"Why did your mother move to the East Coast? Does she have family back there? Did she remarry?"

What the serious fuck? She's relentless. A dog with a meaty bone. "Uh, she... yeah, my mother grew up in Scarsdale, and has family back there. She's never remarried, but she does have a serious boyfriend. This guy named Lee. They live together."

"Oh, how saucy. Good for her." She laughs. "I think it's wonderful for your mother to have a companion later in life. Do you like Lee? Is he nice? Does he join in when you and Mom do yoga?"

Seriously, how the fuck am I talking about this with Georgina? I've had that same goddamned framed photo on my desk since I moved into this house five years ago, and nobody has ever noticed it or asked me about it. Not *once*. But in walks Georgina Ricci, the Intrepid Reporter, and in a matter of minutes, she's sniffed it out—and then pushed and pushed for more and more. I thought telling Georgina that story in the garage about my father and golf would more than satisfy her hunger for personal details. Is she going to be on my ass for stories like this about my life all week?

I want to say, "Enough about this. Moving on." But I'm positive that will only backfire on me. Spur her on more. Put her on the scent. So, instead, I say calmly, "Lee is a nice enough guy. He's really quiet, though, so it's hard to get to know him. But my mother loves him, and that's all that matters to me. And, yes, he occasionally joins in on yoga. But just barely."

Georgina giggles. "I love hearing you talk about your close relationship with your mother. Does she come visit you in California? I bet she's so proud of you and all you've accomplished."

Jesus Christ. When will this torture end? If Georgina loves mothers so much, maybe she should call up hers and have a nice, long chat, and leave mine alone. But there's no way I'm going to let Georgina know this is a sensitive topic for me. If I do, my gut tells me she'll only be *more* intrigued—which would make this one hell of a long week for me.

"My mother visits me occasionally," I lie. "I've actually offered to set her up in a place in Malibu, right on the beach, but she prefers living at her current place with Lee. Lee's got family in the City, apparently. Plus, he's got some health issues that prevent him from traveling, so they've decided to stay put in Scarsdale for the foreseeable future."

Georgina glides to me, wedges herself between my thighs, slides her arms around my neck, and nuzzles her nose against mine. "You want to hear something super kinky?"

"There's no need to ask me that question. My answer to it will always be a resounding yes."

She giggles. "The fact that you keep that photo on your desk, and visit your mom regularly—and do yoga and play Scrabble with her, and make her happiness your top priority..." She physically swoons in my arms with a heavy, happy, sexy sigh. "Oh, God, Reed. All of that *really* turns me on."

The butterflies in my stomach turn into a hard-on—one that's giving me instant amnesia about the annoyance I've been feeling about this topic. I slide my arms around Georgie and smile broadly at her. *"That's* what turns you on? What kind of sick fuck are you, Georgina Ricci?"

She giggles. "Maybe when you go back East on your next business trip, I could come with you to meet your mom? I'd love to chat with her about what you were like as a little boy."

Well, that's a nonstarter, obviously. But she feels so good in my arms, and smells so damned good, I find myself lying to her face. "Maybe. We'll have to see how scheduling works out."

Squealing, Georgina kisses my cheek, and then proceeds to lay soft kisses up and down my jawline that harden my thickening dick to steel. Her lips against my ear, she whispers, "I'm so glad I'm staying here with you, instead of at a hotel. Seeing you in your natural habitat has been a huge turn-on for me."

I turn my head and bring my mouth to hers, and when my tongue slides into her mouth, fireworks explode inside me. We kiss for several delicious minutes, our tongues dancing, our lips devouring, our bodies becoming more and more ravenous. Finally, when we disengage, Georgie looks as aroused as I feel.

"Come on, baby," I say, running my thumb over her bee-stung lower lip. "Let's take this house tour upstairs."

Chapter 4
Georgina

Freshly showered and clad in a white tank top and soft, pink shorts with "Sassy Pants" on the ass, I knock on Reed's bedroom door.

"*Entrez,*" his sexy voice calls from behind the door.

Clutching Alessandra's demo, I open the door and step inside the vast room... and gasp at the sensuous scene before me. As expected, Reed is wearing nothing but briefs. Sexy black ones, to be exact. But expecting him to be nearly naked, after previously seeing online photos of him in swim trunks, is a very different thing than seeing this god among men nearly naked in person. He's mouthwatering, this man. Scrumptious. Delicious. An erotic work of art.

He's lying atop his bed. Also, as expected. But this isn't any normal bed. It's a massive wood-carved four-poster that's, not surprisingly, fit for a king. Its frame is imposing and masculine. Its mattress covered in a ruby-red duvet and sumptuous pillows of gold, blue, and purple. If Henry VIII were alive today, he'd sleep in this bed.

And the cherry on top of this fantastical cake? Or, rather, the *mirror*? Reed's got one on his ceiling. A mirror. Directly above his porno-king bed. It's a feature that turns me on and amuses me in equal measure.

"Nice mirrored ceiling," I say, my tone bursting with snark as I walk across the room. "I didn't know that was an actual thing, except maybe in music videos and porn."

"Hey, don't knock it till you've tried it."

"I'm not. I'm *mocking* it before trying it."

He chuckles. "Trust me, little kitty. Watching yourself having sex is gonna get you off like crazy. It's like watching yourself in a live-action sex tape. So fucking hot." He pats the mattress next to him, his eyes blazing. "Come here, kitty-kitty."

I do as I'm told. I climb onto the bed next to him, still clutching the demo. But when he leans in to kiss me, I hold out the flash drive, sensing one kiss, and I'll quickly forget about the demo for the rest of the night. "I look forward to watching myself getting fucked by you in your mirrored ceiling *after* you listen to *this*. All three songs. A minute each. A deal's a deal."

Reed eyes the demo in my hand, but takes it, although he's looking at it with downright disdain.

My stomach flip-flops. "You promised, Reed."

"Yes, I know." He exhales. "But we need to set some ground rules. Before I listen, I need you to promise that, whatever my ultimate opinions on that demo might be, you're going to react calmly and with maturity."

I roll my eyes. "Remember that thing I said about you coming off as condescending at times? Yeah, well, this is one of those times."

"It needs to be said, Georgie. This is business for me. Nothing personal whatsoever. I want you to promise you won't react emotionally if things don't go as you're hoping. Whatever happens, I don't want this demo to get in the way of us having a great time tonight and during this entire week."

"I'm an adult, Reed. *Of course*, I know this is business for you. Whatever happens, I'll handle it calmly and in a mature fashion, and *without* letting my emotions run wild. Unless, of course, you fall head over heels for her, at which point I'm going to attack you with so much *wild* emotion, I might accidentally snuff the very life out of you. I apologize profusely in advance, if I wind up ending your life out of pure, unadulterated joy." I giggle, but he remains steadfast and serious. Which makes my stomach somersault again. "Reed, all of this is a moot point. I'm *positive* you're going to absolutely love what you hear. But, in the event you're on the fence, I promise to hear you out and respect whatever you say, as long as you're being honest with me."

"Of course I'll be honest. One hundred percent honest."

My stomach seizes with nerves. All my bravado leaves me. Holy shit. *This is it.* I'm ninety-nine percent certain Reed will love Alessandra... but what if he doesn't? I can't fathom having to call Alessandra and tell her Reed finally listened... and wasn't impressed. Making that call would break my heart. But there's no going back now.

"I'm ready," I say. "Go ahead."

Nodding, Reed pushes the flash drive into the side of his laptop. And a moment later, there she is. Alessandra. In a video. Sitting in a small studio, strumming her guitar, and singing from the depths of her soul.

I hold my breath. Wring my hands. And watch Reed as he watches Alessandra's video. I think I'm pretty good at reading him, but he's completely unreadable to me now. Indeed, just this fast, he's flipped into full-throttle business mode, despite the fact that we're lying together, almost naked, on top of his bed. Indeed, just this fast, we might as well be sitting across from each other at his desk at River Records.

I peek at the counter at the bottom of the video and my spirit cautiously surges. Reed's now watched Alessandra's video a solid forty seconds longer than he listened to Bryce's sister! That's got to be a good sign, right? But I've no sooner made that observation than Reed pauses the video.

"Okay," he says, his voice devoid of emotion. "Which file do you want me to play next?"

Shit. Fuck. He stopped Ally's video at exactly the one-minute mark—precisely the length of time he'd promised to listen. If he loved her, wouldn't he listen longer, despite what he promised? "That one." I point to his screen. "It's an audio file. No video. But her voice on this one is especially—"

"We'll let the song speak for itself," he says bluntly. "The time to try to charm and sell me is over, Georgie."

Holy fuck. I shoot him a look that says, *Well, shit. No need to be rude about it*. But he's not looking at me. Indeed, without so much as a glance at me, Reed clicks on the file I've indicated. And, once again, Alessandra's voice is wafting from his laptop speaker.

It's rinse and repeat. Reed listens, stoned-faced and impassive, for exactly one minute, before pausing the song and moving on to the third file. Another audio file. Which he then listens to for exactly one minute, without giving away a damned thing.

And that's it.

The room is filled with nothing but the sound of my anxious breathing now. Reed has listened to all three songs on Alessandra's demo, as promised. And he's right: the time for scheming and negotiating and flirting and middle fingers raised to the sky is over. Alessandra's music must now speak for itself, without any help from me. I let out a slow exhale, feeling nervous and frayed.

Reed slowly closes his laptop. He purses his lips. And, finally, looks at me, his dark eyes intense and giving nothing away. "She's talented," he says matter-of-factly. "She's got good vocal control. A nice texture to her voice. There's no doubt she deserved her spot at Berklee."

I nod, feeling like I'm going to pass out.

"One day, when she figures out who she is as an artist, as a person, I'm sure she'll blossom. But, as things stand now, she's not there yet. Not even close, if I'm being honest. I'm sorry, Georgie. She's a pass for me."

It's worst-case scenario. Way worse than I could have imagined. A truly gut-wrenching disappointment. Without meaning to do it, I whimper and then clutch Reed's arm with urgency.

"If you saw Alessandra perform live, I know you'd be able to see how special—"

"No, Georgie. Don't. It's over. I'm not on the fence about her. Not in the least. She's not for me."

I can't believe my ears. I feel physically sick. Like the room is spinning. "But... when you listened to Bryce's sister, you said young artists always need room to grow and develop." Tears begin welling in my eyes, unbidden, despite my fervent desire to keep my eyes dry as a bone. "Ally just needs a little professional guidance. If she could get some coaching to help boost her confidence, I know—"

"Georgie, stop. Please. My answer is no."

I blink and the tears welled in my eyes squirt down my cheeks.

"Aw, Georgie. I knew this would happen." He reaches out to wipe my cheek with this thumb, but I jerk my face away, too ashamed at myself for crying in front of him, for doing exactly what I promised I wouldn't do, to let him comfort me. Actually, he's the last person I want comforting me right now. I hate that I'm reacting like this. In fact, I'm livid with myself for it.

But when I jerk away from Reed, it's immediately clear he's misinterpreting my body language. He doesn't know I'm angry with myself. He thinks I'm punishing *him*. Taking my proverbial ball from the playground after not being chosen for a team and marching home.

"So predictable," he says, his tone turning acidic on a dime. "I don't get to touch the merchandise if I didn't pay your *price*?"

I'm shocked. Disgusted. *Pissed.*

Shaking his head, Reed retracts his hand from me and says, his voice low and intense, "Yes, Georgina. I told you young artists often need time to grow and develop. You might recall, however, that I made that comment when I *thought* we were having a conversation about music scouting *in general*. When I didn't have a clue we were *actually* talking about your stepsister, specifically. If I'd been privy to that information, then I would have clarified that, yes, I'm willing to help a young, wild bucking bronco of an artist learn to rein him or herself in a bit. To control their wildness. There's nothing better than barely contained chaos. But what I'm not willing to do, Georgina, *ever*, is try to coax a painfully shy pony who's afraid of her own shadow to poke her goddamned head out of the barn and take a fucking risk."

I gasp. *Asshole.*

"Life is too fucking short to try to coax someone out of their shell."

I'm aghast. Flooded with a whole bunch of emotions. Anger. Shock. Regret. Disappointment. Embarrassment. But, yeah, mostly...*rage*. At Reed, for being a dick right now. He doesn't want to sign Alessandra? Okay. Fine. No need to be a prick about it.

I know this is business to him, but I'm lying next to him on his bed in my pajamas, while he's nearly naked. It's not like we're sitting across from each other at his office! It's not like I'm some stranger off the street, like that poor girl who asked him to listen to her demo at the bar—but he's treating me exactly like her! After fucking me—after eating me out—am I seriously *no* different to him than that poor girl at the bar? Would it kill him to soften his rejection, just this once, so as not to decimate me?

But I'm equally mad at myself, as well, for being stupid enough to say the words "painfully shy" to Reed about Alessandra the other night. Obviously, I doomed my poor stepsister in Reed's eyes before he'd even heard her first note. Why was I so stupid?

Reed exhales. "Look, I know this is disappointing to you, but that's life. You promised you'd handle my opinion maturely, and that's exactly what I expect you to do."

Adrenaline surging inside my veins, I leap up from the bed and barrel toward the door. If I don't extract myself from this situation for a bit to cool down, I'll surely say something I'll regret.

"Goddammit," Reed barks from behind me. "Don't be so dramatic, Georgie. You promised you wouldn't let my opinion affect our time together."

I whirl around at the door. "Okay, first off, I'm not being *dramatic*, Reed. This isn't an act, designed to get a reaction out of you. I'm sincerely, genuinely crushed and in need of a minute to process my overwhelming and unexpected emotions." I'm shaking. Flailing. "Gee, I'm so sorry if my pesky emotions are screwing up your plan to get laid tonight, but that's life. Yes, it's true I said I wouldn't let your opinion affect our time together, but that was before I knew you'd talk to me like you're *entitled* to my body. You're *not*. You don't want to sign my stepsister to River Records? Fine. Whatever. Your opinion is obviously wrong and stupid, but you're entitled to it. But there's no excuse for you to be a flaming prick about it, especially when I'm sitting next to you barely clothed."

He throws up his hands. "Oh, for the love of fuck. You're going to make this about me, when you're the one who wouldn't let me touch you because I didn't give you what you wanted."

"You don't know what you're talking about. Not everything is about you."

"I'm running a for-profit record label in a cutthroat industry, Georgie. Not the Make-A-Wish Foundation."

I flip him off with my right hand—with the middle finger wearing my mother's wedding ring. And I truly believe she's cheering me on from heaven for doing it.

"So mature," he says. "And so predictable."

"Oh, I'm sorry. Was that too 'dramatic'?" I say mockingly. "Am I play-acting in my mommy's heels? Well, guess what, Reed? I wish I were play-acting in my mommy's heels. Unfortunately, I haven't had the pleasure of wearing my mommy's heels, whether to play-act in them, or just dress up for a special night out, since I was nine. Which is when she died in a car accident. So, don't say a fucking word about my mommy's heels ever again!"

He's stricken. Pained. Full of regret. "Oh, Georgie. I had no idea."

"And then my father married Alessandra's mother, and it felt like my mother had died a second time." I wipe my eyes, but it's no use. I'm a hot mess. "I was so full of rage about the wedding, Reed. Crushed. Confused. Betrayed. But Alessandra was sweet about it, even though *her* father had just died. She had every reason to be as angry as I was. She had every reason to lash out, the way I did. But, see, that's not Alessandra Tennison. Whereas I've always lashed *out* when I'm hurt, she's always lashed *in*. Yes, I'm too quick to flip someone off. I own that. But at least, I get it out. That poor girl has struggled her whole life with anxiety and self-doubt and crippling shyness. But she's come so far. She went to that audition for Berklee and *nailed* it. She's come so far out of her shell, you have no idea. And do you know why? *Because of her music.* So, yes, she might still be a sweet little pony who's afraid of her own shadow sometimes. But she's well worth the time and effort to lead her out of the barn. I know, because for years, I was the only person she played her songs for. The only one. She knew I was going through so much, and she'd sing those songs to me and make me feel better. She was my angel. And all I wanted was for something wonderful to happen for her. I just wanted to pay her back for all she's given to me, through her music, and her love, and kind heart, over the years."

"Georgie," Reed says. He gets up from the bed, clearly intending to comfort me.

But I hold up my palm. "Stop."

He stops in the middle of the room, mere feet away from me, his bare chest heaving.

"I get that you couldn't possibly love Alessandra's music the way I do. And I know in your world nobody gets a gold star for progress, only results. But that doesn't mean I don't feel crushed in this moment, to hear your brutally honest opinion. It doesn't mean I'm not allowed to feel whatever I honestly feel, and give myself time to process it and try to move past it. I'm sorry you're not getting laid tonight, like you planned. Like you think you're *owed*. But you should know I'm not withholding my body from you because you didn't give me the result I wanted on the demo. I'm not a spoiled brat. And I'm not a whore. I'm withholding my body from you because I'm pissed at the way you spoke to me. The way you assumed I'm so quick to trade on my body." I take a deep breath. "Now, I'm going to my room to be alone for the rest of the night, to process my emotions and anger, because, if I don't, I'm going to say something I regret. Or, quite possibly, punch you in the face." With that, I swing open Reed's door with gusto, tossing over my shoulder, "See you in the morning, Mr. Rivers. *But only because you're my fucking job.*"

Chapter 5
Reed

After Georgina slams my bedroom door shut behind her, I stride to it, every fiber in my body urgently wanting to fling it open and follow her. But I stop myself. Indeed, I stand at the door and press my forehead against it and force myself to stay put.

Goddammit. Why did Georgie have to push so hard about that demo? I knew listening to it would lead to nothing good. *I could feel it in my bones.* But she pushed and pushed. And now, here we are.

Doesn't she know I went in wanting to love Alessandra's music? Doesn't she know nothing would have given me greater pleasure? But I had to be honest. Brutally honest. I'll lie and fudge a little about certain things. But not about my professional judgment. Not for friends or family or anyone else. Not even for the most electrifying girl I've ever met in my life.

Fuck. I thought I'd be tying sexy Georgina's limbs to my bedposts tonight, and then fucking her to bliss like she's never been fucked before. Not making her hate my guts. Yeah, making Georgina storm out of my bedroom tonight most definitely wasn't the plan. Neither was making her cry.

For the love of fuck, how was I supposed to know about Georgina's mother? Somewhere in my brain, I vaguely remember Georgina saying something about Alessandra losing her father as a kid... I think? But Georgie's never said a word about her own mother. How was I supposed to know Georgina's

31

grief about her mother, and her love for Alessandra, and for Alessandra's music, are all tied up together inside her? I mean, if I'd known that, it wouldn't have changed my opinion in any way. It wouldn't have changed the ultimate result. But *maybe* I would have phrased things slightly differently. With a touch more, I don't know, gentleness? Am I even capable of doing that, though? I sincerely don't know.

Shit!

I want so badly to march into Georgina's room and explain myself. Or maybe, just try to comfort her. But I know I can't. Georgina said she wants to be alone, and I can't chase her. Long before she stormed out, when she was perfectly calm earlier, she requested a separate room, much to my dismay. Which means she didn't want me the way I want her, even before this latest fiasco.

Sighing, I straighten up from the door, drag my exhausted ass back to bed, and turn off my lamp. God, I'm exhausted. This has been a long damned day. I close my eyes and command my body to sleep. But, soon, it's clear my body isn't going to obey. I'm way too wound up.

Muttering expletives, I grab my laptop and click into a licensing agreement requiring my review. But I can't concentrate. Because... *Georgina.*

Goddammit! I knew she'd fly off the handle about the demo. I knew it, without a doubt. Because underneath all that beauty beats the heart of a fucking psycho. There. I said it. She's beautiful and sexy and smart and funny. And the most exciting woman I've ever met. But all that comes with a price. Namely, that she's also a fucking psycho.

I sit up in bed and drag a palm over my face. God, she's sexy as hell when her psycho peeks out. I shouldn't get turned on by her flashes of anger the way I do, but, oh, God, I do. So fucking much.

I sit up, grab my phone, and text Owen: *You up?*

Two seconds later, I get his reply: *No, I'm asleep.*

Calling now.

Oh, yay.

Of course, Owen dutifully picks up after one ring. Because he's Owen.

"Hello, boss," he says. "How lovely to hear from you at midnight after I worked all day and night."

"Yeah, don't you mean after you fucked up? You're the one who let Georgina out of your sight, just long enough for C-Bomb to get her alone."

"I let Georgina out of my sight because she was with Leonard and his daughter, and you texted me a *demand* to meet you outside the VIP door."

"Okay, we're wasting time. Moving on. I need a favor."

I explain what I want and Owen tells me what I'm asking for might as well be the moon and the stars, thanks to the short turnaround time I'm demanding.

"If anyone can work a miracle, it's you," I say.

Owen mutters something under his breath.

"I'll pay triple market price," I toss out. "I don't care how you make it happen. Just do it."

He sighs. "Okay, I'm sure I know someone who knows someone who can help me. I'll see what I can do. No promises, though."

I smile to myself. When Owen Boucher says he'll "see what he can do," the task is as good as done.

"So, based on this 'favor,' I'm assuming Georgina's interview of you is either going very, very well... or you've somehow *really* pissed her off?"

I roll my eyes to myself. Fucking Owen. Nothing gets past him. "It's door number two, unfortunately. She's in my guestroom down the hall at the moment, trying to resist her stated desire to 'punch me in the face.'"

Owen chuckles. "Oh my. What did you do, Reed? And is it wrong I'd kind of like to see her follow through with that threat?"

"I did something monstrous." I flap my lips together. "I didn't sugarcoat my opinion regarding her stepsister's music demo."

"Oh, the horror."

"I know."

"Were you harsh about it?"

"No, I was honest."

"You were harsh."

"No. Well, maybe a little bit. I got pissed for a second there, so maybe I didn't word things as nicely as I should have."

He chuckles. "Was she already planning to sleep in the guestroom before you listened to the demo, or is she freezing you out *because* of the demo?"

"She was already planning to sleep there."

"Well, that's good, right? At least, you know she already hated you, even before you pissed her off."

"There was never any question she'd sleep in a guest room," I lie. "Georgie and I have a purely professional relationship, Owen."

"Oh, really? Then why wasn't I allowed to let C-Bomb get her alone?"

"Which you fucked up."

"And why am I moving heaven and earth to arrange that delivery for first-thing tomorrow morning?"

"For your information, I had the idea to give Georgie this present hours before she wanted to punch me in the face. I just didn't get around to asking you to arrange it before now."

"Uh huh."

"I can give a gift to a woman I'm not romantically interested in. Look how many gifts I've given to CeeCee over the years, to celebrate a birthday or whatever accomplishment."

"CeeCee isn't a twenty-something-year-old fireball who's built like a brick house. And CeeCee isn't staying at your house for a full week, at your invitation, when a hotel would have been perfectly convenient. And CeeCee isn't a woman you won't let tour with RCR, or party with C-Bomb, even though both things would have made for an awesome article, and you know it. Should I go on, or are you going to cut the bullshit?"

"No, don't go on. In fact, shut the fuck up."

He chuckles.

"I'm already cranky, thanks to Georgie hating me and wanting to punch me. Why are you actively piling on?"

Owen laughs uproariously. "Wow, she's really gotten under your skin, hasn't she? Good for her."

I drag my palm over my stubble and say nothing. Because, what is there to say? It's obviously true: Georgina has gotten under my skin. In fact, I think she's done a whole lot more than that, not that I'd admit it to Owen. I'm pretty sure, just this fast, the girl has infiltrated my bloodstream. How the hell did Georgie do that? I've had all my usual guards and defenses up... But, somehow, she keeps finding ways to slither around and through and over them, like they're not even there.

"I've gotta go," Owen declares. "My cranky boss wants something unreasonable, so I've got to move heaven and earth to make it happen. I wouldn't want to get fired."

"You're lucky I didn't fire you tonight, after I found Georgie with C-Bomb."

"I'm counting my lucky stars. I'll call you if I manage to get a delivery scheduled. So leave your ringer on."

I smile broadly. "Thanks, O."

"Just think of me as your personal genie in a bottle."

"Oh, I already do."

We hang up, and I force myself to open up that licensing agreement from before. But I've barely made it through two paragraphs when I hear a splash outside my window that makes every hair on my body stand on end and my skin tingle with anticipation.

I scramble to my floor-to-ceiling windows on the

opposite side of the room, and my heart leaps and bounds, every bit as much as my cock twitches. It's Georgina. Swimming laps in the moonlight. Giving me a glorious view of her naked backside.

Chapter 6
Reed

My cock is hard as steel and pulsing as I watch Georgina's naked form swimming laps two stories below. Back and forth across the length of my moonlit pool, she goes, her toned legs and arms working furiously. Back and forth she goes, torturing me. Have I ever seen a more perfect ass? I'm certain I haven't. I'm physically aching to bite that ass. To lick it and fuck it. I lean my forehead against the window, breathing hard. Feeling consumed with lust. Yeah, she hates me right now. But, even so, she obviously came outside to give me a show. Which means hating me isn't keeping her from wanting me. Unless, of course, she only came out here to torture me—to dangle what I can't have in front of me. Which, knowing her, is probably the case.

After a while, Georgina stops in the middle of the pool, flips over, and floats on her back. And I'm gone. Jolted with carnal, unadulterated, white-hot lust and desire like nothing I've felt before. I saw swaths and peeks and segments of her gorgeous body earlier tonight at the stadium, but this is the first time I'm seeing her fully nude, all at once, although the dark water lapping at her sides is doing its damnedest to impede my view. And, good lord, she's a wet dream. A goddess. The most beautiful creature I've ever beheld in my life, without a doubt.

My eyes trained on Georgina, I slowly pull my briefs off, freeing my straining cock, and toss them onto the floor. My breathing heavy and tortured, I bound over to my nightstand, open the top drawer, and quickly sift through the accoutrements I keep there—soft cuffs, cords, and various vibrating toys—until I locate a bottle of lube.

After briskly wetting my palm, I return to the window. And with my forehead pressed against the glass, and my eyes trained on Georgina's floating form below, I grip myself and get to work. I move my palm slowly, not wanting to get myself off too rapidly. But that's easier said than done, when your visual is Georgina Ricci floating naked in a moonlit swimming pool.

All too fast, I'm hurtling toward release. I feel my balls tightening. Tingles shooting through my core and cock and balls. I lay my free palm flush against the window, to the side of my forehead, and give myself permission to lose it. But just before I come, Georgina opens her eyes, turns her head, and looks straight at me, shocking the hell out of me and stopping my hand mid-pump.

There's a split-second pause, where neither of us reacts.

I'm a thief. She's a cop with a flashlight.

And then... Georgina smiles. And, thankfully, it's a bold, brazenly sensuous smile. A smile that tells me she likes what she sees. *A lot.*

My eyes locked with Georgina's, I resume my work—this time, far more slowly than before, just in case Georgina gets the bright idea to join me.

Biting her lip, Georgina glides to the side of the pool, hoists herself onto the ledge, and stands underneath my window—giving me my first wholly unimpeded view of her naked body. And she's glorious. Her curves are an hourglass in the moonlight. Her nipples erect. Her wet hair is slicked back, showcasing her high cheekbones and full lips. She's a goddess. A fantasy come to life. And... Oh, God, I think I'm gonna come.

Condensation begins pooling on the glass in front of my face. I'm a caged lion, an unruly beast trapped behind glass, being teased with a slab of meat. Oh, fuck, I'd pay her any amount of money if she'd come to me now and suck my dick. If only she'd get her hot ass up here and let me touch and lick every square inch of her and then fuck her every which way.

"Touch yourself," I mouth to her. And then again. And again. And again. Until, finally, her face lights up with understanding. Her body trembling with arousal, she sits on the ground, spreads her smooth legs wide, and touches herself, right where I'm dying to lick her.

Oh, God, this is so fucking hot.

With a loud groan, I lick at the glass, wishing my tongue were licking her sweet pussy. And that does it for her, apparently. Her eyes roll back into her head, her body stiffens and then quakes with her orgasm.

As my balls tighten and ripple, I grip my cock and aim it right at her tits, and, two seconds later, I'm streaking the glass with the physical evidence of my need. When the deed is done, and my painting complete, I press both palms against the glass, yearning to touch her. It's a good thing I don't do coke anymore. Because, I swear to God, if I were high on blow in this moment, I'd grab that armchair from the corner, crash it into this window, and leap through the jagged, gaping hole to get to her naked body two floors below. Which, obviously, wouldn't be good.

"Come to me," I mouth.

And she immediately responds by rising to her feet, her tits aimed right at me, and lapping at the air with the full length of her tongue, like she's licking up every last drop of my cum off the window.

"Oh, Jesus Christ," I murmur, every cell in my body exploding with desire. *"Come. Here. Right. Now."*

A naughty smile breaks free across her sultry face, telling me she's understood my command perfectly. To my thrill, she moves from her spot... but not to come to me, as instructed. No. Georgina is having too much fun torturing me to do that.

She grabs a towel off a nearby lounger and returns to her spot, which is where she begins drying herself off, for my benefit. Slowly, Georgina towels off her arms and shoulders. Slowly, Georgina dries off her perfect tits and stomach and pussy. And, finally, with a little wink, she turns around, bends completely over—thereby giving me a view that nearly gives me a heart attack—and *slowly* proceeds to towel off her feet and shins and calves.

"Oh my God, you evil woman," I whisper, pressing my forehead against the glass. "You're the devil."

Her task complete, she straightens up and turns around to face me again, her tits pushed forward and her nipples erect. And then, with a little swish of her hips, she strides across the patio toward the French doors... and disappears from my line of sight.

My heart crashing with anticipation, I race to my bedroom door and press my ear against it, awaiting the sound of her footsteps in the hallway. She's got to be coming to me now, right? She wouldn't be so cruel as to leave me alone tonight after *that.*

Finally, after what feels like half my lifetime, I hear movement in the hallway. But the sound stops before it gets to my door. Is Georgina standing at the far end of the hallway, deciding whether to come all the way to the end, to my room? Or is she summoning the resolve to head to her own room, just to emphasize her point that, although she's staying here with me, she's far from a sure thing?

Yeah, I know exactly what's going on inside that glorious, devious mind of hers. She's standing at the end of the hallway, deciding which she wants more in this moment: to fuck me... or punish me?

I spear my fingertips into the door, wishing I could physically claw my way through the wood to get to her. Frankly, I'd wear my fingers down to bloody stumps to get to her, if I thought it would convince her to come to my bed tonight. I'd open a vein and give her every last drop of my blood, if it would mean she'd open her thighs to me tonight. I'd pay her any amount of money. The only two things I won't do? Lie about that fucking demo. Or beg. I begged her once, that very first night, right before she double-flipped me off and peeled away in an Uber. And I swear to God, I'll never do it again.

There's movement in the hallway again. Footsteps, as plain as day. I hold my breath and wait. And pray. But the brief footsteps are followed by the distinct sound of a door opening and closing at the other end of the hall. And that's that. The house is silent now. Apparently, Georgina decided she'd rather punish me, than fuck me, tonight.

Chapter 7
Reed

At a quarter past eight, wearing cycling shorts and nothing else, I greet two deliverymen at my front door, lead them upstairs, and direct them where to unpack their big box. Most mornings, I get up quite a bit earlier than this to fit in my workout, but after yesterday's marathon day that began in Manhattan and ended with me jizzing against my bedroom window, I fell into a deep slumber until about twenty minutes ago—which was when Owen called and woke me up with the news that my delivery was about twenty minutes away.

I rap on Georgina's closed door. "Wake up, Bobby Fischer," I call out. "Rise and shine." Georgina moans softly behind the door, sending arousal streaking through me. Because, apparently, any moan from this girl, no matter the context, registers as something sexual to my brain. "Wake up, Georgie girl." I knock again. "Even if you hate my guts, you're going to be my shadow today. And right now, I'm heading into my gym for a workout."

"I'm up," she croaks out. "Just give me twenty minutes."

"You've got five. Throw on workout clothes and meet me in the gym."

In the gym, I do core blasters and plyometrics for a full twenty minutes before Georgina finally appears, her form-fitting short-shorts and sport bra instantly making me forgive her completely for keeping me waiting so long.

"Sorry, I..." she begins. But the second she notices a

second Peloton bike set up next to mine, her words trail off. She rushes to the sleek stationary bike and grips its handlebars, like she's confirming it's not a figment of her imagination. "This wasn't here last night during the tour! How did this get here?"

I smile. "You said you wanted to try one. So, I decided to get you one. This way, we can ride together."

Her jaw hits the floor. "This is for *me*?"

I chuckle at her adorable expression. "Yes. It's my gift to you, with an assist from Owen. I know you don't have a place of your own yet, so I'll have it delivered to your father's place after this week, if you like. If not, you can leave it here as long as you need, until you get a place of your own with enough room for it."

"Thank you!" With an effusive squeal, she breaks into an effervescent happy-dance—a sexy, jiggling display that makes me want to give her a month's worth of exercise equipment, if it will guarantee I'll get this same reaction every time.

"I've only got one request," I say. "I'd like you to be my personal spin instructor this week."

"Hell yeah! With pleasure!" She shakes her ass with glee... but then freezes. "Shoot. I don't have any—"

"Shoes?" I point to a shoe box on the floor next to her bike. "Put on your new shoes, saddle up, and let's sweat."

Like a kid on Christmas, Georgina tears into the shoe box while I get my own cycling shoes on, and soon, we're both clicked into our pedals and ready to begin.

"Let's get warmed up," she says, and we both begin pedaling at a fairly easy pace. "So, how hard do you want to work this morning?"

"A ten out of ten," I reply, without hesitation. "Annihilate me."

Georgina snickers. "Careful what you wish for. I taught advanced spin for the past two years. I'm pretty good at this, if I do say so myself."

"Hit me with your best shot, Ricci. Make me pay."

"There is a God."

She cues up a thumping playlist, barks at me to gear my bike up to twenty-two, and then proceeds to lead me in a solid hour's worth of torturous sprints and savage climbs and relentless anaerobic drills that leave us both gulping for air and dripping with sweat. Well, correction: we're both dripping with sweat, but I'm the only one gulping for air. Somehow, Georgina's not only performing every drill and maneuver alongside me, she's *also* barking nonstop orders at me in a clear, smooth voice—something I couldn't pull off right now, if I tried.

Finally, Georgina declares our private spin class over, and I crumple over my handlebars in relief.

She giggles. "Wimp."

"You're the devil... The devil with perfect tits."

She laughs. "Of course the devil has perfect tits. How else do you think she gets stupid mortals to sell their souls to her? Now, pedal at a ten for a few minutes to get your heart rate down, Old Man. And then I'll lead you through some stretching on the floor."

Gratefully, I gear down as instructed, and slow my pedaling to an easy, cool-down pace.

"Seriously impressive, Georgie."

"Back at you. You kept up with me the whole time."

"Yeah, but I wasn't *also* barking orders the whole time. I'm only the Fred Astaire of spin. You're the Ginger Rogers."

She looks at me blankly, and, immediately, I know she's as clueless about Fred and Ginger as she was about Bobby Fischer.

I flick the end of my towel at her in mock annoyance. "Are you *trying* to constantly remind me how young you are?"

"No. Just how old you are."

I laugh. "Would it kill you to *occasionally* know one of my pop culture references?"

"Would it kill you to *occasionally* make a pop culture reference that someone under fifty would know?"

"Everyone knows about Fred Astaire and Ginger Rogers. They're way before my time, too. They've transcended their era to become cultural icons. You should know about them for your writing."

"Okay, Obi Wan Kenobi. Educate me."

I give Georgina a quick primer on Fred and Ginger as we continue pedaling slowly, including the fact that, in modern times, Ginger is generally credited with being the bigger badass of the duo. "And you want to know *why* everyone says Ginger was the bigger badass?" I pause for effect. "Because Ginger did everything Fred did... only backwards and in high heels."

Georgina laughs uproariously, without holding back in the slightest. And that's when I know she's truly ready to move on from the crushing disappointment of last night. Yeah, I'm sure she's still hugely disappointed things didn't work out the way she'd hoped, simply because she loves her stepsister and wants the world for her. But thanks to the belly laugh Georgina is gracing me with, I know for certain she's ready to put last night's fiasco behind us. And I couldn't be more relieved about it.

After a little more chatting, Georgie orders me off my bike, and begins leading me in some stretches on the floor. But a few minutes in, as Georgie is leaning over one of her legs, she shocks the hell out of me by whispering three little words I never expected to drop from her sultry mouth in a million years.

"I'm sorry, Reed."

At the sound of her whispered apology, I don't flinch, even though I feel like I need the crash cart. "Sorry, did you say something?"

She clears her throat. Exhales. "I said I'm sorry. About last night. For how emotional I was." She winces. "And for flipping you off."

"It's okay. I kinda like it when you flip me off."

She leans against her bike. "I couldn't sleep last night for hours after I came back up from the pool, so I had plenty of time to think. And I realized you gave me your honest, professional opinion. And no matter how wrong and stupid it was, I should have respected it." She shrugs. "I had a tantrum. Plain and simple. And I'm sorry."

Holy shit. Who the hell is this humble, contrite woman before me? I don't recognize her, except for the part where she called my opinion wrong and stupid. Whoever she is, she's making my heart squeeze, every bit as much as the fiery, tempestuous, bird-flipping version of her makes my pulse race.

"I understand why you got so emotional," I say. "You love your stepsister and want the best for her. Plus, obviously, your feelings regarding Alessandra are tied up with your feelings about other things, too." I touch her shoulder. "I'm deeply sorry about your mother, Georgie."

"Thank you." She pauses. "Honestly, until I started melting down like a lunatic last night, I didn't even realize how interconnected certain things are inside me. But, regardless, I shouldn't have freaked out on you. That was crazy-pants and bananas and unfair to you, and I promise I'll try never to do it again. No promises, but I really will try."

Oh, my heart. "Hey, lose your fucking mind, if you need to, baby. Let your freak flag fly. I certainly didn't help matters with some of my harsh word choices. When it comes to doling out my professional opinions, I'm used to being brutally honest, without a filter. But I should have appreciated the unique context a bit more. I'm sure it was confusing to you to have me turn into Business Reed on you, while we were lying in bed together in our underwear."

She flashes me a crooked smile that tells me she appreciates my concession. "So, we're good, then?"

Every atom in my body sighs with relief. "We're good." I open my mouth, as if to say more, but close it.

"But... ?" she prompts.

"Before I let this moment pass, I just want to address something. At the stadium last night, you said you hoped I'd want to help someone I love, the same way you wanted to help Alessandra. You said if I don't have that same impulse regarding the people I love, then I'm an even bigger dickhead than you thought."

She grimaces. "Sorry. Wow. I really do fly off the handle sometimes, don't I?"

I chuckle. "No need to apologize. I'm only bringing it up because I want you to know that I *do* have that impulse, Georgina. I won't compromise my business judgment for anyone—as you've learned firsthand—but, other than that, I truly would do anything for the short list of people I love."

Her face softens. She touches my hand. "I don't doubt that for a minute, Reed."

"You don't?"

"No."

I sigh with relief. "I'm so glad."

She takes a long sip of water. "Let's keep stretching."

We hit the floor and she directs me into a runner's lunge.

"So, tell me," she says, bending over her bent front leg. "Who's on this 'short list' of people you love—the ones you'd do anything for?"

And there she is. The Intrepid Reporter has re-entered the building. But it's an innocuous question. One I don't mind answering, actually. So, I do. "Well, my family, of course. My mother, sister, nephew, and brother-in-law. Also, Josh and Henn. I consider them family. Their wives and babies, too. CeeCee, as well."

"CeeCee said the same thing about you. She said she loves you."

"She did?"

"Yep. She said she loves you and would never want to trick or trap you in relation to your interview."

I nod, feeling touched. "I love CeeCee, too. She gave me my first big break and changed my life. I'll be grateful to her forever."

Georgina instructs me to sit on my ass for a new stretch, and I comply.

"How did you and CeeCee meet?" she asks.

"I crashed CeeCee's black-tie birthday party. I knew a guy who knew a guy working the door, so I bribed my way onto the list, rented an Armani tux and a limo, and then waltzed into the party like I was the goddamned guest of honor."

She giggles.

"It was the embodiment of 'fake it till you make it.' I even posed for photographers on the red carpet outside, like they were all there for me."

We laugh together.

"So, what'd you say to CeeCee that made her want to give you that first big break?"

"Nothing particularly ingenious. I told her about Red Card Riot, and I guess my genuine passion was evident. She said, 'Send me the album and I'll give it a listen.' And the rest is history. I think the main thing was we just genuinely liked each other. There was an instant connection."

"I felt that with her, too," Georgie says. "When I had coffee with her, I immediately felt like I'd known her for years."

"Yeah, CeeCee has that effect on people. So do you."

She blushes. "Thank you." She draws her knees up to her chest. "So, is that everyone on your short list?"

I pause to consider. "No, I'd put Amalia on the short list, too. Also, Owen. I'd take a bullet for Owen, but, for the love of all things holy, don't put that into your article, or he'll demand a massive raise."

Georgina looks surprised. "Oh. I wasn't thinking about the article. I'm just enjoying getting to know you."

Oh, Georgina. She's such a liar. A beautiful one. But a liar nonetheless. "Isn't everything we talk about this week fair game for your article?" I ask. "Are you saying this conversation is off the record?"

She ponders that. Or pretends to, anyway. "No, I can't promise that. I guess I was just thinking I'd get to know you this week, organically, and have faith the article will take care of itself."

I take a sip of water. "Sorry, I don't think that approach is going to work for me. At the end of this, I don't want to open the special issue and read something I thought I'd said to you during a private, intimate moment, like during pillow talk or whatever. If you really want to get to know me, then I'm going to need the ability to designate certain conversations as off-limits."

She sighs. "Aw, Reed. So sure everyone is out to get you." She crawls like a cat across the floor, opens my bent legs, and crawls between them onto her knees. She shoves her gorgeous face into mine. She's so close, I can see every pore in her smooth, olive skin. The gold flecks in her hazel eyes. She puts her hands on my cheeks. "Reed Rivers, I hereby promise I'm not here to trick or trap you. I'm here to get to know you and use whatever I learn to write an amazing article about an amazing man that will blow you, and everyone who reads it, away."

I shake my head. "Georgie, you have to understand, I haven't read a single interview or article about me that got everything exactly right. There's always something that gets lost in translation. Every time."

"Well, that sucks." She twists her mouth, considering. "All right. Here's what we'll do. You'll promise that anything you say to me this week, and whatever I might observe, will be fair game for me to *write* about." She puts her fingertip to my lips, silencing me. "But *I* promise to let you see my article before showing it to anyone else, even CeeCee. And if there's *anything* you don't want in there, anything I've gotten wrong or you don't particularly like, then I'll take it out. It's as simple as that."

I squint. "What's the catch?"

"There isn't one. This way, you'll feel free to say whatever you want around me, no matter how stupid or arrogant or condescending it might be." She winks playfully. "And you won't have to worry it might make you look bad later." She slides her arms around my neck and kisses my cheek. "Now you have no excuse not to let down your guard with me."

Let down your guard. I can't believe it. Normally, when a woman says this sort of thing to me, I get hives. Or feel the urge to run away. Or shut down. But hearing those words from Georgina, I'm feeling nothing but excited and turned on.

"My only request?" she says. "When you read my ultimate article, just remember I'm not out to get you. Give it a chance. Please."

I pause. "You've got yourself a deal." I kiss her, and, just like that, those damned butterflies are going to town inside my belly again. Rippling and flapping like crazy. I smile. "Now that we've got that figured out, let's celebrate."

She motions to the massive bulge behind my shorts. "Gee. Do you have a particular kind of celebration in mind, Mr. Rivers?"

"As a matter of fact, I do." I grin wickedly. "You mentioned you like being weightless..."

"Oooh, after last night's torture, you're dying to fuck me in your pool, aren't you? I'm definitely in favor of that."

"Yes, but another time. I've got something else in mind right now." I jut my chin over her shoulder, toward a harness hanging from the ceiling in a corner. "I was thinking you should slide into that contraption right there and let me fuck you into oblivion."

She turns around to look where I've indicated. "What is that thing? Some sort of yoga swing?"

I stand and pull her up. "No, little kitty. It's my sex swing."

Her eyebrows ride up.

"And, I promise, you're going to love it."

Chapter 8
Reed

I'm naked and hard as a rock, standing before Georgina's naked, suspended body. Her thighs, calves, back, and ass are supported by the hanging straps of the swing. And, thanks to my meticulous adjustments, her hips are now positioned at the precise height and angle to ensure maximum G-spot stimulation with every thrust. Which means, before I'm done with her, Georgina is going to get a huge, wet, and incredibly pleasurable surprise. An orgasm like nothing she's experienced before. And I can't wait.

I take a deep breath to control my spiraling excitement. "Lean back and relax," I coo, trying to keep my voice soothing and calm, even though my cock is already seeping with wetness.

Georgina leans back and visibly melts into the harness. "*Whoa*. This is wild."

"Comfortable?"

"Very. Although I've never felt more like a fly in a web."

I make another minor adjustment. "You're not a fly in a web, sweetheart. You're a butterfly in a net."

"Oh, well, that's so much better."

I stroke her thigh and she shudders with anticipation.

"It is. The spider only wants to destroy the fly. But the butterfly hunter wants to *possess* and *admire* the beautiful butterfly.*"

"Yeah, and then tack its wings to paper and enclose it in an airtight frame."

"The price of beauty, baby." My cock straining and wet, I open her thighs and stroke her slit gently. "You're about to discover there's incredible freedom that flows from being trapped like a butterfly in a net. When there's no option but to lean back and surrender to the pleasure, when there's nowhere to go, mentally or physically, when you can't pull away from the intensity of the pleasure you're experiencing, you're forced to let go completely and surrender. And it's in that moment of complete surrender that you're finally able to experience a new level of pleasure you had no idea existed."

I begin massaging her clit now, manipulating it firmly, back and forth, and she sighs and coos and sinks deeper into the harness.

"Take deep breaths, in and out," I instruct. "That's it. Relax. Don't fight the pleasure. There's nowhere to go. So, you might as well embrace it."

I kneel between her suspended thighs, and get to work on her with my tongue and fingers, and, in no time at all, she's rocking and jolting in the swing with a powerful orgasm.

Even before she's come down from her climax, I rise and plunge myself inside her, and Georgina growls ravenously at my delicious invasion. My hands firmly on her hips, I thrust in and out, hard, over and over again, the head of my cock slamming her G-spot without fail. Methodically. Precisely. Mercilessly. And, clearly, she's rapidly losing her mind.

But I don't let up.

Not for a second.

I pound her rhythmically, with no variation, until she's growling and begging me not to stop. I keep fucking her when her eyes roll back into her head. And when she lets out a long, animalistic growl. I fuck her when she's so wet, each thrust elicits a sloshing noise. And when her innermost muscles begin clenching and unclenching in delicious, rhythmic waves around me. I don't let up on beautiful Georgina's G-spot, even when it's clear she's been reduced to a feral animal. When her body goes slack and her head lolls to the side and the only sounds out of her sensuous mouth are groans and growls, peppered with my name and shrieks of "yes."

I fuck Georgina Ricci until she can't imagine fucking anyone else, ever again. Until *I* can't imagine fucking anyone else. Until we're both sweating and moaning and quaking and on the cusp of literal exhaustion.

I fuck her until, finally, I reach the finish line—the moment when Georgina lets out a scream of ecstasy that's so primal, so tortured, I know it can only mean I've finally hit the motherlode. Two seconds later, every muscle of hers surrounding my cock tightens like a vise around me. She throws her head back into the swing... and creams around my cock. Clearly, she's having the orgasm of her life. A wet, all-body climax that will change the way she thinks of sex—and her body—forever.

At the sensation of the warm liquid squirting from Georgina's body all over mine, I feel the most intense pleasure I've ever experienced, hands down. It's better than any drug—which isn't a figure of speech. My eyelids flutter at the injection of Georgina's drug into my vein. My eyes roll back. And I come inside her with the force of a rocket. Like I'm seeing God. Like I'm immortal.

As I come down, I crumple over her, quaking and sputtering. And she grips my sweaty hair and babbles incoherently about how amazing that was.

When I've caught my breath, I lift my head and gaze at Georgie's gorgeous face, and what I see there is sheer perfection: my own bliss reflected back at me. I'm on fire. High like never before. I pull her up, cradle her back, and devour her full lips with unfettered passion.

"Did you see what happened to me?" she sputters. "Oh my God, Reed. That's never happened to me before."

In reply, I kneel between her legs and begin licking up my sweet trophy. And she coos and sighs and laughs through it all.

"Oh, God, Reed. You're amazing. That was beyond incredible."

I smile and say nothing. What is there to say? I've done exactly what I set out to do. I've shown her what her body can do. *But only with me.*

She's an addict now.

Newly created.

A junkie hooked on a powerful drug. And that powerful drug... is *me.*

Chapter 9
Georgina

Freshly showered, I bop into Reed's kitchen to find him standing at his stove, dressed like a baller, and listening to blaring music. I wrap myself around his free arm, inhale the faint scent of his musky cologne, and swoon from the depths of my soul.

"A man who cooks me breakfast?" I purr. "I can't think of anything sexier. Well, yes, I can: a man who cooks me breakfast *after* giving me supernatural orgasms in a sex swing."

"Oh, you think you're getting some of this?" he teases, indicating the food he's stirring in his pan. "Fend for yourself, Ricci. This is all for me."

I giggle like a fool.

"Someone's in a good mood."

"What the hell did you do to me? I feel *high*."

He kisses the top of my head. "That tends to happen after a girl has the best orgasm of her life."

"*By far.*" I inhale deeply again. "God, that smells amazing. What is it?"

"Scrambled eggs with turkey chorizo, onions, jalapeños, and spinach."

I give his arm a little squeeze. "I meant your cologne, Tiger. But breakfast smells amazing, too."

"Did you do a couple shots of tequila before coming down here?"

"Nope. I did a couple shots of Reed Rivers. I'm punch

55

drunk on nothing but you, sexy man." I give his ass cheek a playful little pinch. "Knowing I'm going to get to be a butterfly caught in your net all week long is making me giddy."

Reed turns off the burner and reaches for a pepper shaker. "Don't get too attached to the sex swing. I get bored easily. I like mixing things up."

"Yes, I've stalked you online, remember? I'm well aware you get bored easily and like mixing things up." It's a reference to the many different women photographed on Reed's arm, as I'm sure he realizes—and I instantly regret saying it. Yes, I've kept my tone flirty. But it doesn't take a PhD in psychology to know the comment is borne of insecurity, an uncertainty about the rules of engagement here. After the life-changing sex we just had, I can't help wanting Reed all to myself. Is that an unreasonable expectation?

Reed puts down his spatula and grabs my shoulders gently. "Georgina, don't go psycho on me, okay? I meant I'm going to be mixing things up with *you,* and only you. The mere thought of you kissing another man while you're working on the special issue makes me want to commit murder."

I'm tentatively elated. But I can't help noticing Reed didn't make that last comment mutual. "And what will you be doing while I'm kissing only you for the entire summer? While I'm working on the special issue, will you be all mine, every bit as much as I'm all yours?"

He looks stern. "Georgina, I told you, quite clearly, the first night we met at the bar: it takes *a lot* to get me to agree to exclusivity."

I press my lips together, and he bursts out laughing at the expression on my face.

"Georgina, of course, it goes both ways! Yes, it takes a lot to get me to agree to exclusivity. But, baby, to put it mildly, you're... *a lot.*"

I giggle and throw my arms around his neck. "This is going to be so fun."

He kisses my cheek enthusiastically. "What your body did in the swing this morning was just the beginning. Oh my God. I'm gonna have so much fun with you."

He kisses me again before we reluctantly disengage from our embrace.

"I've instructed Owen to clear my calendar of all nighttime engagements this entire week," he says. "So I can focus all my attention on you."

I blush. "Thank you."

"Don't thank me. There's no place I'd rather be, every night this week, than with my butterfly, showing her all the amazing things her body can do."

I kiss him enthusiastically, and he squeezes my ass with equal fervor, making me squeal. But, finally, it's time to eat. Reed turns off the blaring music, grabs two plates, and divides the contents of his pan, and then we sit down at a small table in the corner of the kitchen to devour our feast.

After complimenting the meal, I ask, "So, what's on your schedule today, Music Mogul?"

"A meeting at my attorney's office, followed by my weekly Monday afternoon meeting with my team."

"Is your attorney that guy I met with his teenage daughter last night at the concert?"

"Yep. Leonard Schwartz. We've got some stuff to go over regarding a frivolous lawsuit." He tells me briefly about the lawsuit—basically, that some band has claimed Red Card Riot stole their song, based on a common chord progression that can be found in a million other songs.

"Can I come to the meeting with Leonard?" I ask. "I'd love to ask him about you."

He chuckles. "Sure. You might have to leave the meeting at some point, if we're going to talk about something that's attorney-client privileged. But you can certainly join the meeting at the beginning to interview Leonard."

"Great. I want to get an overview of what it takes, from a legal perspective, to run your empire."

"Knock yourself out."

We eat and talk, falling into easy, comfortable conversation. In response to my questions, Reed tells me a bit more about the copyright infringement lawsuit and I agree it sounds incredibly stupid.

"I took a class called Journalism and the Justice System this past year," I say. "It covered the intersection between journalism and the law. Like, how to report on trials and court cases and stuff. I learned so much. My professor said ninety percent of all lawsuits wind up settling—that only about ten percent of court cases ever go to trial."

"Those are probably national statistics," Reed says. "I think the rate of settlement is even higher in California, where litigation is like breathing. Either way, those numbers would be reversed for me. I wind up settling only five to ten percent of the cases filed against my various companies, and fighting the rest with everything I've got."

"Why are your numbers so upside-down like that?"

"Most companies think of settling cases as a cost of doing business. They've determined they'll spend less money on a settlement than on protracted legal fees. Or, they're risk averse and scared to death of losing, so they pay out."

"But you don't think that way?"

He shrugs. "I have a different philosophy. I can't stand legalized extortion, so I only settle when I'm sure a case has merit. Or, at least, when I think a *jury* will think a case has merit. Yes, I might pay a ton in attorneys' fees to fight a case, but it's worth it to me, so I can sleep at night." He takes a sip of his cappuccino. "Plus, I firmly believe the long-term deterrence value is worth something, though I can't prove that. You can't prove the cases *not* filed against you because you've scared away unscrupulous plaintiffs' attorneys with your big swinging dick."

I laugh.

"If someone has a legitimate beef with me, fine. Let them

bring it, and I'll settle the case like a man. Otherwise, they'd better brace themselves for a long, hard fight, that will ultimately lead to their resounding disembowelment."

I grimace. "Yikes."

"But enough about all that. Tell me about you, Georgie."

"What would you like to know?"

To my surprise, Reed launches into asking me a bunch of questions. He asks how I knew I wanted to pursue journalism. And then about my family and childhood. And, finally, about my mother and father. And to my surprise, he seems genuinely interested in my answers.

"You took it really hard when your dad remarried, huh?" he says.

I nod. "But when my father got cancer, I knew I had to let it go. Life is short, you know? I realized I love him with all my heart, unconditionally, and that's that. All that matters to me now is making sure my father stays cancer-free and keeps a roof over his head." I smile at Reed through my lashes. "Which is why I'm so grateful to you and CeeCee, for everything you've both done for my father and me."

Reed stiffens. "I haven't done anything. It was all CeeCee. She hired you. She's your boss."

I tilt my head. Shawn always made the exact same face Reed is making now, whenever I told him he was acting kind of weird and suspicious. "No, you've been amazing, Reed. You're letting me stay here this whole week, expense-free, remember? And you've also said you'll give me a hotel room after this week, too. Which means I'll be able to give almost all my salary to my father this whole summer, to help him try to catch up on his mortgage payments. And on top of all that, you're also throwing a party to end all parties on Saturday night *and* letting Alessandra come with me. I'd say all of that is a whole lot more than nothing. I was just saying I'm grateful."

Reed runs his finger down the handle of his fork. "Your father is behind on his mortgage payments?"

I blush. Why did I admit that? "I shouldn't have mentioned that to you. It makes me sound ungrateful for everything you and CeeCee have—"

"It's fine, Georgie. Tell me what's going on. He's behind on his payments?"

I press my lips together. I can't believe I let that slip.

He grabs my hand. "Did your father get behind when he got sick?"

I exhale and nod. "He hasn't returned to work since he was sick. He's a carpenter by trade, and chemo left him with some problems with his hands. But it'll be okay. I'm going to give him as much of the grant money as I can. It won't solve the problem completely, but it should buy him some time until we figure out what else we can do."

Reed rubs his forehead. But before he says a word, an older woman walks into the kitchen—a woman I immediately recognize from the photo on Reed's desk as Amalia. His housekeeper and second mother. Reed gets up and hugs Amalia in greeting, and then turns to me.

"Georgie, this is Amalia Vaccaro, my housekeeper. Amalia, this is Georgina Ricci. She'll be staying here for the summer."

My heart stops. Did Reed just say I'll be staying here... for the *summer*? When did I agree to that?

Reed continues, "I've put Georgie in the blue room upstairs. Make sure she's got everything she needs to feel at home, please."

"Of course. Hello, Georgina. Nice to meet you."

"And you." I stand and shake Amalia's hand, my mind racing about Reed's shocking comment.

"Please let me know if there's anything I can do to make your stay more comfortable this summer," Amalia says.

"Oh. Uh. Thank you. But I'm good. Just getting to stay here at all is a dream come true. It's a beautiful house."

"Yes, it is."

I look at Reed. "I'm so excited to stay for the summer. It's so much nicer here than any hotel."

Reed's handsome face breaks into a wide smile at my implicit acceptance of his invitation. Beaming a huge smile at me, he says, "Georgie, I just realized your bag isn't nearly big enough to hold everything you'll need this summer. I know you need a bathing suit. Probably some more workout gear. What else do you need?"

I'm buzzing. Tingling. Breathless. "No, no. I'm fine. If I need anything, there's a Target—"

"No, no, I insist. Amalia, do me a favor and give Georgie the house credit card for a shopping spree. Also, let's make her feel at home. Stock up on her favorite snacks and toiletries."

"Of course."

"Reed, I truly don't need anything."

"Georgina. You're staying for the summer. Not a week or a month. You need to feel completely at home. Which means we're going to make sure you have whatever your little heart desires." He winks. "Whether you like it or not."

Chapter 10
Georgina

Reed heads to his home office to make a few calls before it's time to leave for his attorney's office, so I hang back in the kitchen to help Amalia clean up from breakfast. In part, because I genuinely want to be helpful. Reed and I made the mess, after all, and I'd be embarrassed to leave it for someone else to deal with. But, also, because I'm dying to talk to Amalia about Reed. What was Reed like as a little boy? What is he like as an adult boss? And, also, what can Amalia tell me about Reed's relationship with his mother? I can't yet envision all the themes of my eventual article, but Reed's lovely relationship with his mother brings a whole new depth to him that people never see, and I'm thinking maybe I'll use it as a touchstone in my article... if, indeed, it's everything Reed said it was. I was probably imagining it, but I thought I noticed a strange tightness in Reed's demeanor, just for a moment, when he was telling me about his mother's happy life in Scarsdale last night. And I'm curious to know if Amalia might be able to shed any light on the topic for me.

Amalia and I are standing side by side at the sink. She's the washer in yellow rubber gloves. I'm the dryer, holding a towel.

"When we're done here, how about we make your list?" Amalia says, her tone as warm and maternal as her body language.

"I'm sorry... My list?"

She hands me a cutting board to dry. "The list of whatever you'd like to have in the house during your stay. Your favorite foods and snacks and toiletries. Like Reed said."

"Oh, that." I wave at the air. "Thank you so much, but I don't need anything."

Amalia smiles like I've said something amusing. "Reed was very clear. He won't accept 'Georgina said she doesn't need anything' as an answer from me, I'm afraid."

I protest. She insists. So, I say, "How about you do for me whatever stuff you normally do in situations like this?"

She looks at me blankly. "In situations like what?"

I take the pan Amalia hands me. "You know, whenever Reed has a house guest for an extended period. He mentioned he sometimes invites bands to stay here for weeks, even months, at a time, right?"

"Well, yes. But he's never once asked me to roll out the red carpet for a band the way he did for you. Quite the opposite." She chuckles. "When it comes to musicians staying here, Reed pretty much always says, 'They'll take what I give them and like it.'"

I chuckle with her. "That sounds like him."

"Yes, it does. Which makes what he said about you all the more remarkable." She stops scrubbing the plate in her hand and looks at me. "Honestly, this is uncharted territory for me. Reed has never once asked a woman to stay here with him for an extended period. And he's certainly never asked me to roll out the red carpet for one."

My lips part in surprise.

"Oh, goodness. I hope I'm not out of line telling you that," Amalia says.

"No. Not at all." My heart resumes beating again. "Thank you for telling me. It's a wonderful thing to know."

"You've obviously made quite an impression on him." She flashes a sweet smile. "And I can certainly see why."

Color rises in my cheeks. "Thank you. Reed has made quite an impression on me, too."

Amalia clearly likes that answer. Smiling, she resumes her work at the sink. "What do you do, Georgina? Are you in the entertainment industry? An actress or model?"

"Oh, no. I'm journalist." My soul swells with pride to be able to say that sentence. "I write for *Rock 'n' Roll*. The magazine about music?"

"Yes, I know it. How wonderful."

"I'm working hard to get onto the writing staff of this other magazine owned by the same company, a publication devoted to in-depth interviews and investigative journalism."

"Oh, how exciting. Good luck."

Imposter syndrome suddenly hits me hard. "Actually, I should clarify: I'm only a summer intern at *Rock 'n' Roll*. I just graduated from UCLA, and this is my first real job. But I'm going to work very hard, and do everything in my power to nab a permanent writing position after the summer."

Amalia hands me a plate to dry. "I have no doubt you'll get whatever position you desire."

Oh, God. Is Amalia putting two and two together right now—piecing together the facts that I'm a *summer* intern at *Rock 'n' Roll,* a *music* magazine, and, huh, what a coincidence, I'm also staying with Reed, the head of a *music* label, for the entire *summer*? Crap. When I said I was going to do "everything" in my power to nab a permanent position, did Amalia secretly snicker to herself and think, *Everything, including Reed.*

"The magazine assigned me to do an in-depth interview of Reed," I blurt, feeling the need to make it clear to Amalia I got my job because of my writing skills—and not because of any help from Reed. "I'll be following Reed around and writing about him for my article, so he invited me to stay here for the summer to make things more convenient."

She smiles kindly. "Well, that makes perfect sense." She

peels off her yellow rubber gloves. "I hope everything works out for you and your career, exactly as you're hoping, Georgie. May I call you Georgie?"

"Yes, I love being called that."

Shit. Now, I feel like I went overboard making Reed and me seem like nothing but interviewer and interviewee. Clearly, she knows there's more to it than that, seeing as how Reed has invited me to stay here for the entire summer, and he's *never* done that before. I don't want her to think I'm a liar.

"But, you know, besides the interview, Reed and I have also clicked personally," I say quickly. "He's been so sweet."

"I'm so glad," she says. And there's no judgment whatsoever in her tone. She puts her sponge and gloves and dishwashing soap away, and moves to the refrigerator. Which is where she begins pulling out ingredients and putting them onto the island. "Don't feel like you have to stay here with me, Georgie. I love the company, but I'm sure you're very busy."

"I'm not, actually. I'm just waiting for Reed to finish his calls. What's all this for?" I motion to the items she's placing on the island.

"I'm making a big pot of Reed's favorite chicken tortilla soup for dinner tonight. He asked me to make 'dinner for two.'"

I blush at the knowing look in her eye. She's sweet and nonjudgmental, but she's no fool. She knows exactly what's going on between Reed and me. Of course.

"Would you like some help making the soup?" I ask, my pulse pounding. "I'm a terrible cook—the absolute worst—so don't get too excited about my offer. But I can certainly help chop vegetables, if you don't mind a random finger in with your chopped onions."

She laughs. "No fingers, please. And, yes, I'd love your help." She grabs a cutting board and knife for me, and hands me an apron. "Reed likes this particular recipe because my version is filled with super foods. He's usually quite strict about what he eats. Fitness and nutrition are passions for him."

"Yes, he's mentioned that. Not that he needed to say it out loud. His body makes it pretty clear he takes excellent care of himself." I press my lips together again. What the hell is wrong with me? This is Reed's second mother, and I've just implied I've seen him naked? Seriously, I know I grew up without a mother, but this is ridiculous.

Thankfully, though, Amalia seems unfazed by my stumbling. In fact, she seems nothing but charmed—the same way CeeCee was when we had coffee together after the panel discussion.

Without missing a beat, she gives me some instruction, including showing me how to make a claw with my left hand while chopping so I don't cut off my fingers, and then puts me to work. And, in short order, I'm a regular sous chef, chopping away at vegetables while Amalia sautées onions at a burner across from me.

As we work at our stations, we chat easily, and Amalia's maternal demeanor calms me, reassuring me with each passing minute she's not judging me for having a fling with her much older, and powerful, boss. Amalia asks me questions, and, soon, I'm telling her about my life—my schooling and family. And I return the favor, drawing her out by asking her questions about her large family, which, it turns out, includes lots of beloved grandchildren.

Finally, about twenty minutes into our conversation, I feel comfortable enough to broach my primary topic of interest.

"So, Reed tells me you've known him his whole life?"

"Yes, I was there when they brought tiny little Reed Charlemagne Rivers home from the hospital, looking as sweet as can be." She chuckles. "He's not tiny anymore, obviously, but he's still as sweet as can be."

Yes, he is, I think. Followed immediately by, *Wow, what a difference a day makes.* Because, as late as yesterday, I never would have believed anyone would describe Reed Rivers as "sweet." But here I am, thinking that word describes him perfectly, after the whirlwind of the past twenty-four hours. Indeed, just this fast, I'm thinking there might be even more sweetness to Reed than I've seen. More than I ever thought possible.

But back to work.

I've got a job to do.

And I'm pretty sure Amalia, who's known Reed his entire life, is the perfect person to give me insight into this fiercely private man.

I say, "It's clear Reed feels exactly the same way about you, Amalia—that you're sweet as can be. Just this morning, he was telling me about his family, and he explicitly said he considers you a member of his family."

She stops what she's doing and looks at me, floored. "Reed said that?"

"He did. In fact, he said he loves you. And that he missed you so much after his father went to prison, when he was thirteen, he hired you as an adult, ten years later, the minute he was financially able to swing it. He said having you back in his life was so important to him, he hired you even before he bought his first sports car."

Okay, yes, I'm extrapolating and expanding ever so slightly from the actual words Reed said. But why else would Reed have hired Amalia the moment he was able to do so, even before buying a sports car, if he hadn't missed her terribly after she'd stopped working for his family—which Reed did explicitly say, coincided with his father going to prison?

From Amalia's body language, it's clear she's blown away by what I've said. Indeed, if I blew on her, she'd tip over. She leans her hip against the island and puts her hand on her heart.

"It means the world to me to hear Reed said all of that. Thank you so much for telling me this, Georgie."

"You're welcome." My heart skips a beat. It's been a long time since I've hung out in a kitchen with a kind, older woman, and helped her cook a meal. The experience is causing my heart to flutter like crazy. "Reed actually referred to you as his second mother." Am I fibbing? Did Reed say that, or did I? I can't recall. But either way, even if I was the one who said it, Reed certainly didn't correct me. And he *did* say he loves Amalia, and a photo of his mother and Amalia is one of the few personal shots in the house... So, I think it's safe to say I haven't told a lie.

"I love that sweet man so much," Amalia says, more to herself than to me. For a moment, she looks lost in thought. But then she shakes off her reverie, sighs, and smiles. "I'm frankly quite surprised Reed said all this to you. Especially, the part about me being with his family until Mr. Rivers went to prison. Reed is an extremely private person. Especially about his father, and his childhood. I think he doesn't like being reminded of anything unpleasant. He prefers not to think about it."

My heart is galloping. I have a feeling, if I handle this conversation right, I'll walk away with a goldmine of insight into parts of Reed he never shows the world. And I won't have to pull it out of Reed to get it. "Reed actually told me a very poignant story about his father last night in the garage. A story about how Reed used to golf with his father every weekend. The point of the story was to explain to me how devastated Reed was when he realized his father had actually committed the crimes he'd been accused of. So much so, he doesn't play golf now, because it brings up too many bad memories."

Amalia's jaw drops. Quickly, she looks down—and there's no doubt she's getting a grip on her emotions. When she looks up again, she looks pale. "I wish so badly I could

68

have done more for Reed after his father went to prison. But there was only so much I could do."

"Oh, of course, Amalia. I'm sure Reed knows that. From what he said, you've been a very calming, nurturing presence for him his whole life."

Again, she looks shocked. "Wow. Reed really *has* shared a lot with you about his life, hasn't he?"

"Well, I have been assigned to write an in-depth article about him. But even more than that, we've really clicked, maybe because I've shared things about my life with him, too. I told him about my mother, who died when I was nine, and that's something I never, ever talk about with anyone. The same as Reed, I'm a person who prefers not to talk too much about things that make me sad."

"Oh, honey. I'm so sorry about your mother."

"Thank you. I think me opening up about that made Reed feel comfortable to do the same with me."

"Well, that makes a lot of sense. You and Reed have a shared experience. I mean, it's not the exact same thing, but both of you did lose your mothers at the exact same age."

I'm stumped. Reed lost his mother at nine? "Right," I say, like I know exactly what Amalia is talking about... even though, in truth, I haven't a clue. If Reed lost his mother at age nine, then who's the mother happily doing yoga and painting in Scarsdale with her boyfriend, Lee? Also, if Reed lost his mother at nine, why on earth didn't he mention that fact to me after I told him about *my* mother? I mean, not last night, when I was screaming at him like a freaking maniac. But this morning, during our amazing, intimate conversation in the gym, when we were both so open and apologetic and kind?

I'm thoroughly confused.

Did Reed's biological mother die when he was nine, and then his Dad somehow remarried before being shipped off to prison, and the woman in Scarsdale is actually his *stepmother*—a woman Reed always thinks of as his mother? That could be it. But, damn, if that's the case, Reed's father got married after the death of his wife awfully fast. As quickly as my own father did. Which, again, I would have expected Reed to mention when I was telling him about my father and Paula.

My head teeming with thoughts, I chop some carrots for a long moment, and finally cast out my fishing rod. "I'm so proud of Reed for all he's accomplished in his life," I say, "especially after everything he went through as a child."

"Oh, yes. I'm enormously proud of him for that, too. It breaks my heart, just thinking about everything he went through. But he's come out the other side and made all his dreams come true, while still retaining his kind heart. That's the best thing of all, if you ask me—that he's as kind and generous and sweet as ever, despite all his success."

Okay, who the fuck is Amalia talking about? I mean, yes, Reed has been enormously generous and sweet with me, but Amalia is making him out to be a saint.

"He really is so generous and sweet," I agree. "I mean, he didn't simply let Henn throw his wedding here. He paid for everything."

"Oh, I know. But that's Reed. If he cares about you, he'll move heaven and earth to make you happy."

"So I'm discovering. You know what I think? Reed is terribly misunderstood by people who don't know him well."

She stops what she's doing on a dime. "Oh my gosh, yes, he is! I'm so glad you understand that about him, Georgina, so you can show the world the *real* Reed in your article. So many people don't see his heart. They think he's only a shrewd businessman. But he's so much more than that."

"That's what I like about Reed most. That he's got so many layers."

Amalia nods enthusiastically.

And we both fall silent for a moment.

Finally, Amalia says, "To be honest, it shattered me to watch poor Reed's world come crashing down the way it did."

I continue chopping methodically, even though my mind is reeling. Is that a reference to Reed's father's arrest and conviction? Or a reference to whatever happened to Reed's mother when he was nine? "Yeah, from what Reed told me," I say, "it seems like everything was extremely difficult for him." What "everything" am I talking about? Honestly, I have no idea.

"I just felt so powerless to do anything to help him," Amalia laments. "And then his father was arrested, only a few short years later, and I thought, 'Oh my gosh. How much can that poor boy take?'"

"You did everything you could," I say vaguely, even though I still don't have a clue what we're talking about. "Reed knows that."

Amalia exhales deeply and stops what she's doing at the stove, so I stop chopping and give her my undivided attention.

"I tried to take him in when his father went to prison," she says. "But the judge said I wasn't a relative, so I couldn't have him. It broke my heart to watch him get sent to live with some distant relative he barely knew, rather than with me. I wanted to be the one to take him because I loved him like my own. I truly did." She wipes her eyes with her apron. "I still do."

Well, this is new information. When Reed's father was arrested, Reed was sent to live with a distant relative? Why? Where was Reed's mother... or his stepmother, if that's who the happy woman in Scarsdale is? Oh, God, I'm so confused. I move around to Amalia on the other side of the island, and put my hand on her shoulder reassuringly. "I'm sure Reed knows you did your best, Amalia."

Amalia shakes her head. "I cried when I couldn't get custody of him. I cried for myself and for Reed, and for his poor mother, too. Of course, I would have preferred his mother could have taken care of him, but that simply wasn't possible. Truly, it was just a tragedy, all around, for all of us."

"Yes, but you wouldn't be here with Reed now, all these years later, if he felt anything but love and gratitude toward you."

"Thank you. I only want the best for him."

"Of course, you do. I think that's what Reed appreciates about his relationship with you. How uncomplicated it is. When he told me about his mother... and her life in Scarsdale..." I trail off, not sure how to complete the sentence. What the hell are we talking about?

"Yes, I know Reed wishes she'd agree to transfer to the facility in Malibu. But she won't leave the one in Scarsdale."

And there it is. Finally. The truth. The word that explains that tightness I thought I saw on Reed's face last night when he talked about his mother's happy, perfect life in Scarsdale with her boyfriend, Lee. *Facility*. As in *mental* facility?

"Yes, exactly," I say calmly, even though my synapses are exploding. "He said he gets out there to visit as much as he can, but I'm sure it would be easier if she'd transfer to the facility in Malibu."

"Of course, it would. I'm sure it hurts Reed, more than he lets on, that she won't move to a facility closer to him, so he can spend more time with her and take care of her the way he wants to do." She looks toward the door of the kitchen, and then back at me. "I'm not surprised Eleanor won't move closer, honestly. She never put her boys first, right from the start. That was the hardest thing for me to watch, as their nanny. A mother should *always* put her children first, whether she's got a nanny or not."

Holy fuck burgers. My brain is whirring and clacking now, deftly processing the shreds of new information Amalia just supplied to me. *Eleanor*. Note to self: gather every bit of information you can on Eleanor Rivers of Scarsdale. *Boys*. Plural. Amalia said Eleanor never put the *boys* first. And that

Amalia was "their" nanny. But Reed didn't mention he has a brother. Only a sister. And I don't think Wikipedia mentioned a brother.

I put down my knife, every molecule of my skin buzzing. "Hey, Amalia. I'm sorry. I just remembered I have to research something for one of the articles I'm writing. I'm sorry to ditch my duties as your sous chef, but—"

"Go, go. This is my job, not yours. Thank you for the conversation. I've wanted to talk to someone about these things for a very long time." She smiles kindly. "You're absolutely lovely, Georgie. It's no wonder Reed is so taken with you."

My heart squeezes. "Thank you. It's no wonder Reed loves you so much. I'm looking forward to cooking and chatting with you a lot this summer."

Amalia's face lights up. "I have some wonderful recipes I'd be happy to teach you."

"I'd love that." I hug Amalia goodbye, and then sprint upstairs to my room, where I flip open my laptop and hop online. Obviously, there's a whole lot about Reed's life he doesn't want to talk about. Which is perfectly fine. But that's not going to stop me from digging a little deeper... to try to get to know the man *behind* The Man with the Midas Touch... whether he wants me to... or not.

Chapter 11
Reed

I lean back in my chair, my phone pressed against my ear, looking out the window of my home office.

"Hi, boss," Owen says, answering my call. "Did the bike arrive?"

"It did. Right on time. Thank you."

"Did she like it?"

"She went apeshit for it." I smile to myself, remembering Georgie's jiggling happy dance this morning when she found out that second Peloton bike was hers. "Actually, her reaction made me want to give her even more gifts, just to see her lose her shit like that again and again. I was thinking of maybe getting her a car. I'd want to get her something cute and fun and reliable—a little convertible, maybe—but nothing too crazy in terms of pricing."

Owen pauses. "So, his and hers Bugattis are out of the question, then?"

I ignore the obvious snark. "I want something to bowl her over, but not something that will make me look like a madman. If the car is too extravagant, she'll think it implies some sort of commitment past the summer. And that wouldn't be good."

"As opposed to a commitment *within* the summer?"

"Oh. Yeah. Change of plans. Georgina's not staying at my house for a week anymore. I asked her this morning to stay for the entire summer, and she said yes."

He's quiet for a moment. And then, "Wow. That's quite a 'purely professional relationship' you're having with her, Reed."

I smile to myself. "Just do some research for me on cute little convertibles, would you? Tell me what you recommend."

"I already know exactly what I recommend: lay off the blow, Reed."

"I'm not high, Owen. At least, not on coke. Georgina doesn't own a car. Not even a shitty one. Who the hell doesn't own a car in LA? She needs one."

"You don't think maybe *any* car would be too extravagant a gift that makes you look like a madman? It's still *really* early days, Reed."

My spirit falls. I say nothing.

"You gave her a Peloton on day one. Maybe that's enough for now?"

My heart is thundering. He's right. I've let myself get swept away. I'm moving way too fast and I need to slow down. "A Pilates machine, then. She said she taught spin *and* Pilates classes. I don't know anything about Pilates. Isn't there a machine for that?"

"Yes, it's called a reformer. But, Reed. I'm not kidding this time. Do I need to call Promises and see if they've got a bed for you? Are you back on the blow?"

"I don't need rehab, Owen. I'm fine. I'm just... "

In a flash, my mind wanders to Georgie. In rapid-fire succession, I see her happy dance again. And then her floating naked in my moonlit pool. I see her standing naked underneath my bedroom window. And the look on her face when that orgasm in the sex swing shattered her. And, finally, I see the beautiful look of contrition on her face when she apologized to me this morning. The look that grabbed my heart in its iron fist.

And it suddenly occurs to me...

Holy shit.

Georgina isn't the one who's the junkie here. *She's the drug*!

"Reed?" Owen says. "You're just... what?"

I scrub my palm over my stubble. "Fucked." I shake it off. "Moving on. No car. Look into Pilates machines for me, okay? Now, tell me about the party. You've got everything cooking?"

Owen rattles off a brief update. He tells me invitations went out an hour ago. And that everyone who's not on tour knows it's mandatory they come. He says, "And I got your note about us having a stage filled with musical instruments, in addition to a DJ—so musicians can hop up there in random combinations and jam together. Great idea."

I thank him and give him my notes for Watch Party's upcoming album, which I finished listening to this morning while making breakfast, and we end the call.

After disconnecting with Owen, I get a text from Henn, telling me he just heard about the party on Saturday. But rather than text him back, I decide to call him, since I've got a few minutes before I have to head out to my meeting with Leonard.

"Hello, brother," Henn says. "What's up?"

"Nothing much. I'm busy conquering the world. You?"

"Oh, I'm just, you know, living the thug life. Hannah had a big project due at work and the nanny called in sick, so I'm trying to bang out some code for a client while Hazel is taking her morning nap. She's in her crib right now, sleeping butts-up coconut."

I chuckle. "I'm afraid to ask."

"That's what Hannah calls it when Hazel's sleeping with her bottom straight in the air. She smashes her cheek into the mattress and curls her little legs up underneath her, and points her butt straight up. It's the cutest thing I've ever seen."

"Send me a pic."

"Reed, Hazel is my *baby*."

I laugh. "I want to see."

"Are you drunk?"

"I'm just in a good mood. Now, send me a fucking photo of your baby doing butts up coconut before I beat your scrawny ass. My time is valuable, man. I don't beg."

He laughs.

My phone pings.

"I sent it."

"Aw. You're right. That *is* adorable."

"I can't get enough. I've got like nine hundred photos of the same basic shot on my phone." He chuckles happily. "But, surely, you didn't call to hear me gush about Hazel. I'm guessing you're calling about your party? I RSVP'd right before you called. It's perfect timing. Hannah's mom and my parents were already coming into town for the weekend for Hazel's birthday party on Sunday, so we've got overnight babysitting. Same with Josh and Kat."

"Oh, you've talked to Josh? He's coming, for sure?"

"Yeah, he texted both of us. You didn't see? He and Kat changed their flight to come to LA on Friday now."

"Awesome. You guys will have to pre-party at my house on Saturday afternoon."

"Count us in." He pauses. "So, you haven't said a word about Hazel's birthday party being the next day."

"Yeah, I totally forgot about that. Does it start before two?"

"No. It starts at three."

"And you'll be serving booze, I hope—preferably Bloody Marys?"

"Yes, to booze. I'll add Bloody Marys to the menu, specifically."

"Then I'll be there."

Henn pauses. "That's it? You're not going to complain the guest of honor has no idea it's her fucking birthday? Or that we'll be partying till dawn at your place, and that getting up for a baby's birthday party the next day is the last thing you want to do?"

I laugh. "Nope. I'm looking forward to Hazel's birthday bash. My party will be one for the record books, but it'll be crazy and hectic. It'll be nice to hang out with everyone the next day in a chill environment where we can actually talk. Just don't let me down on those Bloody Marys, and we're good."

"Wow. You're in a shockingly good mood."

I can't help smiling from ear to ear. "Yes, I am."

"Is there a specific reason?"

My smile broadens. I bite my lower lip. "Remember that hot bartender from Bernie's the other night?"

"No. Remind me what she looks like."

He's being sarcastic. Georgina is unforgettable.

"She's here. She stayed the night."

"*No.*"

"Yep."

He makes a sound like he's blown away. "Well, that's a twist I didn't see coming. I thought you said she hated your guts. You said she told you to fuck off and die in front of your gate and then took off in an Uber."

"She did." I chuckle. "But I happened to see her at the RCR show last night, and one thing led to another... And now she's here. I just made her breakfast, Henny."

"She's *breakfast-worthy*?" He whistles. "Wow. That was fast. Okay, back up. How did you 'happen' to run into her at the RCR concert? You pulled strings, didn't you? You made her think she'd won backstage tickets in a contest or something."

I smirk to myself. "You think I'm so Machiavellian, so sneaky and diabolical, I'd pull strings behind the scenes to create a situation where I could have a second bite at the apple with a woman who'd rejected me, without her even realizing I'd played God?"

"That's precisely what I think of you."

"Well, you're absolutely right. Thank you for knowing me so well."

I tell Henn the whole story. Georgina's internship, and how it came about. I tell him about the grant and that Georgina has no idea I'm the one who funded it. And, finally, I tell him about the interview I had to throw into the pot to get CeeCee to agree to doing the special issue.

"Wow, that's going to be one hell of a thorough interview when she's through with you," Henn says. "Considering she's got the entire summer to gather information."

"Yeah, especially since Georgina will be staying here at my place the entire summer."

"You're shitting me."

"Nope. I invited her this morning. And she said yes."

He's quiet for a beat. "I'm sorry. Could you hand the phone back to Reed, please?"

I laugh. "I know. It's crazy."

"You invited her for the summer... for the article?"

Anxiety flashes through me. Did I jump the gun? Inviting Georgie for the whole summer was a spur of the minute decision. Seeing her with Amalia, for some reason... it felt so natural and right. Plus, I knew she'd be in my life throughout the summer, regardless, working on the special issue... And, suddenly, I couldn't stand the thought of Georgina staying in a hotel throughout the summer, when she could be under my roof... "No, I asked her to stay for purely personal reasons," I admit.

"That's awesome, Reed. Wow. Plus, the incidental benefit is her interview of you is going to be amazing."

"I'm sure it will be. Unfortunately for Georgie, however, most of what she writes won't see the light of day."

"What do you mean?"

"Georgie made a rookie error. She gave me full editorial

control over whatever she ultimately writes about me. Of course, I'll green light some of it. Whatever's on-brand for *Rock 'n' Roll,* plus a little extra something to give her an exclusive scoop. But beyond that, whatever she might write about my childhood and my family, that shit is coming out."

He sighs. "I know you hate talking about that stuff. But I think you should keep an open mind here, Reed. You never know. You might really like her article. The truth shall set you free, my brother."

"My truth is nobody's fucking business, Henn."

He sighs. "Yeah, I know. But let's think this through for a minute. Imagine she works all summer long on some epic article about you, something she's really proud of and excited to submit to her boss, and you nix ninety percent of it. She'll be crushed. Not to mention she'll hate you."

"She's the one who fucked up and gave me full editorial control. It'll be a life lesson for her."

"A life lesson about not trusting the asshole she's slept with all summer? Reed, implicit in your agreement with her was that she can trust you with her baby. She trusts that you'll give due consideration to whatever she ultimately writes."

I say nothing.

"I'm just saying you sound like you're walking on air today. You made her breakfast, for fuck's sake, and invited her to stay for the summer, just for the fun of it. And you're not even grouchy about Hazel's birthday party on Sunday. Whatever spell she's cast on you, don't fuck it up by sending her on a wild-goose chase this entire summer that will end in her hating you."

He's right.

Georgina's going to hate me at the end of this.

Fuck.

My mind is racing. Calculating. Seeking a solution. And, finally, I've got it. Georgina can't hate me if I've already given her something even *better* than an in-depth interview of *me*. Something that equally accomplishes her goal. At the end of the day, Georgie doesn't even want an interview of me, specifically. She wants to impress CeeCee enough to get hired onto the writing staff of *Dig a Little Deeper*, and my interview is merely a means to an end. Which means I know exactly what to do.

"She won't hate me if I get her an even better interview than mine," I say. "All I've got to do is get her an A-list interview, with someone way better than me, and all will be forgiven."

"I'm not sure it works that way."

"Sure, it does. I've invited a shit-ton of A-listers to my party on Saturday, and I'll tell Owen to invite a shit-ton more. I'll introduce Georgie around on Saturday night, and see who she clicks with and make it happen for her." I smile. "This is actually a great plan. Georgie clicks with everyone she meets. It's like the girl has magical powers. She'll have her pick of the litter on Saturday night."

"If you say so," Henn says half-heartedly.

An idea pings me. "But it certainly wouldn't hurt to get myself some insurance—some proverbial belts and suspenders. I need a favor, Henny."

I tell Henn about Georgie's father—specifically, about his recent cancer battle and the financial troubles he's having because of it. "So, will you do me a favor and hack his bank or whatever, and find out how much he owes on his condo? And while you're at it, you might as well find out how much Georgina owes in student loans. Just find out Georgie's and her father's complete financial situations for me, if you would."

The line is silent.

"Are you still there?"

"Yeah, I'm here," Henn says.

"Can you do all that for me?"

"It should be easy to do. But *why*, exactly, do you want to know this stuff?"

"Just in case I want to play Fairy Godfather at some point."

"In other words, you're worried you're going to piss her off with the article, so you want to have her 'price' ready to go, just in case?"

I frown. My two best friends know me, inside and out. It's a blessing and a curse.

"Reed, listen to me," Henn says. "In all the time I've known you, I've never once heard you sound this jacked up about a woman. You sound like I did when I met Hannah— like you've been struck by a lightning bolt."

I roll my eyes. It's the stupidest thing I've ever heard in my life.

Henn says, "For fuck's sake, Reed, if you break her trust, you won't be able to buy your way out of it. Instead, how about *not* doing anything to make her hate you? How about opening up and telling her about your life and letting her write the article and get to know you. How about enjoying the summer with an open mind and seeing where that takes you. Take a chance on this girl. Take a chance on what might happen if you let down your guard a bit."

"Are you done?"

He sighs. "Yes."

"Thank you for the TED Talk, Peter. It was inspiring. But let me remind you, she's writing an article about me. She's not here to 'get to know me' in a vacuum. She's a shark, this girl. It's my favorite thing about her. Don't get me wrong. But we're not just two people shacking up. She wants something from me. So, 'letting down my guard' completely, as you've suggested, would be a felony stupid thing for me to do."

He sighs. "If you say so."

"I do. So, will you get me the financials I've asked for, or not?"

"Of course, I will. Just send me the names and whatever information, and I'll get it to you in a couple days."

"Thank you. I'll send you a text after we hang up."

"So, will you be bringing this breakfast-worthy girl with you on Sunday to Hazel's party?"

To my surprise, my heart leaps at the idea. I never bring dates to personal events with my good friends. Hardly ever to work events, either. And yet, here I am, eager to bring Georgina to my best friend's house and introduce her to pretty much everyone I care about, all in one fell swoop... Indeed, I can't wait to sit back and smile with amusement as Georgina casts her uniquely powerful spell on every last one of them.

"Yeah, I'll bring her," I say, trying to sound nonchalant.

But Henn's not a fool. He knows this is totally outside the box for me. "Holy shit, Reed," he says. Which is exactly what I was expecting him to say. But then, he goes on to say something I'm not. "For a smart man, you're dumb as dirt sometimes."

"Huh?"

"Don't fuck this up!" he booms. "Be completely honest with this girl. Let her know the real you. In fact, why all the secrecy about you funding her grant? Tell her so she knows what a generous guy you are. I'm sure she'll be thrilled to find out you're the reason her internship is a paid one."

"Are you insane? Henn, when I came up with the idea to donate to the cancer charity, my main motivation was to arrange things behind the scenes so I could get her into bed. You think she won't realize that in two seconds flat? The last thing I need is for her to doubt she got her job on her merits. Which she totally did, by the way. CeeCee was going to hire her, regardless."

"You truly don't think Georgina would be grateful to you for helping her?"

My stomach clenches fiercely. "She's proud, Henn. It means the world to her to be a 'professional writer.' I don't want her to doubt herself."

"But if she finds out you're the source of the grant, later, it'll be ten times worse than if you'd told her on your own, up front. You *not* telling her makes it seem like you did something nefarious and creepy, rather than something generous and kind."

"She won't find out."

"Well, if she does, paying off her dad's mortgage and her student loans won't fix the problem. Trust can't be bought."

I respect Henn's mind more than anyone's, probably. He's a literal genius—the smartest guy I've ever met. But this time, he's dead wrong. "I'm not telling Georgina jack shit about the grant, and she won't find out about it on her own. But, on the off-chance she does, then she'll forgive me because, by then, I'll have gotten her an A-list interview with someone even better than me *and* I'll have the information I need to immediately pay off her debts in full, too." I look at my watch. "I can't talk about this anymore with you. I've got to head to a meeting at my attorney's office. Thanks for getting me that info. I'll text you and everyone about a pre-party on Saturday."

"Hey, Reed. I really think—"

"Drop it, Henn. I've got this. I'll see you on Saturday. Thanks for the favor. Bye."

Chapter 12
Georgina

Have you ever met some regular, nice person, and instantly connected with them in a genuine, easy way... only to find out *later* that regular, nice person was actually a big wig? Someone who would have intimidated the heck out of you, if only you'd known? But by then it was too late to feel intimidated. The easy friendship was already formed. The connection made.

Well, that's what happened when I met Reed's longtime attorney, Leonard. When I encountered him backstage at the RCR concert last night, he was a sweet older dude in jeans and a Red Card Riot T-shirt who was geeking out over watching his teenage daughter and her friends meet the band. But now that I'm sitting across from Leonard in his sleek office, and I can see the impressive diplomas and framed magazine covers and awards on his walls, I'm realizing he's actually a big wig. But it's too late now for me to feel intimidated, because all I see when I look into his smiling face is the sweet, kind dude in jeans and a Red Card Riot T-shirt from last night.

It's a lucky thing for me, actually. It's meant I've been able to dive right into deftly interviewing Leonard about the legal services his firm provides Reed and Reed's various businesses, without feeling hampered by nerves.

Unfortunately, though, all good things must come to an end. When the expert witness Reed and Leonard have been waiting on finally arrives, apologizing profusely for her delay due to traffic, it's time for me to head out and leave the trio to their meeting. She's the same woman who moderated the panel discussion the other day, though—the dean of UCLA's music school—so, before heading out the door, I mention I was in attendance at the panel and thoroughly enjoyed it.

"Oh, are you a music student?" she asks.

"No, I just graduated with a degree in journalism."

Reed pipes in. "Georgie is interning for *Rock 'n' Roll.* She's been assigned to write an in-depth article about me, so she's shadowing me this entire week. I've been told she's a brilliant writer. One to watch."

Goosebumps erupt on my skin, thanks to Reed's amazing words about me, and his tone while saying them. Oh my gosh. Everything Reed just said makes me want to jump his bones the moment we walk through his front door later tonight!

The woman asks me some polite questions about my internship, which I answer, but, soon, it's clear I should run along to let them get to work.

"If you'd like a quiet place to work while you wait for Reed, I can set you up in a conference room," Leonard offers.

"No, thank you," I say. "I think I'll head to a coffee place nearby and plan to come back here . . .?"

"In a couple hours or so," Leonard supplies.

"Perfect. Thank you for all the helpful information, Leonard. It was invaluable to me."

"It was my genuine pleasure, Georgina. Your questions were thoughtful and full of insight."

I blush. "Thank you. Please say hello to McKenzie and her adorable friends for me."

"I will."

I look at Reed and my heart skips a beat at the twinkle in his brown eyes. "Thank you for letting me tag along today. It's been so helpful."

"My pleasure, Georgina. I was also impressed with the

questions you asked. CeeCee told me you're one of the most promising newbies she's ever had the pleasure to hire—if not the most promising. And I can see why."

Biting back a massive smile, I grab my laptop, say my last goodbyes, and head out the door. But I'm not going to a coffee place, like I said. I'm heading straight to the courthouse a few blocks away to do a little research. From what Leonard just explained to me about Reed's legal affairs, combined with something Reed said to me last night, I've got a strong hunch there's a damned good story out there, waiting to be uncovered by the right journalist. I just have to be smart enough, and scrappy enough, to be the one to find it.

Chapter 13
Georgina

While sitting on the courthouse steps with a fish taco, I read the lengthy printout I obtained a few minutes ago from a court clerk inside. Specifically, it's a list of every lawsuit filed against Reed and his various companies over the past ten years.

The list includes the following basic information about each lawsuit, without providing any details about the facts or specific claims asserted: the plaintiff's name, the defendants' names, and the general nature of claims asserted—for example, personal injury, breach of contract, wrongful termination, copyright infringement, etcetera. And, finally, the printout notes the ultimate disposition of the case. For instance, sometimes, judgment was granted, or the case dismissed, by the judge on a motion filed by one of the parties. Occasionally, some of the cases went all the way to trial. And, in rare instances, a given case was dismissed after the parties had reached a confidential settlement.

Of course, it's only the last category of cases that interest me, the ones Reed, or his particular company, settled, seeing as how Reed told me last night he only settles a case when he believes it has merit. Or, at least, when he thinks a jury would think so.

I pull a yellow highlighter from my computer bag and go down the "ultimate disposition" column, marking all the settled cases. But when I go back up to the top and begin going through my yellow markings, I realize this isn't the right approach. My search criteria was too broad, resulting in a list of crap I don't care about in the slightest. A slip-and-fall lawsuit filed against one of Reed's nightclubs, for instance. Another slip-and-fall against Reed's real estate holding company, regarding one of his apartment buildings. A lawsuit filed by a guy against the partnership that owns a nightclub Reed co-owns, claiming the guy didn't get paid his accrued overtime.

Snooze.

Frankly, I don't know what I'm looking for here. But my gut tells me to keep looking . . .

I pull the cap off a green highlighter pen this time, and decide to go down a different column on the printout. This time, I look at only the yellow-marked cases—the ones Reed's settled—but mark in green only the ones filed against River Records, specifically, as opposed to one of Reed's many other businesses. And, lo and behold, when I reach the end of the list this time, and I look at the intersection of my yellow and green markings, I discover the entire universe of cases now only numbers three:

First, a lawsuit filed nine years ago by "ALM Business Properties" against Reed, personally, and River Records, alleging breach of lease. That doesn't sound particularly sexy to me, but I decide to get a copy of it from the court clerk, nonetheless. Why not?

Second, a lawsuit filed eight years ago by someone named Stephanie Moreland against Reed, personally, and River Records, alleging wrongful termination, breach of contract, and sexual harassment. *Whoa.* Sexual harassment? Yeah, I'm definitely getting a copy of that one.

And, third, a lawsuit filed six years ago by a guy named Troy Eklund against Reed, personally, and River Records, alleging breach of contract, breach of the implied covenant of good faith and fair dealing, fraud, and assault. Another *whoa.*

Fraud? Assault? Definitely another set of documents to order from the court clerk.

I scan the printout one more time, just to be thorough, and then shove my green and yellow highlighters back into my computer bag, throw away the empty wrapper from my delicious fish taco, and race into the courthouse. After making it through security at the front door, and then waiting in line at the clerk's office, I finally make it to the counter, coincidentally, getting the same guy who helped me with the printout earlier.

"Hello again," he says, shooting me a wide smile.

"Hello there. I've been through the list you gave me and figured out which lawsuits I'd like to copy." I plop the printout onto the counter between us. "The good news for me is that I only need three lawsuits on this huge list."

"Easy peasy. I'll have copies delivered to you in three to five hours. Just fill this out." He slides a form across the counter to me.

I bite my lip. "Is there any way I could get those records from you now—like, within the next hour?" I lean forward and flash him my most charming smile. "It'd be a huge help to me. My boss said she wants this stuff 'right away.' And it's my first week on the job, so I'd really like to impress her."

The guy's eyes flicker to my chest, ever so briefly, before drifting back to my face. "Yeah, okay. But just this once. Don't tell anyone I bumped you to the front of the queue, okay?"

"I promise. Thank you so much." I look at his nametag. "*Charles*. I'm grateful."

I read off the case numbers of all three cases, and Charles inputs them into his computer.

"You're in luck. All three cases are here in this building, in storage," he says. "I'll just have to go into the records room to grab whatever is there and make copies. It shouldn't take me more than thirty minutes or so, depending on how many documents are in each file."

"Wow. You're a life-saver."

He turns to go.

"Actually, before you go. While I'm waiting, I'd love to look at another printout. This time, regarding all the lawsuits filed against a different defendant."

"Sure." He returns to his keyboard. "What's the defendant's name?"

"Eleanor Charpentier Rivers."

It was easy to locate Reed's mother online this morning. Eleanor Rivers of Scarsdale, New York, whose address matches up with a high-end mental facility in the heart of the posh community. But, other than Eleanor's full name and address, and a passing reference to her name in a few of the articles written about Reed's father, I wasn't able to learn any details about the woman.

"Spelling on Charpentier?" Charles says.

I spell the name for him, and he clacks on his keyboard.

"It looks like there's only one lawsuit naming Eleanor Rivers or Eleanor Charpentier Rivers as a defendant or respondent. A 'Dissolution of Marriage and Custody of Minor Child' case, filed by one Terrence Rivers."

My heart lurches into my mouth. "Would you add that to my copy order, please? I'd like everything in that case file."

"Sorry, no can do," Charles says. "Family law cases are a different animal, stored separately. But since this one was from over ten years ago, I doubt they'd even have it on-site anymore. Plus, since the case involved the custody of a minor child, I'm sure the records would be sealed, anyway."

"Shoot. I really want to read that one."

Charles shrugs. "Sorry."

I twist my mouth, thinking back to what I learned in school. Specifically, a class called Journalism and the Justice System. "Do you think maybe there's some roundabout way I could get my hands on it? Like, some motion or deposition that might at least refer to it or summarize it?"

Charles considers my question for a long beat before his face lights up. "Hold on. I've got an idea." He clacks on his computer keyboard, and then smiles like a Cheshire cat. "Bingo. I searched for any case involving Eleanor Rivers, even if she was the *plaintiff,* and hit pay dirt. A year after the dissolution and custody dispute, Eleanor sued her divorce attorney for malpractice."

I look at Charles blankly, not understanding how this information helps my cause.

Charles smirks. "It means you're in luck. Apparently, Eleanor didn't like the result of her divorce and custody battle, and thought her attorney in that case botched the job. So she sued her for malpractice. It's not guaranteed you'll get *all* the details of the underlying divorce and custody dispute by reading the malpractice lawsuit that came a year later, but I'm guessing you'll at least get the gist."

"*Oh,*" I say, a lightbulb going off. "Because, in order to explain how her attorney messed up in the divorce case, Eleanor would have had to summarize that underlying case?"

"Exactly." He clacks on his keyboard for a moment. "Okay, the malpractice lawsuit is something I can get for you. It's general civil litigation, not family law. But it was filed twenty-two years ago, so you'll have to fill out a form for that one, so it can be retrieved from the archives or microfiche, or whatever. You'll probably have the documents in about a week or so."

I'm giddy. "Thank you so much, Charles. Oh my gosh. You're a rock star."

I fill out the form he gives me, listing the address for delivery of the documents as the offices of *Rock 'n' Roll*—not River Records—even though Owen has kindly set me up with a cubicle down the hallway from him. I don't know what, of interest, I'm going to find in Eleanor Rivers' twenty-two-year-old malpractice lawsuit, if anything. But, whatever is in that file, I sure as hell don't want Reed walking in on me in my cubicle and discovering that I'm reading it.

"Thank you again for all your help, Charles. You're the best."

"No problem. I'll be back in a jiffy."

When Charles leaves, I take a rickety chair in a corner, pull out my laptop, and make furious notes. But a few minutes into my note-taking, I get a phone call from Reed.

"Why, hello there, Mr. Rivers," I say.

"Hello there, Miss Ricci. My meeting just ended. Where are you?"

My stomach tightens. "At a coffee place."

"Which one? I'll pick you up."

I glance at the empty spot at the counter, where there's still no sign of Charles. "Actually, um, the writer assigned as my mentor at *Rock 'n' Roll*—this woman named Zasu—happens to be downtown, so I'm going to hook up with her for a bit. I'll grab an Uber after that and meet you at your house."

"I can hang around and do some work in a conference room at Leonard's, if you won't be too long. I know you're excited to sit in on my weekly team meeting."

"Oh, I am. Will you be having another weekly meeting next Monday?"

"Yes. But won't that fall outside the week you've earmarked for shadowing me? Are you sure you want to keep following me around after your obligatory week is up?"

Reed's tone is flirty and fun, so I throw back more of the same.

"Hey, whatever it takes to write the best possible article about you, I'm willing to make the sacrifice. Although, to be clear, an extra day of following you around will be a *huge* sacrifice."

I can hear his smile across the phone line. "The Intrepid Reporter strikes again."

My stomach somersaults. I look around the clerk's office, feeling guilty as hell. But why? I'm not doing anything wrong. I'm only doing exactly what I was hired to do: *dig a little deeper*. Exactly what Reed *knows* I was hired to do. I mean, come on, as fun as this surprising romance with Reed is, it's not like it will lead to anything serious. It's fun, yes. So fun, it should be illegal. But I can't let it sidetrack me from my higher purpose, which is writing the most kickass article I can, and getting myself my dream job.

"I think I'll catch the weekly meeting next week," I say. "And meet you back at your house later, after I'm done with my work."

"Okay. Work hard. Play hard. And I'll do the same." He chuckles. "Although, I must admit, I'm gonna have a bitch of a time trying to get you off my mind during my weekly meeting. I could barely do it during my meeting with Leonard and the expert witness."

My heart skips a beat. He's so freaking yummy, I can barely stand it. "Yeah, I can honestly say I've been thinking about you, pretty much nonstop, since I left Leonard's office. How was the meeting with the expert, by the way?"

"Couldn't have gone better. She agrees the copyright infringement lawsuit is total and complete bullshit—nothing but a meritless money-grab by an unscrupulous plaintiffs' lawyer."

"Oh, that's great news."

"It is. I already knew the lawsuit is bullshit. But the legal system is such a crap shoot sometimes. It's nice to hear an expert confirm what I already know."

"I bet. You've been sued a lot, huh?"

"Oh, God, Georgie. So many times, I've lost count. It would boggle your mind if you saw an actual list of all the times one of my companies has been sued for one thing or another over the years."

I look down at the printout of lawsuits that's coincidentally sitting on my lap at this very moment, and my stomach tightens again. Why do I feel like I'm doing something terribly wrong by having this printout? Why do I feel like I'm doing something disloyal by being here at all, and not telling Reed about it? Truly, I need to take a chill pill, keep my eye on the prize, and my mouth shut—at least, for now, until I know what's in the documents I've ordered. For all I know, I'll read the entire stack and think, *Yeah, so what?*

"Hey, maybe I should come to the coffee place and meet this other reporter," Reed says. "I could reschedule my team meeting..."

"No!" I take a deep breath. "Don't do that. Just go about your normal life. I don't want to be a disruption."

He chuckles. "Well, it's too late for that. You've already knocked my world off its axis, Georgina."

My breathing halts. "You've knocked my world off its axis too," I whisper. I cup my hand to the phone, so nobody else waiting in the clerk's office will overhear me. "I feel addicted to you, Reed. So horny for you, I think I might be losing my mind."

He lets out a slow exhale. "Amalia's leaving at five today. Be at my house at five-oh-one."

"I'll be there. I can't wait to be alone with you again. Now that I'm hearing your voice again, I'm physically craving you."

His breathing has become audible. "I can't wait to make you scream again. I can't stop thinking about the way it felt to fuck you in my swing."

"Georgina?" a male voice says, and I abruptly swivel my head toward the counter, bug-eyed, like a thief caught with two bags of money. Charles, the clerk, is approaching the counter.

"I've got to go," I blurt to Reed. "The... barista just called my name for my coffee order. I'll see you at five-oh-one."

"Don't be late."

"I won't."

My heart racing, I hang up, feeling like an asshole, a liar, a scumbag for lying to Reed, and stride to the counter. "Wow, that was fast. Thank you."

Charles puts a large cardboard box onto the counter between us. Its side is imprinted with the words *Courthouse Copy Service*. "This is everything," he says. "There weren't a lot of documents in each file. Just the plaintiff's complaint, the defendant's answer, and a notice of settlement."

"Perfect." I pay for the copies and reach for the box, but Charles doesn't let go of it. "Why don't I carry this to your car for you? It's kind of heavy."

"I'm strong. I can handle it. Plus, I don't have a car. But, thanks."

"Well, how about we grab a coffee, then? I'm due for my break."

Shit. Seriously? I don't have time for this. "Thanks for the kind offer. But I've actually got a boyfriend, so..." I physically yank the box from Charles' grasp. "Thank you so much for expediting this for me. You're a prince. Bye now. Have a great day." And off I go, as fast as my legs will carry me, while lugging a pretty heavy cardboard box.

When I get outside, I put the box down and pull out my phone. "Siri, where is the nearest coffee place?"

"I think I've found what you're looking for," Siri replies, showing me several nearby choices. I pick one, rest the box of legal documents onto my hip, and head off, excited to find a quiet spot where I can sip an iced coffee and devour as much of the contents of this box as possible before heading to Reed's house... where, God willing, he'll take me to heaven again, the same way he did in his swing this morning... only, this time, perhaps while tied to the four posters of his bed.

Chapter 14
Reed

Me: **Where the hell are you, butterfly? It's 5:18 and my net is rock hard and ready to capture you (so I can thereafter tack your wings to paper and enclose you in an airtight frame).**

Georgina: So sorry! I lost track of time reading something at a coffee place downtown, and then got stuck in traffic. My navigation app estimates arrival time of 5:49. Don't you dare touch your butterfly net before then. Save yourself for me.

Me: I'll stay locked and loaded for you, baby. Gate code 874593. I'll be in my bedroom.

Georgina: Can't wait. PS I'm starving. Is there food?

Me: Amalia's soup.

Georgina: Oh yeah! So excited. Don't eat without me! XO

Me: Of course not. See you soon. XO

Smiling like a goof, I toss my phone onto my mattress next to me. For the love of fuck, I just texted her "XO." I've only ever texted that sardonically to Josh. What is this girl doing to me?

My phone on the bed next to me rings, drawing me from my thoughts, and when I glance at the screen, I see it's Isabel calling me. Fuck. She's been calling me all day, without ever leaving a voicemail. Sighing, I pick up my phone.

"Hi, Isabel."

"Finally!" she shouts. "I've been trying to call you all day. Why haven't you picked up?"

"I've been in meetings. Why didn't you send a text or leave a voicemail?"

"Because what I've got to say has to be said in an actual conversation."

My heart stops. *No.* In a flash, my brain hurtles back to that drunken night in the Hamptons. How long ago was that? I wore a condom that night, didn't I? I'm positive I did... Oh, God, *please* tell me I wore a condom... and that it didn't break.

"I'm getting married," Isabel declares, and every hair on my body wilts in relief.

"Did you just sigh with relief?" Isabel shouts, going from zero to sixty on a dime.

"I sighed, but it was with happiness for you. So, who's the lucky guy?"

"Seriously?"

"What?"

"I call you, out of the blue, to say I'm getting married, and *that's* your reaction? *I'm happy for you, Isabel, who's the lucky guy?*"

I chuckle. "How should I have reacted? I know you've always wanted to get married."

"To you, dumbass!"

"Well, we both know that was never going to happen, so it's good you've found your Plan B. Now, are you going to identify the lucky man you're going to pledge yourself to for eternity, or not?"

She pauses for a long beat, before saying, "It's Howard."

"*Devlin?*"

"Obviously, Reed."

Holy fuck. Even lying here on my bed alone, I make a face like I've just swallowed a bite of rancid yogurt. Howard Devlin is a sixty-something-year-old blow-hard billionaire movie producer/studio head who thinks his shit doesn't stink. He's always had an obsession with Isabel. That's not a secret. Ever since she first met him at her first big audition. But she's never given him the time of day. And now, suddenly, she's agreed to marry him? It was Howard's studio that signed Isabel to her four-movie deal a couple weeks ago. Did Howard make this engagement a condition of the deal? Is this a PR stunt? It's got to be. Isabel can't possibly love him. And she certainly doesn't need his money. She'll probably net upwards of fifty million by the time those four pictures are done, assuming they hit as big as hoped. Was fifty million Isabel's price to slip a ring on her finger? Or did Howard sweeten the pot, on top of that, to coax her into saying yes to his proposal?

"I didn't want you to find out online," Isabel says. "I'm going to post a photo of Howard and me tomorrow, with my rock on full display."

"You're making it 'Gram official, huh? Wow. This is serious."

"I want you to comment on the post. It's important people see we're still good friends, and you've got no hard feelings about me dumping you and moving on."

I chuckle. She didn't dump me. And I definitely don't have hard feelings. But what I say is, "Fine with me."

She sighs. "Thanks."

Oh, shit. I shouldn't do it. I don't give a fuck what she does. But that "thanks" sounded so damned defeated, I can't resist. "Are you okay, Isabel?"

"Of course, I'm okay. I just got engaged. I'm on Cloud Nine."

She sounds resigned. Detached. Just plain sad. But, unfortunately, I'm not the guy who can make her happy. Surely, Howard Devlin isn't, either. I'm not sure anyone could make Isabel happy, actually. Her online avatar is the happiest woman alive. But the real Isabel? She's got a gaping hole in her soul she's never been able to fill—though, God bless her, she keeps trying.

"So, Gary said you're throwing a party on Saturday night," she says, referring to Gary Pembroke, her agent, the top guy at the top talent agency in Hollywood. A guy who represents the highest echelon of A-listers, some of whom have already RSVP'd for my party.

"Yeah, my entire roster will be there, other than RCR and a couple others. Plus, a pretty impressive crowd from your world will be there, too."

"Yeah, Gary said it's going to be the coolest party of the year."

Well, clearly, she's trolling for an invitation. Which isn't going to happen. Hell no. Indeed, I open my mouth to say as much, when an idea slams me. *Georgina.* I bet she'd give her right arm to interview Isabel for *Dig a Little Deeper*! In fact, I bet Georgina would pick the world's current "It Girl" as an interview subject over me, any day of the week, if she were forced to choose only one of us. Granted, CeeCee sent Georgie to peel *my* onion, but I can't imagine CeeCee would complain if Georgina came back, instead, with an in-depth interview of the world's biggest movie star!

The only problem with this plan? Isabel's a notoriously wooden interview subject. She's renowned in the industry for giving great soundbites—which is a skill in itself—but, otherwise, giving rote, formulaic interviews filled mostly with PR talking points. It's actually a fantastic thing when Isabel's on a press junket, where she's tasked with answering the same questions over and over to plug her latest movie. Or on a talk show, where the goal is being superficial and fun. But ask the woman to let down her guard and provide thoughtful, honest answers to less predictable questions, and she's a fucking train wreck.

But, still, I think this idea is worth a shot. I can't imagine a better "get" for Georgina than somehow managing an exclusive, in-depth interview of Isabel Randolph. Talk about something that will take the sting out of Georgina's disappointment at the end of the summer, if I wind up nixing most of her article about me. Of course, I'm not stupid. I'm only willing to invite Isabel to the party—a party attended by Georgina—if Isabel will be bringing the great love of her life as her plus-one, to ensure Isabel isn't all over me like a cheap suit.

"Hey, why don't you and Howard come to the party on Saturday?" I suggest. "If you want buzz about the engagement, then this party is the perfect place to get it. Photos of you two partying with rock stars and Hollywood A-listers will go a lot more viral than an Instagram post."

"Oh, that'd be great. Thanks."

I decide to give myself a bit of insurance that Isabel will actually show up to the party *with* Howard. "I'll even say a toast to you and Howard."

"Oh, that would be awesome. Thank you."

"You know what? I just got a great idea for an invaluable PR opportunity for you. Are you familiar with the magazine, *Dig a Little Deeper?*"

"Yeah. My PR woman keeps trying to nab a cover feature for me in that one, but no dice. Apparently, I'm not 'forthcoming enough' for the kinds of interviews they feature, especially for the cover slot."

"Did you know *Dig a Little Deeper* and *Rock 'n' Roll* were both founded by CeeCee Rafael?"

Isabel gasps. "Oh! Will CeeCee be at the party? I'd love to chat her up and convince her to give me that cover slot."

"No, CeeCee won't be there. She's out of the country this week. But just the other day, CeeCee told me, in confidence, she's considering a 'Women in Hollywood' special issue of *Dig a Little Deeper.*" It's bullshit, but sometimes, the end justifies the means. "Don't tell her I told you about this, Isabel. CeeCee hasn't fully decided to do it yet. If she does, though, she said she's leaning toward putting Gabrielle LeMonde on the cover."

"Gabrielle?" She scoffs. "That's so inside the box. Yes, Gabrielle has three Oscars. But she's never secured a four-picture deal like mine. Nobody has. I'm a trailblazer, Reed."

"I couldn't agree more. That's exactly why I brought it up. You should be on that cover."

"Damn straight."

"This is confidential, too, but I happen to know CeeCee has assigned *one* of the two *Rock 'n' Roll* writers coming to the party, CeeCee's personal favorite, to gather content for *Dig a Little Deeper*. How about I introduce you to her, and you can charm the hell out of her—so much so, she wants to do an in-depth interview of you she could submit to CeeCee? If the interview is kick-ass enough, I'm sure CeeCee would want it as her cover feature for a 'Women in Hollywood' issue."

Isabel squeals. "I love it!"

"Apparently, this writer is some sort of phenom. Fresh out of college, and yet CeeCee said she's the best writer she's ever hired. I'm positive she'll be able to cook up something spectacular with you."

Isabel starts babbling about how excited she is. But as she talks, I hear Georgina's footsteps in the hallway—and, instantly, just knowing Georgina is in the house is making my dick buzz like a neon hotel *Vacancy* sign that's just been flipped on

"Hey, I've got to go, Isabel. I'll see you and Howard on Saturday."

"Thank you so much for always having my back, Reed. When push comes to shove, you're the one person—"

"You bet. I gotta go."

"Hang on. Are you planning to have a pre-party at your place before the party? I'd love to—"

"Nope. No pre-party. I'll see you at the party. Owen will text you. Congrats on your engagement."

Click.

Chapter 15
Reed

I fling open my bedroom door after hanging up with Isabel, bursting at the seams to see Georgina. But she's not in the hallway. Shit. Did I imagine her footfalls a moment ago?

But I've no sooner had the thought than Georgina emerges from her bedroom door. When she sees me, her face lights up. Squealing, she barrels toward me, leaps into my arms, and wraps herself around me like a monkey in a tree.

And that's it. Without delay, we're a frenzied blur of lips and tongues and hungry, groping hands. I clutch her ass, kneading it frantically, as she grips my neck and hair and grinds her center against my aching bulge behind my pants.

Still devouring her, I turn around and bump and thump my way through my bedroom doorway, somehow making it across my room and to my bed without toppling over or sending a lamp crashing down.

Like a man possessed, I lay Georgie down on my bed and begin frantically peeling off her clothes and mine, while she gasps and purrs and goads me on. When we're both naked, I open her smooth, trembling thighs, crawl between them, and begin eating her with unbridled enthusiasm.

When I glance at her face, I find her looking enraptured... but with her eyes closed.

"Look in the mirror," I say. "Watch me eat you."

Her eyes flick open and train on the ceiling above us, and I get back to work, even more turned on to know she's watching me. And soon, she's losing her mind. Writhing, moaning, clawing at the bed. Until... *bliss*. I'm gifted with a screaming climax from Georgie that makes me dizzy with arousal. Panting, I crawl up the length of her writhing torso, place her thighs on my shoulders, and plunge myself deep inside her.

My thrusts are hard. Animalistic. Deep.

And Georgina responds by digging her nails into my forearms, screaming my name, and finally, coming hard. Not surprisingly, when I feel her innermost muscles constricting— milking me ferociously—it's more than I can withstand. With a loud groan, I release along with her, blurting her name like a prayer. I feel dizzy with my pleasure. Momentarily blinded by it. Blissed out like I've mainlined a brick of cocaine.

When we finally come down, I heave myself onto my back next to Georgina, trying to catch my breath, and she gasps at the air alongside me.

"That was amazing," she says.

"I told you not to knock the mirror till you tried it."

She smiles. "You have the most gorgeous ass."

"You have the most gorgeous everything."

I stroke her arm. "I've got some great news to tell you. Isabel Randolph called me today."

Georgina stiffens.

"To tell me she's engaged," I quickly add.

Georgina lifts her head and looks at me, but says nothing.

"To this guy named Howard Devlin. He's one of the most powerful movie producers in Hollywood. He actually owns a studio." I tell her a bit about Howard and the mega-successful studio he owns, concluding with, "His studio churns out blockbuster hits and Academy Award contenders, in equal measure. The guy can't miss."

"So, what you're saying is he's the Reed Rivers of the movie industry?"

I chuckle. "The reason I brought it up is that, while Isabel and I were talking about her happy news, I got an idea. What if you interviewed Isabel for *Dig a Little Deeper*? You know, in-depth, as one of the 'audition' pieces you submit to CeeCee?"

Georgina gasps. "Oh my God. I would love to do that! Do you think she'd say yes?"

"If you meet her and charm the hell out of her, I sure do. Which is why I invited Isabel and her new fiancé to the party on Saturday night. I figured it would be the perfect opportunity for you to get her to say yes to an in-depth interview."

Georgina bolts to a sitting position in the bed. Apparently, she's too excited about this idea to remain horizontal. "So, Isabel said she'd come to the party?"

"Yup. She also said she's excited to meet you and talk about a potential interview."

Georgina squeals. "You've already floated a possible interview with me?"

"Yep. To be clear, it's not a sure thing. You're going to have to convince her you've got the chops to write something worth her investment of time and image. And even if she winds up giving you an interview, you're going to have to finesse her to get something that will be on-brand for *Dig a Little Deeper*. For all her social media presence, Isabel is actually an extremely guarded person. Very curated, if you know what I mean. Too image-conscious for her own good. But if anyone can break down Isabel's walls and peel her onion, it's you, Georgina Ricci."

Elation washes over Georgina's face, followed immediately by determination. "By God, I'm going to make this happen."

I chuckle. "I don't doubt that for a minute. The way you handled Leonard today blew me away. If today had been a music demo, I would have signed you on the spot."

She leans down and kisses me. "Thank you for saying that."

"It's the truth."

"And thank you for trying to arrange this incredible opportunity for me. I can't believe it."

"You're welcome. I cracked the door open for you, baby. Now, kick that fucker wide open."

"Oh, I will." She bites her lower lip for a moment, her mind visibly teeming with thoughts. "Are you surprised she's getting married?"

"Yes and no. It's sudden. But she's always wanted to get married."

Her eyes narrow. "How do you feel about it?"

"About her getting married? I'm happy for her. Of course."

"No, but I mean... aren't you a tiny bit upset?"

"About . . .?"

"Isabel getting married."

I pull a face like that's an asinine comment. "Not at all."

She stares at me for a beat, like she's a psychic, trying to read my mind. And then, "You know that feeling when someone is driving away, and you suddenly realize you forgot to tell them something important? So you yell and wave at the car and maybe run after it down the street, but they don't see you... and then, the car is gone? You don't feel the tiniest bit like that?"

I smirk. "Is that your clever way of asking me if I feel like Isabel is my 'one that got away'?"

She looks like she's holding her breath.

I grab her hand. "Georgina, no. Isabel and I are more like brother and sister than exes at this point. I still care about her as a person, and want the best for her. If I can help her out with something in some way, without too much effort or annoyance on my part, I'll always do it. But I know I'm not even close to the guy who can make her happy, and she knows it, too. So it's for the best she's found the guy who can."

Georgie lets out a long exhale, like she just made it to the ledge after a long walk across a high wire. "Do you have any tips for me, for when I talk to her at the party? Anything at all to help me close the deal?"

"Well, for one thing, I wouldn't mention you're fucking me."

Georgina rolls her eyes. "Yeah, I figured that one out all by myself. Engaged or not, no woman would ever want to give an in-depth interview to her ex's..."

Georgina trails off, apparently not sure of the appropriate word to finish that sentence. And I don't blame her. I have no idea how she should finish it, either.

"Here's a tip for you," I say. "Something that will work like a charm on her." I pull on Georgina's arm, guiding her to lie in my arms. "Tell Isabel you heard her franchise deal set a record in terms of salary for a female lead. Tell her she'll go down in history as breaking new ground for women in Hollywood. Call her a 'trailblazer' for women in Hollywood."

"Ooooh, that's good."

"Actually, that's a great hook. Tell her you're going to pitch the idea of a special 'Women in Hollywood' issue of *Dig a Little Deeper*, with Isabel as the cover interview."

"Ooooh!"

"I'm positive both CeeCee and Isabel would *love* that idea. In fact, if you want to guarantee Isabel will give you a pound of flesh in an interview, rather than her usual guarded talking points, then dangle her possibly being the face of a prestigious issue like that... only if her interview is in-depth and revealing enough."

"Holy crap. You're a genius! My Fairy Godfather!" She grabs my face and lays an enthusiastic smack on my mouth. "Thank you so much for this!"

"I only planted the seed. You're going to have to go in, guns blazing, and close the deal."

"ABC, baby!" Georgina says enthusiastically. "That means 'always be closing.'"

"Yes, I know. *Glengarry Glenross* is one of my all-time favorite movies. Finally, a pop culture reference we both know."

Georgina looks at me blankly, and I know she's a broken clock that happens to be right at the exact right moment.

"Aw, come on, Ricci! You can't say ABC, if you've never seen *Glengarry Glenross*!"

She giggles. "I just thought it was a cute thing hustlers say."

I pull her to me, laughing, and kiss the top of her head. "What am I going to do with you?"

She pinches my nipple. "I'm sure you'll think of something."

"Seriously, though. How do I even tolerate you, let alone like you so damned much?"

My heart lurches into my mouth. Oh, shit. What did I just say? Panic. It's rising inside me. Too much. Too soon. She's gotten under my skin way too fast. And way too deep.

Sighing happily, Georgina lays her palm on my chest and shoots a wide, glorious smile at me, her hazel eyes sparkling. "I like you so damned much, too, Reed. So damned much, I feel like I'm going to burst when I'm with you."

And, just like that, my rising panic disappears... supplanted by butterflies in my stomach. No, bald eagles this time. Fucking condors.

Georgina's stomach rumbles loudly, making her giggle.

"Was that *you*?" I say, laughing.

She blushes. "I'm *hungry*."

"Well, damn, let's get you fed, before the alien living inside your stomach bursts out and eats my face."

She laughs, but, again, I know she's clueless.

"You have no idea what movie I just referenced, do you?" I say.

"You referenced a movie?"

Oh, God, I can't get enough of this girl. I touch her cheek. "What am I gonna do with you?"

"In the immediate future, feed me," she says. "After that, do whatever you please."

I kiss her full lips gently, my heart soaring around the room. "Come, come, little kitty. Let's get you some food."

Chapter 16
Georgina

I can't believe how good this is," I say, eating another mouthful of Amalia's amazing soup.

"It's my all-time favorite," Reed says. "The word 'soup' doesn't do it justice."

We're sitting across from each other at Reed's small kitchen table. I'm wearing a tank top and a pair of soft shorts. Reed is shirtless and in sweats, looking like a god. And for the past twenty minutes or so, I've been peppering him with follow-up questions about what Leonard told me at his office today. I've asked my questions out of genuine curiosity. But also, they've been my way of easing into asking Reed about an even greater topic of interest: the lawsuits I got earlier today at the courthouse.

Thus far, I've read two out of the three lawsuits the court clerk copied for me. I ran out of time to read the third, before it was time to head back to Reed's house. But what I've read so far in the first two lawsuits has raised some serious questions for me. Well, actually, not the first one involving a lease dispute. That one was a total snoozefest, as expected.

But the *second* lawsuit, the one filed eight years ago by a former employee of River Records claiming sexual harassment and wrongful termination? Yeah, I've got some burning questions about that one. All of which I plan to ask Reed about during this meal. Just as soon as I muster the courage.

In her lawsuit, Stephanie claimed Reed pressured her into having a sexual relationship for several months, and then fired her when she refused to continue. Which means, if her claims were true, then Reed was, and *is*, an asshole of epic proportions. A dirtbag who'd shamelessly abuse his power.

But Stephanie's version of Reed doesn't ring true to me. Yes, he's harsh at times. And arrogant. But the kind of boss who'd force an employee into a sexual relationship? Reed himself told me he never has sex with his employees. Also, when I toured River Records with Owen, back when Reed was still in New York, it was clear to me everyone on Reed's staff, including a bunch of women, respect their boss. Yes, they said he's exacting and tough and pulls no punches. Yes, one person laughingly said Reed can flash-freeze a room with one withering glare. But it was obvious to me they all admire their fearless leader, and would follow him to the ends of the earth.

I mean, I recognize I might not be the best person to accurately assess Reed on this topic, since the man started hitting on me the second he saw me. But he's not my boss. And, in fact, expressly told me he wouldn't have agreed to the special edition if it meant he would be.

Plus, I've never felt taken advantage of by Reed, even when we've gone toe to toe. For instance, backstage at the RCR show, when we were engaged in hard-nosed "negotiations," Reed stopped me several times, when I made a misstep, to tell me I'd said the wrong thing—basically, to give me a free pass—because he knew he's got far more experience at negotiations than I do.

Frankly, if it weren't for the fact that Reed settled Stephanie's case, and has told me his philosophy regarding settlements, I'd be thinking Stephanie's complaint was almost certainly a pack of lies, every bit as much as the copyright infringement lawsuit against Red Card Riot. But Reed *did* settle it. And Reed *did* tell me he only settles cases when they've got merit, or he thinks a jury will believe it.

The bottom line? I'm dying to ask Reed what the hell happened between him and Stephanie Moreland. Will Stephanie's lawsuit make it into my article? It's unlikely. But, either way, Reed is the man I've been sleeping with. The man I've been swooning over. Feeling addicted to. The man who gives me butterflies like crazy. If it turns out he's an asshole who'd force an employee into a sexual relationship, then, regardless of my article, I want to know about it.

I eat the last spoonful of my soup and push my empty bowl to the side.

"Would you like another bowl?" Reed asks.

"No, I'm good."

"Another beer?"

"Yeah. Thanks."

Reed gets up and heads to the stove with his empty bowl.

"So, I did something kind of clever today," I say.

"Oh, yeah?"

"After you said I wouldn't believe it if I saw the list of lawsuits you've had to deal with over the past ten years, I popped over to the courthouse to see for myself."

It's a little white lie. In truth, I'd already had the printout when Reed made that specific comment this afternoon. But Reed already thinks I'm freaking Bobby Fischer, and I don't want to give him more reasons to think that. Let him think I'm smart and sneaky, sure, but not *that* smart and sneaky.

Reed returns to the table, puts down his refilled bowl, and hands me a beer bottle. "And? The list is as thick as a phone book, right?"

"Well, I've never actually seen a phone book, but I get your meaning. Yes, it was crazy-thick. I don't know how you sleep at night with so many people gunning for you, claiming you've done them dirty."

Reed takes a swig of his beer and shrugs. "Getting sued is one of the costs of doing business, especially in California. I don't take it personally."

"I was amazed at how many different kinds of lawsuits there were," I say, my pulse quickening. I'm circling the runway, getting ready to land. "There was everything from personal injury to breach of lease to copyright infringement to wrongful termination."

I watch him closely at those last words... but he doesn't flinch. Indeed, he smoothly takes a bite of food, as relaxed as ever.

"I've got a great team of lawyers," he says. He swigs his beer. "Also, I rest easy knowing almost all of it is total bullshit. The truth shall prevail, right? And if not, then I pay what needs to be paid, and move on."

My breathing hitches. *Does that mean Stephanie's lawsuit was the truth?* But I don't have the courage to land the plane yet. I'm still circling like a coward. "The printout noted you'd settled a lease dispute?"

He takes another bite of food. "Yeah. That was years ago. At my very first office space, I'd stupidly signed for way too long a lease period, thinking my business would expand much more slowly than it did."

At my urging, he tells me about the case. And, as expected, it's a big ol' nothing-burger. In summary, Reed's business blew up like crazy, way faster than he thought it would, and the space he'd been renting became way too small for his operations. So, he vacated that space, in order to rent a much bigger one—the one he's in now, actually—thereby breaching his lease.

"I never denied I'd broken the lease," Reed says. "I told the landlord I was willing to pay him what I owed him. But he wanted to gouge me. So I said, 'Here's what I rightfully owe you. Sue me for the rest, motherfucker.' And he did."

"And?" I say. "Did the guy get everything he'd wanted in the settlement?"

"No. Not even close."

"Was it all worth it in the end?" I ask, still trying to figure out how to broach the topic of Stephanie Moreland.

Reed's eyes light up. "Oh, God, yes. I had to act fast when the space I'm in now became available. It was the exact one I used to drive by in college and dream of occupying one day. Every day I get to walk into my lobby at River Records, every day I get to see my name above the door on *that* particular office space, every day I get to see all those framed gold and platinum and diamond records on those walls, I feel like I've made all my dreams come true."

Goosebumps erupt on my arms. Not only about what Reed just said, but how lit up he looked while saying it. "Hold that thought," I say, grabbing my phone. "I've got to make some notes. You just gave me goosebumps."

He laughs. "Knock yourself out, Intrepid Reporter."

I make a bunch of notes. Ask him to repeat a few things. And when I finally put down my phone and look up, I find Reed smiling broadly at me.

"What?" I ask.

He bites back his smile. "Nothing."

"Why were you smiling like that?"

"If I tell you, are you going to get angry?"

"It depends what you say."

"Are you going to flip me off?"

"No. I'll refrain, no matter what you say."

Again, he bites back a smile. "I just find you incredibly entertaining. And adorable. And, yes, amusing. And sexy. And smart. And, on occasion, all of that just makes it impossible for me not to smile."

I return his wide, beaming, beautiful smile. "Oh."

"Does any of that make you want to punch me in the face?"

"No. It makes me want to kiss you."

He laughs. "Progress."

"I'd say so."

I take a sip of beer. Shit. If I don't ask about this now, the moment will pass and I'll fall hopelessly under his spell again. It's now or never.

"So, one of the lawsuits on the printout caught my eye, in particular." I take a deep breath. "One you settled. The case was filed by a woman named Stephanie Moreland. She said you sexually harassed and wrongfully terminated her."

Boom.

Reed's demeanor changes. His jaw sets. His posture stiffens. And I know, without a doubt, I've stumbled upon something Reed doesn't want to talk about.

Chapter 17
Georgina

W hat happened with Stephanie Moreland?" I ask. "You settled it. So, that means there was some truth to her claims... or you thought a jury would believe her... right?"

Reed drags his palm down his face. He takes a long sip of his beer. Puts down his bottle. And exhales. "If I tell you about this, Georgina, you have to promise me this conversation will be off the record. I know what you said about me being able to nix anything I don't like in your article. But this particular thing..." He shakes his head. "It's the most humiliating thing that's ever happened to me, besides my father's arrest and conviction. And I don't want to have to read about it, or think about it, or see it reflected back to me through your eyes. I'll talk about it with you, to ease whatever doubts I'm assuming you're now having about me. But I'm only going to tell the woman I'm sleeping with this story. Not the reporter who's trying to get herself a permanent position at *Dig a Little Deeper*."

I feel short of breath. Sick to my stomach. What choice do I have?

I exhale. "Okay."

"Off the record?"

I nod. "Yes."

Reed takes another long swig of beer. Takes another deep breath. "Stephanie was my first full-time hire at River Records. A marketing manager I hired right after RCR's debut rocketed up the charts. Early on, I could tell we had chemistry. But I never made a move on her because I was her boss. But then one night, Stephanie comes into my office and closes the door. This was right before RCR's second album was set to come out, and I was totally stressed out. Sophomore albums are notoriously dicey, and I was determined to catch lightning in a bottle again. So, I was working round the clock. Sleeping on a couch in my office. Doing way too much coke."

My eyebrows ride up.

"I don't do that anymore. Ever. But I was a big fan back then, especially in times of extreme stress. So, anyway, Stephanie comes in and says she knows I've been stressed out, and she wants to help me relax."

I cringe.

"Yeah, it's what you're thinking. I was sitting in my desk chair at the time, and she kneels in front of me and gets busy. I hadn't come on to her in the slightest before then, so it was totally out of the blue. And I was shocked. I knew I should say, 'No, Stephanie. Bad idea.' But I didn't. She was hot, and I was high as a kite. And I thought, 'Fuck it. She's the one coming on to me. What could go wrong?'" He rolls his eyes at himself. "Well, from that moment on, she owned my ass, although I didn't know it at the time." He shakes his head, rolling his eyes at himself. "For the next few months after that first BJ in my office, we'd fucked around at the office. I never saw her outside of work. Never took her on a date. Never took her to my place or went to hers. But we had some fun, now and again, after everyone else had gone home. But then things got out of control. Every time I turned around, even during normal working hours, she was unzipping my pants, or begging me to fuck her over the copy machine. It was like she wanted us to get caught. Like she wanted everyone to know she was fucking the boss. And then, *boom.* RCR's second album comes out and it's a global smash. I mean, holy shit, Georgie. I'd thought their first album was big, but that sophomore album took things to another level. And then came the debut of Danger Doctor Jones, which hit top ten. And then 2Real hit number one with 'Crash.' And I swear to God, I thought I must have made a deal with the devil, without remembering it. Which, it turns out, I did. Thanks to my coked-out pecker. A devil named Stephanie Moreland."

"Oh, Reed."

"She comes into my office and closes the door. She wants to give me a blowjob to celebrate 2Real's number one. But by then, I was sick to death of her. Sick of messing around. Sick of the distraction. Sick of myself. I wasn't even physically attracted to her anymore. Just disgusted. So I told her it was over. That we had to go back to being completely professional. And, to my shock, she said, 'You think you can get rid of me that easily? Guess what, asshole? I *own* your fucking ass now.' So, I said, 'I'm not getting rid of you, Stephanie. You're good at your job. I just mean I'm done *fucking* you. I've been an idiot to mess around with an employee, a coked-out idiot, and I've decided to clean up my act and never do it again.'" He shakes his head. "It turned out, she was recording that conversation, and a whole lot of others. Plus, every sex act. Every bit of dirty talk."

I grimace with him. "No wonder you settled the case."

"No, the recordings weren't the reason I settled, actually. I knew they were illegal. Both parties have to consent to recording in California, thank God. But what they made me realize was she'd totally set me up. From day one, I'd been her mark. She came into *my* office to give me that BJ, knowing she was ultimately going to come after me. And that freaked me out. I knew it was going to be her word against mine, if she accused me of something. And normally, I'd take on that challenge. But what would someone like *that* be willing to say about me?"

"Why didn't you turn her in for making those illegal recordings? That's a crime, right?"

117

"And let the police hear all that shit? Ha! No, thanks. Plus, I knew I was guilty as shit. I was her boss, and I'd fucked her. No getting around that."

"So what happened? Did she demand hush money?"

"Not at first. Instead, she decided her job duties had become 'optional.' For a couple months, she came and went as she pleased. Never made deadlines. Took days off, without calling in. I knew she was daring me to fire her, so she could sue me. Obviously, I didn't want a lawsuit. I just wanted to move past the sex thing and have her do her job, as required. But then she went MIA for a week, without a word, so I fired her, and she sued my ass a day later, making me sound like a monster. But guess what? Under California law, I *was* a monster, and I fully acknowledge that. When you're the boss, you can't fuck your employees. Period. There's no gray area. It's a strict liability state, meaning there's no defense. No saying, 'Hey, it was consensual.' No saying, 'Hey, she came onto *me*.' If you're the boss, and you've fucked an employee, then you've committed sexual harassment."

"Oh, Reed."

"It's actually a fair system, ninety-nine percent of the time. Sociopaths like Stephanie are rare. I've thought about this quite a bit."

"I'm sure you have."

"And I've realized something big. As the boss, I can never know, for sure, if an employee genuinely wants to sleep with me, or if she's only saying yes because she's afraid of losing her job if she says no. She could say yes. She could even come on to me. But I've realized there's no way to separate the fact that I hold all the power, when it comes to my employees. So, in the end, I've got no quarrel with the way the laws are written. The rules are clear and there for a reason. Just because I'm an idiot who let myself get played by a con artist, doesn't mean the laws aren't fair. Which is exactly what Stephanie was, by the way: a con artist.

Leonard's investigator did some digging and found out she'd done the exact same thing twice before."

"No way."

"Yep. She'd slept with her boss, made secret recordings, and then threatened a sexual harassment lawsuit to get herself paid. I was the only one who didn't pay her off right away, so she'd never filed anything before. But, still, it was the same MO."

"Why the heck did you settle when you realized she's a con artist? Surely, the jury would have believed you, when they found out she'd done it before!"

"That's exactly what I said to Leonard. But he and his team convinced me those other instances wouldn't get into evidence, and I'd get reamed at trial. He said, even without the recordings being admissible against me, any jury would hate my guts for fucking around with an employee. Leonard said my cocaine use would come out. And that would make them believe Stephanie's version of events. He said I could get hit for ten million or more in punitive damages, given how my company had just skyrocketed. So, I caved." He rubs his forehead, looking distraught. "I paid her off in a confidential settlement that required her to destroy all the illegal recordings she'd made of me, got my ass to rehab, and tried not to think about Stephanie fucking Moreland, ever again."

My heart is physically aching at the expression on Reed's face. "You haven't done coke since then?"

"No. Never."

"How much did you wind up paying her?"

Reed pauses. "It was a confidential settlement, so I'm technically not allowed to talk about it, any more than she is. I'll tell you the number, but only if you swear you're just Georgie right now. Not the Intrepid Reporter. Not playing me, in any way. Look me in the eye, and promise this will stay between you and me, forever, and I'll tell you."

My heart is thumping. "I promise, Reed. I'll never tell a soul."

"You're not recording this conversation?"

Oh, my heart. This poor man. "I'm not. I'll never record anything you say without your knowledge and express permission. I promise."

He looks down at his hands on the kitchen table. "I paid that bitch a cool million."

"Wow. An expensive life lesson."

"Yeah. Honestly, the whole thing screwed with my head. Before Stephanie, I'd already had a hard time trusting people. Women, especially. I was always positive they were out to get something from me. But after Stephanie, my paranoia with women went to a whole new level. Ever since then, I'm just super careful. Always on guard."

Oh, my heart. I rise from my chair and go to him. I slide into his lap and touch his cheek. "I'm sorry she messed with your head."

"I've never told anyone about her," he whispers. "Well, other than my lawyers."

I press my forehead against his. "Not even Josh and Henn?"

"No. I was too embarrassed to tell them. I fucked up. Royally. In the end, it was my fault for being so stupid and reckless."

My heart feels like it's going to burst from my chest. I feel so close to him right now, so connected. So much so, I feel the need to reciprocate. To tell him something I've never told anyone, as well. "I've got my own Stephanie Moreland," I whisper, my heartbeat increasing. "I've never told anyone this story. But it's something that's made it really hard for me to trust. Something I can't stand thinking about. Something I want to forget." I swallow hard. "But I want to tell you about it. I want to tell you, because I feel really close to you right now."

He strokes my hair and looks deeply into my eyes. "You can tell me anything, Georgie."

I open my mouth... determined to tell him the thing I've never told anyone. Ever. But I close my mouth, too nervous to begin my story. "I think I'm gonna need some liquid courage to do this." I motion to my beer. "Something a bit stronger than that."

Chapter 18
Reed

We're sitting on barstools at the bar in my game room. Holding our second shots of Patrón.

"On the count of three," Georgina says. And when she counts us off, we both throw the tequila back.

"Beer chaser?" I ask.

"Hell yeah."

I grab bottles for both of us from a mini-fridge behind the bar, and she takes a long swig as I resume my stool.

"Okay. I'm ready to tell you my story now," she says, shaking out her hands. "I can't feel my face or toes."

I laugh. "You don't have to tell me this story, you know."

"I know, but I want to." She takes another long swig of her beer. Laces her fingers together on top of the bar. And exhales. "In high school, I wrote for the school newspaper the first three years. And I absolutely loved it. At the end of my third year, Mr. Gates, the teacher who supervised the paper, selected *me* to be editor-in-chief for the next year, over this total brainiac guy who'd also wanted the position. I was so freaking excited and proud to be selected, I could barely keep it together. I'd worked my ass off for three years, unlike the brainiac guy. He was way smarter than me, but he'd just phoned it in."

"Hustle beats talent, when talent doesn't hustle," I say. I grab her hand. "Although you've got both talent and hustle, so never mind."

She squeezes my hand. "Thank you." She pauses. "As it turned out, some of the kids at the newspaper—particularly, this group of mean girls—didn't think I deserved the editor position. So, they started a rumor that Mr. Gates had only selected me because he wanted to sleep with me."

"Oh, Georgie. Those girls were bitches."

She looks down at her beer, and it's immediately clear those mean girls aren't, collectively, her Stephanie Moreland, like I was just thinking. No, apparently, there's more to this story. I wait, my pulse thumping.

"I just tried to ignore the rumors and gossip and put my head down and work harder than anyone else, you know? I was so embarrassed they'd say that. I just wanted to work extra hard to prove them all wrong about me. To show them I *had* deserved the promotion." She looks up from her hands. "And then, one day, in the middle of my senior year, when I was working after school in the newspaper room, all by myself... Mr. Gates came in... and he..." She takes a shallow breath. "He cornered me, and he... pinned my arms behind my back, and he... he kissed me."

I'm flooded with rage. Disgust. A fierce urge to protect. I need to fix this. Protect Georgie. *Kill that motherfucker.*

Georgina wells up. "He said all this crazy stuff about me teasing him and flirting with him. He said I wore sexy clothes to turn him on. But I swear I didn't!"

I get up and hug her and she collapses into me. "Of course, you didn't. No matter what you wore, no matter what you did or said, ever, he had no right to touch you. Georgie, he was a fucking monster and you did absolutely nothing wrong."

"I was so shocked and scared... So ashamed."

"*Ashamed?* You had nothing to be ashamed about. He assaulted you."

"Yeah, but those girls were right about me the whole time. He picked me over the brainiac only because he wanted to sleep with me!"

"Oh, sweetheart."

"You want to hear the craziest part? That's what I was thinking when he did it. 'Those mean girls were right.'"

"Did you report him?"

"No. I knew nobody would ever believe me. Plus, I was embarrassed. The same as you with those illegal recordings. "

"You had nothing to be embarrassed about. He *assaulted* you, Georgie. You should have reported him."

"You don't understand. Mr. Gates also coached football, and the team had won two championships in four years. Everybody loved Mr. Gates. If I thought those mean girls were on my ass before, I couldn't even imagine what would happen to me if I told anyone about what Mr. Gates did. Plus, there was no way I wanted those girls to find out they'd been right. It was the most humiliating, embarrassing, horrifying thing I could imagine."

I'm losing my fucking mind. A hair's breadth away from jumping in one of my cars and driving in a blind rage to the Valley to find this Mr. Gates and wrap my bare hands around his throat and squeeze the fucking life out of him.

"I quit the paper the very next day," she says flatly. "I knew I couldn't tell anyone what he'd done. And I didn't want to be in the same room with him, ever again. Thank God, I'd already gotten into UCLA, and my second-semester grades didn't matter. Because the entire rest of the school year, I couldn't concentrate. I was always on edge. If I saw Mr. Gates across campus, I ran the other direction and hid in a bathroom. At first, my father thought my grades plummeted because I was having boy problems. Then, he figured it was because I'd gotten into college and had senioritis. But the truth was, I was a wreck the entire rest of the school year because of Mr. Gates and this horrible secret I was keeping."

"You poor, poor baby." I wipe her tears. "I'm so sorry this happened to you." I stroke her cheek. "You've never told anyone any of this before?"

She shakes her head. "Not even Alessandra. You're the only person I've ever told."

I pull her to me and hold her tight. My heart is thundering. Aching. Breaking. Bleeding. My blood is boiling. I'm out of my head. "Does Gates still work at the school?"

"Yes. But please don't try to get me to report him. I just can't do it, Reed. No one would ever believe me. You need to trust me on this. He's a god at that school." She breaks free from our embrace and wipes her eyes. "It's okay. I've moved on. Honestly, getting this internship has worked wonders for me. Getting to work for CeeCee. A kickass woman. Knowing, for a *fact*, she offered me this internship based on my talent and nothing else... because she loved my writing, and my personality, not because she wanted to get into my pants. Having that kind of validation has meant everything to me and my confidence and helped me move on so much. But Mr. Gates is part of the reason why I've been so adamant about not wanting your artists to know about us while I'm working on the special issue. I just want everyone I'm interviewing to respect me. I don't want them thinking I got assigned to the special issue, specifically, because you requested me for personal reasons."

Oh, fuck.

I feel physically sick.

On the outside, I might be stroking Georgina's back calmly, kissing her cheek, holding her close... but, on the inside, I'm freaking the fuck out.

Prior to this moment, I didn't want Georgie to find out I'm the one who funded her grant and made it so that her internship is a paid one. But now, all I can think, on a running loop, is: *Georgie can never, ever find out. Never, never, never.*

"You knocked CeeCee out when she met you, baby," I say soothingly. "When CeeCee and I first talked about the special issue, she specifically said she loved your writing samples. And she also said you're the most charismatic and charming newbie she's met in a long time. Maybe, ever."

She squeezes me tight. So tight, in fact, I suddenly feel overcome with emotion.

"CeeCee really said all that about me, Reed? You swear?"

"She really did, baby. I swear. In those exact words."

Holy fuck. I've never been more relieved to be able to honestly quote anybody's exact words in my entire life.

"That's so amazingly wonderful to know. Ever since Mr. Gates, I've been so paranoid and filled with self-doubt. Not only that, I've had such a hard time trusting anyone. The same way you've felt after Stephanie Moreland. I think Mr. Gates is part of the reason why I went so batshit psycho on my boyfriend, Shawn, when I discovered he'd cheated on me. Because I'd let down my guard with him and trusted him. And it's so, so hard for me to do that."

I pause. And disengage from our embrace. "Um. So... how 'batshit psycho' are we talking here?"

She smiles through her tears. "Pretty fucking psycho."

I wait, but she says nothing further. All she does is giggle.

"You're not planning to elaborate?" I say.

"Not really," she says. And then she laughs again, still wiping tears.

I kiss her cheek. "Come on, Ricci. If I've invited a psycho into my home, I think I should know about it."

She twists her mouth adorably. Takes my hand, and kisses the top of it. "Okay, Mr. Rivers. I'll tell you this story, too. Why not? But let's talk about this next thing in the pool. I'm suddenly feeling the urge to float."

Chapter 19
Reed

Georgie, the most beautiful girl in the world, is naked and floating silently in my moonlit swimming pool, while I stand next to her, looking down on her. Feeling like I'm staring at an angel sent straight from heaven. A batshit psycho angel, apparently. She hasn't told me the story yet. We had some champagne while sitting on the pool ledge together. And then peeled off our clothes. Made out a bit. And now, she's floating and in some sort of meditation, while I stand next to her, lightly supporting her naked, horizontal frame, thinking two things on repeat. One, I'll never let anybody hurt you again. And, two, I've never seen anything so fucking beautiful in my life.

Finally, Georgie opens her eyes and stands. Without saying a word, she wraps her arms and legs around my neck and torso, like a monkey clinging to a tree, and nuzzles her nose into mine. "I feel better now."

"Good. That's all I want for you. I want you to feel good and nothing else."

"Thank you. I feel good when I'm with you."

My heart skips a beat. "I feel good when I'm with you."

"Good. Now, walk me around the pool, while I lay my cheek on your shoulder and tell you about the time I went batshit psycho on my cheating ex."

"I can't wait to hear the story."

I begin walking a loop around the shallow end of my pool,

as Georgina tells me about the time she awakened one fateful morning and discovered a string of texts and photos on her then-boyfriend's phone that confirmed her long-simmering suspicions: he was cheating on her like she didn't exist.

"Actually," she says, "confirming Shawn was cheating on me was a huge relief. Twice before that morning, I'd told Shawn he was acting really weird and suspicious and secretive, but both times he said I was crazy and paranoid. So, I was kind of thrilled in a weird way to finally know I wasn't insane—that he was cheating on me. And not just cheating on me. The dude had *four* side chicks."

"Four? Oh my God. No wonder you went batshit psycho on him."

"Right? Who could blame me!"

"So, what'd you do to the guy?"

She laughs. "I'm scared to tell you. I don't want you to be scared of me and send me packing."

Oh, God. She's so fucking adorable. "No worries about that. Your invitation to stay here for the whole summer is irrevocable."

She lifts her cheek from my shoulder and beams a radiant smile at me.

"Come on baby," I coo. "A little psycho won't scare me off. To be honest, I get turned on by a little bit of crazy. It keeps things from getting boring for me."

"Yeah, well, this wasn't a little bit of crazy, sweetie. It was a shit-ton of batshit psycho."

I wince. "Okay, I admit you're starting to scare me a tiny bit."

She giggles uproariously. "One more glass of champagne and then I'll tell you *everything*," she says with gusto, clearly savoring the fact that I'm on the edge of my proverbial seat, waiting to hear this story from her.

But, of course, since her wish is my command, I carry her to the ledge, where I fill our empty flutes from a bottle of Cristal we brought down to the pool with us.

"Aah, that's good," she says after taking a long sip. "Best champagne I've ever had."

"I should hope so. This stuff ain't cheap. It's liquid gold. Now, come on. Tell me what you did to the guy. No more stalling. I know you're enjoying torturing me. But enough is enough."

She looks at me flirtatiously. "Okay, but in my defense, keep in mind that my dad was in treatment at this point. So I was on the brink of a nervous breakdown, as it was. And, like I said, I was more enraged at the betrayal of my trust, in my time of need, than about the cheating itself."

"Just tell me the story already. I'll consider all mitigating factors once I know the extent of your batshit psychosis."

She returns her empty flute to the ledge and leans her shoulder against the side of the pool. We're both standing now. Facing each other. Her hair is wet and slicked back. Her breasts just above the water line. And I can honestly say whatever's about to come out of her mouth won't scare me off in the slightest.

"Okay, so, I saw all those texts on Shawn's phone while he was taking a shower, and I—"

"Hold up. Sorry. How, exactly, did you see those texts and photos? Wasn't Shawn's phone passcode protected? If not, he's the world's stupidest serial cheater."

Georgina snickers. "Yeah, he had it passcode protected. And, trust me, he never punched in the code at an angle where I could peek over his shoulder. But where there's a will, there's a way."

"Oh, shit. His passcode was all zeroes, wasn't it? Or something like 1-2-3-4?"

She giggles. "Nope. It wasn't an obvious code. I'm just a brilliant, devious hacker."

I pause to let her elaborate, and when she doesn't I say, "Come on. Give it up. What'd you do?"

She giggles happily, sounding very much like a woman

with an abundance of beer, tequila, and champagne in her bloodstream. "If I tell you, then I won't be able to hack into *your* phone, when *you* start acting weird and suspicious on me."

Oh, Georgie. I put my palms on her cheeks and her lips part in surprise.

"Sweetheart, I'm a lot of things, some of them not so admirable, but a cheater isn't one of them. I promise."

She swoons in my palms, so I lean down and kiss her bee-stung lips. And, for a moment, fireworks are going off so violently and deliciously inside me, I feel physically dizzy. When our lips break apart, I nuzzle her nose and whisper, "Also, I use facial recognition."

She bursts out laughing, and throws her arms around my neck again. And, just like that, she's clinging to me again... which I don't need to be told means she wants me to walk laps around the shallow end again.

"Okay, so here's how I hacked Shawn's phone," she says. "The night before, when he fell asleep, I cleaned his phone screen immaculately, until there wasn't a single smudge on it. And then, after he'd logged in several times the next morning, I peeked at the new smudges when he was in the shower." She shrugs. "Once I had the pool of numbers to work with, I was able to figure out his code on the third try."

"You're a genius."

She runs her fingers through my wet hair. "Are you scared of me now?"

"Not at all. Just impressed."

"So, anyway, I saw those texts and photos, and lost my shit. I went straight to his closet and grabbed all of his jerseys. Shawn played basketball for UCLA, so he had—"

"Hold the fuck up. 'Shawn' is Shawn *Gordon*? This whole time we've been talking about motherfucking Shawn *Gordon*?"

"Oh, God. Not you, too."

"Georgie, he's been UCLA's top scorer the past two years. He's a freak. A beast."

"Yeah, well, he's also a dickheaded cheater. If you're so in love with him, then *you* date him and see what kind of boyfriend he is to you."

I chuckle heartily. "Sorry. Josh, Henn, and I still follow UCLA sports religiously. Shawn Gordon is one of our favorites."

She glares at me.

"But not anymore. Now, I hate him."

She laughs.

"Continue. Please. You took all of his jerseys out of his closet, and..."

"I went outside to the barbeque set up at the back of Shawn's apartment complex... and I burned them all!"

"Oooh. What a psycho," I say sarcastically.

"Reed. I burned *all* his jerseys."

"Yes. I heard you the first time. But I hate to tell you, that's not batshit psycho. That's just run-of-the-mill anger."

"Yeah, well, I haven't told you the rest. Wait until you hear what *else* I did."

"Can't wait to find out."

She bites her lower lip, relishing whatever she's about to say. "There was a screwdriver sitting next to the barbeque, for some reason. And I picked it up, and marched straight to the parking structure, where Shawn's beloved Jeep was parked. He was so proud of that thing. It was his version of a Bugatti." She pauses for dramatic effect. "And I took that screwdriver and I punctured all four tires on his car! *One puncture for each side chick!*" She opens her mouth wide. As wide as it will go. As if to say, *Can you believe it?*

But I'm not the least bit impressed, and I'm sure my face shows it. "That's *it*?" I say.

"What do you mean, 'That's it'? Reed, I gave his beloved car *four* flat tires! Do you know how expensive tires are? And I made it so he'd have to replace the *entire* set, all at once!"

I can't help laughing uproariously at her beautiful innocence in this moment. Her stunning beauty. I kiss her cheek, still laughing. "Oh my God, Georgie girl. I thought you were going to say you keyed the fucker's car. Maybe scratched 'liar' onto his car doors."

She looks utterly shocked at the suggestion. "Well, first of all, his Jeep didn't really have doors. But, second of all, why would I do that? I could have gone to jail for a very long time if I did something as serious as that. I think that would be a felony!"

I laugh again. "And here I thought you were such a badass."

"I am." She pouts. "I gave him *four* flat tires and burned *three* jerseys. I was proud of myself for that."

I laugh. "Well, yeah. I'm glad you did *something* to the guy. He cheated on you with *four* women. I'm just saying that was your chance to go full-on 'Left Eye' Lopes on the guy, and be perfectly justified. I'm just saying you didn't really seize the opportunity as fully as you could have. That's all."

She looks up from her pouting. "Full-on 'Left Eye' Lopes? I'm sure it won't shock you to learn I have no idea what you're talking about."

I throw my head back. "No!"

She giggles. "Sorry."

I return to her. "Lisa 'Left Eye' Lopes. She was in TLC—the female R&B trio from the '90s."

She grimaces. "Nope. Sorry."

I drag my palm over my face. "Please, at least tell me you've heard of TLC?"

She shakes her head, so I sing the chorus of "Scrubs." And when that elicits nothing, I switch to the chorus of "Waterfalls," which, thankfully, she instantly recognizes.

"I *love* that song," she declares.

"Okay, well, the rap in the middle of that one was performed by Lisa 'Left Eye' Lopes."

"Ooooh. Quick question. What's the point of that song? When they say you shouldn't chase waterfalls, are they saying you shouldn't follow your dreams?"

"No, they're saying you shouldn't engage in self-destructive behaviors."

"Aaaaah. Okay."

"So, Lisa 'Left Eye' Lopes. You need to learn this."

"Yes, sir."

"Lisa 'Left Eye' Lopes had a boyfriend named Andre Rison. He was a pro football player. And one night, after they'd had a huge fight, Left Eye burned Andre's very large house in Atlanta completely to the ground."

Georgina gasps.

"She claimed she'd only intended to burn a pair of sneakers in a bathtub, but that the fire had spread and burned out of control."

"Holy crap."

"Guess how long she went to prison for felony arson?" I raise my eyebrow. "*Not a single day.*"

"What?"

"Andre knew he deserved it, apparently. He supported her in court."

"What the hell did Andre do to her?"

"She said he'd beaten her. He denied it."

Georgina's jaw sets. "Well, if he did, he got off easy, if you ask me."

In a flash, I'm thinking about that fucker Mr. Gates again. "I couldn't agree more," I say, my jaw tightening. I set Georgina down onto her feet, and put my fingertip underneath her chin. "Listen to me, Georgie girl. Listen close. Nobody is allowed to hurt you, ever again. You got that? If any man ever dares lay so much as a pinky on you, that you don't want on you, or if someone you trusted hurts you in any way, then I want you to go full-on 'Left Eye' Lopes on his fucking ass. Or, if you're too scared to do that. If you just want to get away, then you do that. But then, I want you to promise me, no matter how far in the future this scenario might come to pass, you'll come to me. Straight to me. No matter where I am in the world. And you'll tell me what happened, so I can go full-on *Reed Rivers* on the motherfucker's ass."

She's shaking against my fingertip. She nods, her hazel eyes flashing.

"Nobody—*nobody*—is allowed to hurt you, Georgina Ricci. Never, ever again. Do you understand me? *Never.*"

She nods again, just before lunging at me and crushing her gorgeous lips to mine.

Chapter 20
Georgina

My head is swimming. And not just from all the booze I've had tonight. The conversations I've had with Reed... our incredible make-out session in the pool, after I told him about Shawn... All of it has been electrifying. Intimate. Like a fairytale. And the night isn't even over yet.

We're out of the swimming pool now, sitting in the hot tub, gazing at the sparkling view of Los Angeles. And I swear I don't remember the last time I felt this alive—this safe and protected and adored—in my entire life.

I take a long swig from the bottle of Cristal and hand it to Reed.

"Tell me about Isabel."

"I already did. Tell her she's a trailblazer. She'll eat that shit up."

"No, no. I mean, tell me what happened between the two of you. Tell me about your relationship. Why did you break up?"

Reed takes a long sip from the champagne bottle. "Because our relationship ran its course, as these things always do. We realized we'd be better as friends. So, we called it quits. The End."

"'We' called it quits? Or *you* called it quits?"

"If you put Isabel into the article about me, I'm taking her out."

"I'm not asking you about her for the article. If I'm going to meet her and try to convince her to let me interview her in-depth, I should know about potential landmines. I should know what happened between the two of you."

"Bullshit. You want to know because you're jealous."

I bat his shoulder. "That's so absolutely... *not*... false!"

Reed laughs uproariously, and so do I.

But when his laughter dissipates, and it's clear he has no intention of answering my question, I slide into his lap and flash him my most charming, drunken smile.

"Aw, come on, Mr. Rivers. I told you about my ex, Shawn *Gordon*. Tell me about your ex, Isabel *Randolph*."

He shrugs. "There's not much to tell. We had fun for a while, but it eventually ran its course, so I ended it. And we've remained friends ever since." He takes another swig from the champagne bottle and hands it to me. "And, obviously, that turned out to be for the best, for both of us, seeing as how she's now marrying the man of her dreams, and I'm here with you."

My heart stops. *Holy crap.* "Where did you and Isabel first meet?"

"At that black-tie birthday party for CeeCee. The one I told you about already. The one I crashed, so I could meet CeeCee and convince her to write about RCR."

I giggle. "Just think. Ten years later, I crashed a music school event to meet CeeCee and convince her to read my writing samples. We're equally diabolical."

"Yes, we are." He kisses me. "Okay, it's my turn to ask a question. And I want your brutally honest answer this time, okay?"

My stomach clenches in anticipation. "Okay."

"This is important, Georgina. No fibbing." He puts his fingertip underneath my chin and looks at me sternly. "Georgina Ricci, did you *truly* have a poster of C-Bomb on your teenage wall—or did you tell me that to fuck with me?"

I burst out laughing, both in amusement and relief, and shake my head. "I was totally fucking with you."

"I knew it!" Reed says, joining me in laughter. "You're evil!"

"I really did love RCR as a teenager, though. That part wasn't a lie."

"You'll say or do *anything* to get what you want, won't you? You're shameless. Shameless and evil."

"You can't blame me for lying about that. I had to make sure you wouldn't let me walk out that door and go to C-Bomb. I didn't want to be Caleb Baumgarten's Penny Lane for a week." I nuzzle my nose against Reed's. "I wanted to be *yours*."

Reed runs his palm down my arm, before it disappears into the warm water of the hot tub and rests on my tailbone. "I was never going to let you go to Caleb, baby. Over my dead body." He kisses me passionately, sending my spirit swirling through the night sky. "What the hell are you doing to me, Georgina?" he mutters.

I'm drunk. On all the alcohol I've ingested tonight, and on Reed himself. "I don't know," I whisper back, my smile hurting my cheeks. "All I can hope and pray is it's half of what you're doing to me."

Chapter 21
Reed

I lay Georgina's sleeping, drunken frame onto the bed in her guestroom. Oh, how I wish I were laying her naked body down onto the four-poster in my room. But, of course, that's not an option. When she was perfectly sober last night, she asked for a room of her own, much to my extreme disappointment. And she didn't retract that request before passing out in my arms in a lounger by the pool.

I get her situated comfortably in bed underneath a sheet, and then move to the foot of the bed to grab a folded blanket... when my foot bumps into something hard on the floor by the bed. The room is too dark for me to make out what I've bumped into, but it's definitely not Georgina's suitcase, the outline of which I can see across the room by the door.

Curious, I head to the nightstand and flip on a small lamp. Momentarily, when the lamp illuminates, I worry the light will awaken Georgina. But a quick glance at Drunken Sleeping Beauty tells me, no, this girl is out for the night.

I return to the mysterious obstacle at the foot of Georgina's bed and discover it's a cardboard box emblazoned with *Courthouse Copy Service* on its side. The exact same kind of box Leonard always has in his office. And, instantly, even before I've peeked inside the box, I know what I'm going to find inside. Stephanie Moreland's lawsuit. But, still, just for kicks, I look anyway. And, yep. No surprise. There it is. Stephanie's complaint, sitting right on top a stack of documents.

A puff of air escapes from my nose. I should have known Georgina had it. There's no way Georgina would have seen reference on that printout to a *settled* sexual harassment lawsuit and not beelined to the clerk's office to get a copy of it. But why didn't she tell me she'd read it, when she asked me about the case? *Because she thought, if I didn't know she'd already read it, then I might lie to her about Stephanie. And she wanted to catch me in a lie.*

For a moment, I feel betrayed. Hurt. Angry. I feel the old familiar urges bubbling up. The ones I feel whenever a woman gets too close. When I feel my walls being threatened. The urge to run away, push away, shut down. That's what I'm feeling. As usual.

But then, I take in Georgina's beautiful, sleeping face... and I remember the secret she shared with me tonight. The way she laid herself bare to me. And the panic inside me vanishes. The urge to run away, push her away, shut down subsides.

Okay, so she got the printout of lawsuits and noticed I'd settled a sexual harassment case. Considering what that asshole Mr. Gates did to her, it's no wonder she was especially determined to find out everything she could about Stephanie's claims. At least, to Georgie's credit, she came straight to me and asked me for *my* side of the story, rather than jumping to conclusions and instantly believing Stephanie's lies like they were gospel.

My heart rate is slowing again.

This is not a problem.

Georgina is simply doing her job.

And doing it well.

After what she's been through, I can't blame her for wanting to know what kind of man she's been sleeping with. Good for her for following the breadcrumbs. She might be young. And she might be smoking hot. But Georgina Ricci is nobody's fool.

I grab the blanket from the foot of the bed and gently cover her with it. I bend down and kiss her cheek gently, and turn off the light. Goodnight, Intrepid Reporter.

I stare at her for a long moment, not wanting to leave her side. But, finally, I drag my ass to my room. Which is where I brush my teeth, shower, and, finally, blessedly, crawl into my bed with an exhausted groan. But before flipping off my light, I grab my phone and send a text to Henn:

I need another favor, brother. Find out where Georgie went to high school. It's in the Valley somewhere. A guy named Gates is the football coach. They won two championships in four years. I need you to hack into his phone and computer and dig around. See if you find a vulnerability. I don't know exactly what I'm looking for. All I know is I want you to find something, anything, I can use to go Left Eye Lopes on the guy's ass. I want to burn this motherfucker's entire life to the ground, Henny. Just like Left Eye burned Andre's house. No mercy.

Chapter 22
Georgina

"Good afternoon," I chirp to CeeCee's personal assistant, Margot. She's seated at a desk, holding down the fort while CeeCee is still on vacation in Bali.

"Georgie!" Margot replies warmly. She hops up and gives me a hug. "How are you?"

It's a standard question, obviously. One I've been asked in polite conversation countless times in my life. One that *should* be answered with a simple, "I'm great! And you?" And yet, today, upon hearing that simple question, every fiber of my being wants to shout maniacally, "I think I'm falling for Reed Rivers!"

It's the same maniacal reply I wanted to shout at Amalia this morning, when she kindly asked if I'd slept well. And the same thing I wanted to scream at the top of my lungs at the barista in Starbucks, who asked if I wanted my coffee drink hot or cold. Truly, I don't know how many more times I can be asked how I'm doing or how I slept or how I want my coffee, and be expected to *not* shout in reply, "I think I'm falling for Reed Rivers!"

Because... I think I am.

Hard.

Obviously, I don't want to fall for Reed. Indeed, I'm trying very hard *not* to do that supremely stupid thing. But it's a hard thing to resist doing, after the amazing conversations we had last night, followed by the magic of this morning.

This morning, after Reed woke me up (and kindly gave me a couple ibuprofen for my slight hangover), he led me into his home gym for our morning workout... and then shocked the living hell out of me by giving me yet another piece of exercise equipment. This time, a top-of-the-line Pilates reformer! Which I happen to know costs around four grand. I protested, of course. Said I couldn't possibly accept it. But he insisted and wore me down. Obviously, I'll never collect it from him. As far as I'm concerned, that thing will stay in Reed's home gym forevermore. But just the thought that he bought it for me? *Swoon.*

But the amazingness didn't end here. After our workout, and after some delicious sex on my new machine, Reed and I headed to a recording studio in Hollywood. Which was where 2Real, aka Will Riley, was hard at work on his third album. Apparently, Will had asked Reed to swing by the studio today, saying he desperately wanted Reed's input on a particular track that was giving him fits. So, of course, Reed dropped whatever he'd been planning to do today, and headed straight there, with his eager shadow in tow.

And, oh, God, it was mind-blowing to watch those two work together. After brief introductions, I sat quietly in a corner for three hours that felt like three minutes, and watched in awe as they played a portion of the track in question. Stopped it. Went back. Talked. Tried something else. Talked again.

I came away from the experience with even deeper respect for Reed. Clearly, he's a meaningful partner to his artists. A genius at far more than business and marketing, or music scouting and strategizing. He's a genius at pulling the best out of his artists, as well.

Granted, I didn't understand most of what Reed said to Will during those three hours. For example, at one point, Reed said: "What if we were to saturate the vocals and make them extra dirty?" And I was like, *Huh?* Another time, Reed said, "We could turn up the flux on the Echo to around 300, playback level at zero. Let's try that and see if it makes our balls vibrate." It was another *huh*? But even without understanding the conversation, I could plainly surmise, thanks to Will's reactions to Reed's comments, Reed was making a powerful contribution to Will's art.

But our amazing day together didn't end after the studio. From there, Reed spoiled me by taking me to lunch at the nicest restaurant I've ever been to—a hotspot frequented by the Hollywood elite. And when we ran into several movers and shakers, all of whom Reed knew and introduced me to, he said to each one of them, "This is Georgina Ricci, a brilliant new writer for *Rock 'n' Roll*. CeeCee hand-picked her to write an in-depth feature on me, so she's following me around to get the goods." Of course, I swooned at that introduction, each and every time.

After lunch, Reed had a meeting with his business partners on a bunch of nightclubs. He said I could come, but I decided to use the time to head over to *Rock 'n' Roll's* offices for a few hours.

"I'll drive you over there," he said. "It's not too far out of my way."

And that's when I said something awkward and embarrassing... that would have been mortifying to me if it hadn't led to Reed saying something so swoony, it made an egg pop out of my ovary.

The thing I said to Reed was this: "Thanks for the ride over there. I don't know how long I'll be there, though, so I'll plan to grab an Uber back home afterwards."

Back home.

I called Reed's house my home.

Of course, I was instantly mortified I'd let that word slip out. So, I quickly stammered, "I mean, back to *your* house. I'll take an Uber back to *your* house afterwards."

At first, Reed didn't even acknowledge my slip. He simply opened the passenger door to his Bugatti and gestured for me to get in. Which I did, and then promptly covered my face in embarrassment as he walked around the back to his own door.

But when he dropped me off in front of *Rock 'n' Roll*'s offices, and called to me as I got out of the car, I forgot all about my embarrassment. Because that's when Reed called out, "I'll see you back home around five, baby! Don't keep me waiting this time!"

Yeah. I swooned pretty hard in that moment. It's when I knew *not* falling for Reed was going to be a tall order. Which brings me to this moment with Margot. To her question, "How are you doing?" and my raging impulse to shout, "I think I'm falling for Reed Rivers!"

Somehow, though, through sheer force of will, I manage to take a deep breath and reply, in a calm voice, "I'm great, Margot. How are you?"

"I'm swamped," Margot says dramatically. "It's always bananas when CeeCee is out of the country. But this week, especially, has been insanity. Are you here to see Zasu?" She's referring to the veteran reporter who's been assigned as my mentor this summer. "She just left."

"No, I texted with Zasu earlier today. I'm actually here to see if a box of documents I've been waiting on from the courthouse has arrived."

"I haven't seen anything addressed to you. I'd be happy to text you if something arrives." Margot makes a note on a pad. "Is it legal documents?"

"Yep."

"What is it, out of curiosity?"

"Just an old court case that might have some interesting information in it. To be honest, I'm probably just chasing a wild goose. Speaking of which, do you guys keep old issues of *Rock 'n' Roll* on the premises?"

"Of course. We have every issue ever published, filed in chronological order, in a storage room."

My heart leaps. "May I take a look?"

"You bet. Follow me."

***

I look around me, taking in the small storage room, its shelves filled to bursting with back issues of *Rock 'n' Roll*. I don't know which issue I'm looking for—from which month or year. Or, for that matter, if there will be anything of value in the article I've got in mind, if it exists at all. But not knowing what I'm doing has never stopped me before, and it won't stop me this time, either.

I head to Wikipedia on my phone and discover that CeeCee turned sixty a few months ago, in March. Which leads me to conclude the birthday party Reed crashed, where he met both CeeCee and Isabel, must have been CeeCee's fiftieth. I can't imagine CeeCee would have thrown herself a huge, black-tie affair for her forty-ninth or fifty-first.

So, that line of thinking gives me the *year* of the issue I'm looking for. Also, a two-month window, since my mentor, Zasu, told me the production cycle of most *Rock 'n' Roll* issues is thirty to sixty days. If an article about CeeCee's fiftieth birthday party, thrown in March, was printed in *Rock 'n' Roll* at all, I'm assuming it would have appeared in the April or May issue.

Obviously, it's a long shot to think such an article exists. And that, if it does, it includes a photo spread. But Reed did say he posed in his rented tux for "all the photographers" on the red carpet outside the party. So I think it's *possible* the magazine featured an article about the party, including photos... although I'm sure it's equally possible those photographers were only there to snap photos for CeeCee's social media or personal memories.

And why am I looking for this, at all? For several reasons, I think. The one I keep telling myself is my primary motivation is that any photos, if they exist, would allow me to trace Reed's professional path to glory, starting from the very beginning. Which, in turn, could lead to me painting a better portrait of Reed in my article. And, actually, I think that rationalization—that this wild goose chase is legitimate journalism—is plausible.

Unfortunately, though, I think the *higher* truth here is that I'm shamelessly stalking Reed. Dying to see a photo of the wildly successful man who's knocked me flat on my ass, from when he was nothing but a hungry, twenty-four-year-old hustler in a rented tux. Not too long ago, I crashed an event to meet CeeCee in an effort to change my life. And I can't deny I'm dying to see a photo of Reed on the night he did precisely the same thing a decade ago. In truth, I think I simply want to feel closer to Reed. To get to know him, inside and out.

But that's not everything, and I know it. There's one more reason I'm here, looking for a needle in a haystack like a St. Bernard looking for a skier buried beneath an avalanche. A reason I'm not proud of. But one I simply can't deny. *Isabel.*

I know the odds are slim I'll find a photo of the pair on the night they first laid eyes on each other. Neither of them had yet become famous or important that night. So, why would the magazine include a photo of either of them, let alone the two of them together? But I can't help thinking it's *possible* they were snapped in a group shot, or maybe in the background of someone else's shot, perhaps dancing together on the dance floor. If so, then I want to see the shot. I want to see what kind of electricity coursed between them in those first moments after they'd laid eyes on each other. I want to know how Reed's chemistry with Isabel compared to his chemistry with me. I want to know if Reed looked at me in the lecture hall the same way he looked at Isabel at CeeCee's birthday party.

Okay, yes, I know. Obviously, I have zero chill. I'm a psycho bitch who's jealous of one of the most beautiful, glamorous, famous actresses in the world. A woman who shagged the man I'm falling for, for years, and also, I suspect, snagged his heart at some point, too. I know she's engaged to the love of her life now. And that Reed has said he wouldn't want her anymore, regardless. But, still, I'm almost positive Reed loved Isabel at some point. And maybe still does. And I guess I'm grasping at straws here, irrationally trying to figure out if, maybe, Reed could one day, possibly, love me, too.

After some poking around, I figure out the filing system used in the storage room, and five minutes later, hit pay dirt.

The magazine in my hand has George Michael on its cover. On the left side of George's head, a small headline reads, "Meet your new obsession: Red Card Riot." In larger print above that, another headline reads, "CeeCee Rafael Knows How to Throw a F*cking Birthday Party!"

My heart in my mouth, I flip to the article about the birthday party, and squeal loudly when I see *five* full pages of photos.

"Jackpot," I whisper, my voice cutting through the air of the empty storage room.

Ravenously, my eyes search and scour. But, not surprisingly, I don't see any photos of Reed or Isabel. But then I see it. In a shot of Justin Timberlake. He's arriving at the party. He's just gotten out of a limo, and he's starting to traipse down the red carpet. And what I see in the background of the photo, behind Justin, snatches the air out of my lungs.

What the hell?

I pull out my phone and take a photo of the photo. And then I spread the background image on my phone wide with my fingers to zoom in. But it's no use. Thanks to the camera's focus on Justin, the background image is slightly blurred. Which means I'm only ninety percent sure of what I'm seeing. But, still, that's pretty damned sure.

Holy fuck.

If this photo shows what I think it does, then that could mean only one thing: Reed lied to me. Right to my face. About something I would have thought was totally innocuous.

And, for the life of me, I can't understand *why*.

Chapter 23
Reed

Georgina is late, once again. Caught up in traffic. This time, because she lost track of time while reading a bunch of articles at *Rock 'n' Roll*'s offices.

To distract myself while awaiting her return, I've been sitting on my couch with my laptop, going over the marketing plan for Fugitive Summer's upcoming release. As I've been working, I've been sipping a glass of Bordeaux. Occasionally, glancing up at the sunset painting the floor-to-ceiling windows on the far side of the living room.

Surely, if someone were to see me right now, not knowing anything about Georgina, they'd think I'm the perfect portrait of a man in relaxation mode. But it couldn't be further from the truth. If Georgina doesn't get here soon, I'm pretty sure I'm going to die from anticipation. I'd probably feel that way, regardless. Just because I'm physically craving her after being away from her for several hours. But my impatience is amplified by the flat, square box hidden underneath my couch cushion at the moment. The box I hid there when I got home, so I can give it to her at just the right moment tonight.

Georgina won't keep my gift. Not this one. Not for long, anyway. She'll take it from me with a beaming smile and turn around and sell it, the first chance she gets. But that doesn't mean I don't want to give it to her. Or see that beaming smile of hers when she first opens the box and sees the sheer perfection of what's inside. Whether Georgina winds up keeping my gift for a day or a week, her gift to *me* will be the look on her face when she first opens the box.

Finally, just as I'm reaching the end of Fugitive Summer's release package, I hear my front door open. When I turn my head, it's just in time to see Georgina bursting into the expansive room. And, just like that, every cell in my body simultaneously jolts with a tsunami of reactions. Arousal, joy, relief. *She's home. She's safe. She's mine.*

"Sorry, sorry, sorry," Georgie says adorably, barreling over to me, her computer bag clanking against her hip as she moves. "I got caught up reading a bunch of stuff, and totally lost track of time."

Frazzled, she kisses me in greeting, and I calmly rise and hand her a goblet of wine.

"What were you reading?" I ask, settling next to her on the couch.

"Every past article I could get my hands on about every River Records artist," she says. "Including the article that started it all—the one CeeCee wrote about Red Card Riot's debut."

"Oh, wow. I haven't seen that one in forever. I'd love to read it, for old time's sake."

"I thought you might say that..." Waggling her eyebrows, she reaches into her computer bag and pulls out a sheet of paper. "So, I made a high-resolution color copy for you!"

"No way," I say, as she hands me the page. "This is amazing, Georgie! Thank you." I kiss her cheek. "That was awfully sweet of you."

"Well, you're awfully sweet to me, so... "

Oh, Jesus Christ. Those condors in my belly are back again, full-force. I read the entirety of the short article, stopping once to make a comment to Georgie, and, finally, place the page on the coffee table. "What a walk down memory lane. Wow."

"I was actually thinking you might like a framed copy for your home office," Georgie says. "You have all your major 'firsts' in there, so I thought..."

"That's a fantastic idea. Thank you. I'll give this to Amalia to get framed."

"Oh. No. I was thinking I'd get it framed for you, if that's okay." She smiles shyly. "I know a framed article isn't much of a gift, but you've given me so much. I'm dying to give you something special. Something that might be meaningful to you."

My heart skips a beat at the sweetness in Georgina's expression—even as my heart leaps and bounds at the perfect segue she just lobbed to me. I'd planned to give Georgina my gift after dinner. But after a segue like that, how could I possibly resist giving it to her now?

"Speaking of gifts, I have one for you."

"Oh, Reed. No."

"Just listen. My meeting this afternoon was in Beverly Hills." I take a deep breath. Holy shit, my heart is racing. "And when I was walking the couple blocks back to my car afterwards, I happened to pass a store window that was displaying something that instantly reminded me of you. So, I walked inside the store and bought it for you."

"Reed, no. No, no, no."

Ignoring her protests, I reach under the couch cushion and pull out the box I've been dying to give her. "This is for you. I hope you love it."

Her wide eyes dart from the blue box to my face and back again. "I can't accept that, whatever it is. Thank you so much for thinking of me, but it's way too much."

"Why don't you decide what's 'way too much' after you see it?"

"Reed, it's from Tiffany's."

"So what? It could be a bottle opener."

She's frozen. In shock.

150

"Come on, Georgie. Open the box. Are you going to deny me that pleasure?"

She looks deeply conflicted. But, still, she doesn't move.

"Aren't you the least bit curious what item in a store window reminded me of you so much, I felt called to buy it for you, on the spot?"

That does it. Her curiosity gets the best of her. With a trembling hand, Georgina takes the box from me and slowly opens it—and then sucks in a sharp inhale when she beholds the stunning treasure inside: a baroque-style ruby necklace set in Spanish gold, its multitude of deep-red gems cascading down in golden dripping, chandelier settings.

"Oh my God," she whispers. She puts her free hand on her heart. "Reed. This is... *exquisite.*"

And so are you, I think. And it's the truth. The look on her face is everything I dreamed it would be and more. Even though I know she's going to sell it, this moment made buying the perfect piece of jewelry for her, rather than some placeholder that happened to be of the right monetary value, well worth it.

Georgina's eyes prick with tears. "It's the most beautiful thing I've ever seen," she whispers. She's shaking. Flushed. *Beautiful.*

"The crazy thing is," I say, my chest heaving every bit as much as hers, "I didn't even know rubies are your birthstone when I first saw it. The saleswoman inside the store told me about rubies after I asked her to show me the necklace. Did you know rubies are called 'the king's gem'?"

Georgina shakes her head, looking like a teary-eyed deer in headlights.

"It turns out, the king's gem is highly symbolic. They symbolize power and blood. Passion, desire, and fire. All of which is perfect for you, Georgina, because you're passion and power embodied. A human flame." *And you've infiltrated my blood.* I grab Georgina's limp hand. "Ever since I first laid eyes on you, I've wanted to tie you to my bed and show you what your body can do, if only you're willing to surrender completely. But then I got to know you, and I realized I had to wait to do that with you. I knew you'd enjoy it and have fun, to be sure, which is good enough for some... but with you, I didn't simply want to show you a good time. I wanted to show you something that would transform you." I squeeze her hand. "Tonight's finally the night, Georgina. You're ready to let go completely. You're ready to trust me. And I can't wait another night. Tonight, you're going to wear that necklace for me—a necklace dripping in the king's gems—and let me worship you as my queen."

I've rendered her speechless.

"Say yes, Georgie."

She swallows hard. She looks deeply conflicted. Which is exactly as expected. Indeed, I fully expected and counted on Georgina's conflicting emotions when I bought this necklace in the first place. "I can't," she says. "I mean, yes, tie me up. *Please.* I've wanted you to do that since you mentioned it the other night in front of your gate. But I can't accept this gift from you. It's too generous."

"I won't take no for an answer."

She frowns. "The truth is, I can't own thousands of dollars in rubies when my father is on the brink of losing his condo, any day now. If I took this necklace from you, I wouldn't be able to resist selling it behind your back at my first opportunity, so I could give the proceeds to my father."

I force myself not to smile. *Damn, I'm good.*

When Henn called this afternoon to give me the grand total of what Georgie's father owes on his condo, and also to tell me that a third notice had just gone out to him from the bank—meaning the guy is mere days away from being foreclosed upon, I knew I had to act fast. But I also knew paying off the guy's loan would be a bit tricky.

Georgie would never accept a straight-up check from me.

That much I know. Nor could I anonymously pay off the loan. Georgie would instantly know who'd paid it... and then, quite possibly, quickly put two and two together, and think, "If Reed covertly paid off Dad's loan, maybe he also covertly paid for Dad's medication... *and my salary.*" Which, obviously, isn't something I want Georgina to be thinking, especially now that I know the story of Mr. Gates.

But, still, there was no question I had to pay off that damned mortgage somehow, as soon as possible, but in a way that didn't lead Georgina straight back to me. I needed a creative solution... a way Georgina would accept the money from me, in the first place, and also that wouldn't make her suspect my prior "donations" to her and her father.

And then it came to me. A perfect solution. *Don't rich men impulsively buy the women they're fucking sparkling baubles all the time? Isn't that a trope nobody ever questions?*

Now, granted, *I've* never bought a single piece of jewelry for any woman, other than my mother. Who, by the way, never wears the thing I bought her. But Georgina doesn't know that. Indeed, as far as she knows, I'm the kind of rich dude who sees a sparkly ruby necklace in a window at Tiffany's and buys it for his flavor of the month on the spot, just because he can. Georgina has no idea I'd never actually do that.

Although, come to think of it, maybe I *would* do that. Because, hell, I did. Today. Yes, my ultimate plan was to give Georgina a gift she could sell off, a gift that would yield the perfect payday for her and her father, without Georgina suspecting my endgame. But if paying off the mortgage had truly been my only motivation, then why did I buy *this* particular necklace—a piece of jewelry with almost triple the price tag of Georgina's father's debt? Why ask the saleswoman to see whatever pieces they had in the range of eighty grand, but then immediately ignore all the pieces she'd laid out for me the instant I happened to notice this particular ruby necklace, worth over two hundred grand, sitting in a display case on the opposite side of the store?

Obviously, when I bought the necklace, instead of one of the options in the range of eighty grand, I wasn't thinking about the loan any longer. I wasn't thinking about my brilliant plan. All that mattered to me in that delirious, impulsive moment was seeing Georgina open the box that held *that* particular necklace. All that mattered to me was seeing *that* particular necklace on Georgie's slender neck, if only for one night, and having the pleasure of fucking her in my bed while she wore it. I knew Georgie wouldn't keep the ruby necklace for long, exactly according to plan. But, in that moment, I knew seeing Georgina wearing the *perfect* necklace in my bed was worth far more to me than my two hundred twenty grand.

"I'm sorry," she whispers. "I feel terrible admitting I'd sell it. Please forgive me."

I'm quiet for a long moment. Partly, because I'm pretending to process Georgina's "shocking" confession. But also because I'm genuinely shocked. Not by the content of Georgina's confession, but by the fact that she's making it to me at all. Yes, I knew she'd sell the necklace. That was the point of me giving it to her in the first place. But I thought Georgina would take the necklace from me and then sell it behind my back.

I clear my throat. "I didn't realize things were so dire for your father."

Her shoulders droop. "He just got a third notice from the bank. I don't know what that means, exactly. But I know it can't be good."

"How much does your father owe, if you don't mind me asking? Because, whether you like it or not, this necklace is yours, to do with as you please, even if that means you're going to return it to the store for cash."

"Oh, gosh, no, Reed. I couldn't possibly—"

"Yes, you could. Unfortunately, the necklace probably

won't cover your dad's full debt. It only cost me eighty grand. But it might help."

She's flabbergasted. "Reed. Oh my God! You're not going to believe this, but... *my father owes exactly eighty grand*!"

I palm my forehead. "No."

"*Yes!*"

"Holy shit." I shake my head in disbelief. "Well, that settles it, then. You have to return it and use it to pay off the mortgage. Now, I *really* won't take no for an answer. Me seeing this necklace in the window was fate!"

She chokes back a sob, and then another, but then loses her battle. She bursts into big, soggy, beautiful tears and throws her arms around my neck. "Thank you, thank you," she murmurs into my shoulder, her body wracking as she weeps.

"You're welcome." I pull back from our embrace, apparently struck by an idea. "Actually, you know what? I should return it for you. I have another meeting in Beverly Hills tomorrow. I'll return it and immediately wire the money straight to his bank. The loan will get paid off more quickly this way. And it sounds like time might be of the essence here."

It's a pack of lies, of course. I don't have a meeting in Beverly Hills tomorrow, any more than I had one there today. My meeting today was actually in Century City, and I left midway through to head to Tiffany's in Beverly Hills, the minute I got my brilliant idea. But I can't let Georgie walk into that store with a ruby necklace worth over two hundred grand, when she thinks it's only worth eighty, and find out the truth.

Georgina pulls back from me, her face contorted with anxiety. "I just realized my dad is going to ask me how the heck I got eighty grand. And what will I say? 'Oh, um, the CEO of River Records gave it to me as a gift, Dad!'" She scoffs. "He'll immediately know I'm sleeping with you, Reed. And that's not something I'm eager for him to know. I wouldn't want him to think, even for a second, that you've somehow taken advantage of his precious little girl. No offense, but you're not only rich and powerful. You're also, you know..." She grimaces. "*Thirty-four.*"

"What happened to 'Age is just a number'?"

She pulls an adorable face. "Yeah, well, that may be *my* philosophy, but my father doesn't share it. At least, not when it comes to his baby girl. He thinks I'm far more naïve and inexperienced than I am. If he found out we're sleeping together, he'd think you've been taking advantage of me somehow."

"And he'd be right."

She smiles, assuming I'm joking. But, unfortunately, I'm not. How could I not be taking advantage of this naïve, sweet, inexperienced twenty-one-year-old? I know Georgina thinks she's seen it all, but she's wrong about that. Adorably, amusingly wrong. I keep telling myself the end justifies the means. I tell myself I've helped her and her father immeasurably. That my intentions, in the beginning, weren't *solely* lascivious— I also had other, parallel intentions, that were altruistic and good. All of which means I'm helping her, not taking advantage of her, even if I've also reaped some benefits along the way. It's what I tell myself. But with each passing day, as Georgina's hazel eyes increasingly fill with trust and affection toward me... I'm beginning to worry I might be barreling toward a catastrophe here. One I won't be able to fix.

"I wouldn't blame your father for thinking I'm too old for you," I admit. "To be honest, I'm thinking the same thing. I'm deeply conflicted about how young you are, Georgina. A month ago, I never would have believed I'd be dating a twenty-one-year-old. And yet, here I am."

Her face lights up. "You're *dating* me, Mr. Rivers?"

Shit. What did I just commit to? And how can I get myself uncommitted, if needed, without ruining this good thing?

"I thought you said you're merely 'seducing me,'" she sings out happily, and the look of unadulterated joy on her face instantly shoos away my threatening anxiety, the way a shaken broom shoos away a stray cat.

"Yes, I said that," I say. "But, at this point, I think we can both agree: *seduction complete.*"

She straddles me on the couch and throws her arms around my neck. "I'm glad you're dating me." She bats her eyelashes. "Even if it's got to be a secret for a little while." She gasps. "Oh! I just got a great idea! I could tell my father the money to pay off his mortgage came from that same cancer charity that paid for his medication!"

My heart stops. Shit. Fuck. No. Shit. *This is it.* Holding my breath, I scrutinize Georgina's face for any sign she's figured me out. Is this a test? Is she daring me to confess sins she already knows I committed? Is this the same as when she asked me about a sexual harassment lawsuit I'd settled, when she'd already had Stephanie's complaint sitting in a box in her room? But, no. I don't see anything on Georgina's lovely face except beautiful, blissful ignorance.

"That's a great idea," I say, regarding Georgina's idea to credit the cancer charity. "Do you have your father's account information, so I can wire the funds to the bank tomorrow?"

"I do."

"Great. The loan will be totally paid off by close of business tomorrow."

She can't contain her effusive joy. She hugs me and kisses every inch of my face, making me hard as a rock. I put my palms on Georgina's cheeks. "But before I return that necklace tomorrow, you're going to take off those clothes and slip on that ruby necklace. We're going to dine in the formal dining room. And then I'm going to take you upstairs and give you a night you'll never forget."

Chapter 24
Reed

Georgina rises from the couch and begins peeling off her clothes. So, I peel off mine. When we're both naked, I turn her around, brush her dark hair to the side, and lay soft, sensuous kisses along the nape of her neck before finally placing the necklace around her neck. The necklace in place, I push my cock into her ass and kiss her neck and shoulder. I reach around and touch her breasts. Pinch her nipples. Whisper to her that she's perfect. And, soon, she's so aroused, her knees are buckling.

Still kissing her neck and shoulders, I begin gently stroking her slit, until she's swollen and trembling. Aching for me. Dying for me. Until, finally, I touch her clit. Two seconds later, she cries out, digs her fingernails into my arm, and comes.

"You only get little ones for now," I whisper, pushing my cock into her ass. "To get you excited for the big ones to come later."

She shudders. "I'm so wet for you, Reed."

"And you're going to stay that way. Turn around."

She complies. And, when I see the fire in those hazel eyes, the fire in those rubies dripping off her neck toward her pink, erect nipples, my cock twitches with arousal. The head of my cock is already beaded with pre-cum. Its shaft is straining for her. My skin is hot. But tonight is all about the slow-burn. It's a night to savor, every bit as much as the special bottle of Bordeaux we're going to drink.

"You need to see yourself right now."

I take Georgina's hand in mine and lead her to a nearby mirror, and then stand behind her, the tip of my cock brushing her ass, as she takes in her glorious, glowing reflection.

As she stares at herself, she touches the necklace, in awe of it. "It's so beautiful. Thank you for seeing it and thinking of me."

"I had no choice. It was made for you. It belonged to you, even as it sat in the store window." I kiss her shoulder, making her shudder with arousal. "Amalia left an incredible meal for us in the oven. Eggplant parmigiana. Another favorite of mine. We'll eat at the big table, on opposite ends." I nuzzle my nose into her hair and inhale her glorious scent. "And then, I'm going to carry you upstairs, my queen, and give you a night that will change you forever."

***

Georgina, my queen, is wearing nothing but her ruby collar. I'm wearing nothing but a smile. We're sitting in high-backed upholstered chairs at opposite ends of my long dining table, the air between us crackling with sexual heat. And we're eating and chatting and sipping a bottle of Bordeaux, like all of this is the most natural thing in the world.

In fact, I think it's the apparent normalcy of this meal, while we're both naked and fully aroused, that's making it so scorching hot. It's the calm before the storm, the ultimate foreplay, and we both know it.

Finally, when both our plates are empty and Georgina's second glass of wine is gone, I push my empty plate and goblet aside and rise, showing her my erection.

"Come to me," I say, my eyes locked with hers. "Crawl across the table on all fours and come to me."

She doesn't hesitate. She pushes her plate and glass aside, the way I just did, places her linen napkin onto her plate, and rises. With her eyes trained on mine, she climbs onto the table on all fours, and proceeds to crawl slowly across it, like a cat.

Well, isn't that fitting, I think. Because, since the moment we met, Georgina and I have been engaged in a game of cat and mouse—a game in which both players have thought, at one time or another, they were the cat. But now, watching my glorious feline traversing the length of my table, I feel our roles cementing. Georgina is the cat in our relationship. There's no doubt about it. *And I'm the wolf.*

She comes to a halt in front of my straining cock, licking her lips. Her eyes ablaze, she whispers, "I've been fantasizing about—"

I put up my palm. "From here on out, you won't speak except when given a command or asked a question. When I give you a command, you'll reply 'Yes, sir.' When I ask you a question, you'll answer it fully, but say nothing more."

Her hazel eyes flicker with heat. "Yes, sir."

I run my thumb over her full lower lip. "You never have to do anything you don't want to do, Georgina. Not with me or anyone else. *Ever.* I have no desire to hurt or humiliate you. I only desire to give you the most outrageous pleasure of your life—an extreme form of it you didn't know was possible. If you don't want me to do something, tell me so. It's as simple as that. I don't want to force you to do anything. I don't want to cause you discomfort, let alone pain. If you feel pain, which you shouldn't, tell me so, and I'll immediately stop whatever I'm doing. If you're scared, say so—and, again, I'll stop whatever I'm doing so you can catch your breath and decide if you want to proceed. At which point, you'll tell me so, clearly and without equivocation. Do you understand?"

She nods, looking relieved—and incredibly turned on. "Yes, sir."

"Do you trust me to take good care of you?"

"I do." She softens. "I really do trust you, Reed. I'm nothing but excited."

I hold her trembling face in my hands. "You loved the swing, right?"

"I loved it."

"Then you're going to love this, too. Even more." I trace the contours of her striking cheekbones, before dropping my hand to my side. "Now, suck my cock, kitten. And make it the best fucking blowjob you've ever given."

Unbridled lust washes over her features. "Yes, sir." She dips down, sending her round ass into the air, and her breasts and necklace against the table, and gets to work. And, soon, I'm on the cusp of total Nirvana. Hurtling toward a release my body wants, but the rest of me knows won't serve my greater purpose.

"Stop," I choke out.

She obeys, her chest heaving.

"Come here."

I put my arms out and Georgina comes to me, wrapping herself around me the way she did in the swimming pool. When I've got her firmly in my grasp, I carry her out of the dining room, through my living room, and up my staircase, taking the steps two at a time. Finally, when I reach my bedroom, I lay her down on my bed, the head of my cock dripping, and open the top drawer of my nightstand.

Chapter 25
Reed

I've lost count of the number of orgasms I've pulled out of Georgina tonight. The number of times I've gleefully licked up the evidence of her complete and total surrender. I've marked her tonight. Literally, with my teeth and cum. Figuratively, with the tattoo I left on her deepest desires. Maybe even her very soul. *Property of Reed Rivers.*

She's mine now. Sex with anyone else will never measure up to what she's found with me. I've ruined her for anyone else. The same way I ruined Audrey. And Isabel after her. And then Natasha and Corinne and Veronica, and anyone else who's been fortunate enough—or, perhaps, *unfortunate* enough—to attract my undivided attention for any length of time. The only difference with Georgina is that, for the first time, ever, I'm pretty sure I've been ruined, too.

It's a thought that would terrify me, if I weren't so exhausted. If I weren't so drunk on Georgina and the perfection we shared tonight. As it is, though, in this moment, after this incredible night, in addition to exhausted, I'm feeling high. The kind of high an explorer feels after discovering, and conquering, a new land. I led Georgina to The Promised Land tonight, in a way she couldn't have fathomed. I showed her pure ecstasy, repeatedly, and watched with glee as her flames turned into a raging forest fire, and as that forest fire burned out of control. I watched everything she previously thought about her sexuality, and deepest desires, turn to ash. And, finally, I watched Georgina rise like a Phoenix from those ashes and unabashedly claim her new sexuality, without apology. There's no turning back now. Georgina Ricci will never be the same again. And, almost certainly, neither will I.

After one last, lingering kiss, I remove the soft cuffs from Georgina's ankles and wrists. I sit on the edge of the bed, pull her slack body to mine, and cradle her. And she wraps her legs around me and melts into me.

Still holding her, I lean toward my nightstand and grab a water bottle for her, which she gulps down greedily when I give it to her. I remove her ruby necklace with a soft kiss on her shoulder, and place it on my nightstand, next to her now-empty water bottle. And finally, holding her tightly, I carry her into my bathroom, to the shower, and wash my little kitten in warm water from head to toe.

Our shower done, I dry her off, stopping occasionally to suck her nipples or kiss her belly or thighs, and then wrap her in a thick white towel and carry her back into my room.

I place Georgina in an armchair. Change my bedsheets. Clean and put away my various cuffs and toys. I send a quick text to Owen, telling him to cancel my morning meetings. And then I bring the shades on my large windows down, turning my room into a dark cave. I carry Georgina's sleeping frame from the armchair to my bed, crawl next to her, pull her backside into me. And, finally, I exhale from the depths of my soul.

Holy shit.

I'm sure I'll start panicking tomorrow. Freaking out she's going to start demanding things from me I can't possibly give her. But I can't be bothered to feel any of the usual shit right now. I'm too exhausted. Too relaxed. Too... *happy*. And so, I simply clutch Georgina to me, just a little bit tighter, and revel in the overwhelming desire I'm feeling to *protect, protect, protect* what's mine... and, slowly, drift into the deepest sleep of my entire life.

***

A blood-curdling scream rips me out of a deep sleep, and my eyes fly open. In a heartbeat, my mind clicks into place. Georgina. She's lying next to me in bed. She's safe. Asleep. The scream came from her.

"No!" she shrieks. "No, no!"

I grasp her shoulder. "Georgie, wake up. You're having a nightmare."

Her eyes fly open, and when she sees my concerned face staring back at her, and realizes whatever was terrorizing her is gone, she crumples into my bare chest.

"You're safe," I whisper, holding her tight. "You're here in bed with me. Nothing can hurt you."

She shakes in my arms and whimpers, and with each tortured sound that comes from her, my heart feels like it's physically cracking.

"What was your nightmare about?" I ask.

"Mr. Gates," she says. "Telling you about him... I think it made everything I've been stuffing down bubble up and come to the surface." She pauses. "After he kissed me, he tried to do more, Reed. He tried to do a lot more, but I screamed and kicked him and ran away, as fast as I could."

I'm so full of the carnal urge to kill, I can't speak, so I lay my cheek against hers.

"I was terrified," she squeaks out. "I ran and ran, and never looked back."

I turn my head and kiss her cheek. "You're safe now, baby. You're safe, and I'm not going to let anything happen to you, ever again."

Chapter 26
Georgina

It's finally here! The morning of Reed's party. I'm so freaking excited, and not just about the party. About life! About *Reed.* I can't believe how close I feel to him. How much I've opened up and let him in. I never would have believed it possible, but... I think I'm no longer falling for him. I think the fall is complete.

Which is so stupid, I want to slap myself silly. What sane, intelligent woman would ever let herself fall for Reed freaking Rivers—an intensely guarded, "non-committal" older man music mogul whose every third sentence is a bald-faced lie? The answer to that question is: no sane, intelligent woman would do that. Only an idiot. A felony stupid moron who's clearly let her foolish heart hijack her rational mind.

It's why my mind keeps shrieking at my heart to snap the fuck out of it! But my heart won't listen. And, really, I can't blame it, after everything that's happened in such a short amount of time between Reed and me. How could my heart possibly hold back, after the night of the necklace, and the way he comforted me after my nightmare? I didn't *want* to wake up the next morning and look at Reed's sleeping face on the pillow next to mine and think, "*My love.*" But that's what happened, whether I wanted it or not... and has kept happening, at random moments over the past couple of days, ever since.

My ruby necklace is gone now. As promised, Reed

brought it back to the store the next day and used the proceeds to pay off my father's condo in full. Which, *hello*, is even more reason for my heart to ignore my brain when it comes to my feelings for Reed. But I don't need the physical necklace around my neck to feel its phantom weight against my skin. Surely, I'll feel the power of those rubies, the power of that magical night with Reed, for the rest of my days.

I don't plan to tell Reed any of this, of course. My feelings for him have turned me stupid, but not dumb. I just wish I could stop *feeling* so damned smitten with him all the time. It's actually annoying me to constantly feel like I'm swooning, even when I'm trying to work. I spent most of the morning in my room, researching the first half of the guest list for tonight. But the whole time, I felt physically buzzed. After that, I left my room and, for the past hour, I've been following Reed around the house as he's made sure the various workers are preparing for the party to his exacting standards. I figured watching Reed manage the nuts and bolts of an event like this might be a cool metaphor for his hands-on management style, in general. And it has been. I've made several notes for my article. But, still, even as I've been working, I haven't once stopped feeling that crazy buzz—that simmering in my blood and skipping of my heart that constantly makes me swoon.

"No, no," Reed says to a worker, his voice dripping with annoyance. "The bass rig needs to be set up there, next to the drum kit. Have you never set up a live music performance in your life? Bass and drums. Peanut butter and jelly."

"Sorry, Mr. Rivers."

"Owen?" Reed shouts over his shoulder.

Owen arrives, looking irritated.

"Get someone over here who knows what the fuck they're doing, for fuck's sake."

"I'll handle it, Reed."

Owen pulls the red-faced worker aside, just as a large black man taps Reed's shoulder from behind. Which, of course, makes Mr. Cranky-Pants turn around to see who's dared touch him. But when he sees his assailant, Reed's demeanor instantly brightens.

The two men clap each other on their shoulders warmly and exchange quick pleasantries before Reed turns to me, a wide smile on his face.

"Georgina, this is Barry Atwater, the head of security for both my label and nightclubs. Barry, this is Georgina Ricci, a brilliant writer for *Rock 'n' Roll* who's doing a feature on me."

Ah, it never gets old, hearing Reed introduce me like that. I exchange brief small talk with Barry, and quickly surmise he's a teddy bear underneath all that muscle. And then, Barry and Reed drift into conversation about logistics for tonight.

As the men talk, I check the time on my phone. *Crap.* Alessandra should be here in about an hour to "pre-party" with me, and I still haven't finished going through the names on the guest list. Before the party starts, I want to be sure I know at least the basics about every name on the list, as well as being able to identify each person on sight, without needing an introduction. The last thing I want is to be introduced to some huge A-lister, without me realizing it. Or, even worse, with me asking something stupid like, "And what do you do for a living?"

"Hey, Reed," I say, pulling on his shirt sleeve. "I'm going to head up to my room for a bit to finish going through the guest list before Alessandra arrives. It was great to meet you, Barry. Reed has said wonderful things about you." I return to Reed. "Hey, can I talk to you privately about something for a sec?"

"Don't go anywhere," Reed says to Barry. "I want to finish our conversation."

Reed and I walk a few feet away, until we're in a semi-private spot.

"Is everything okay?" Reed asks, looking mildly concerned.

"Everything's great. I just wanted to let you know I haven't told Alessandra you listened to her demo. I want her to be able to enjoy the party, without feeling self-conscious or awkward around you. I'm going to tell her everything on Monday, before she heads back to Boston."

Reed rolls his eyes like I've said something ridiculous. "One of the conditions of you inviting Alessandra to the party was neither of you talking to me about her music tonight. Remember?" He glances over his shoulder and then, to my shock, reaches around me, and pinches my ass. "God, you turn me on."

I leap out of his clutches and immediately look over at Barry, worried he might have seen our clinch. But, nope, Barry is busy on his phone. I return to Reed and waggle my finger at him. "No more grabby hands, Reed. From this moment forward, until we're safely in your bedroom tonight, I'm nothing but a reporter from *Rock 'n' Roll* to you."

"I'll do my best to control myself." He flashes me a completely unapologetic smile. "The caterer should have a lunch buffet set up in the kitchen by now. I asked for a spread for whatever pre-partiers come by. Why don't you fuel up? I don't want you drinking on an empty stomach."

"There's going to be a pre-party?"

"Yeah, I told a small group to come by early. Not sure who's coming, for sure, beyond Josh and Henn." He looks at his watch. "Shit. I've got a conference call. Get yourself some food, baby."

I glance at Barry, my cheeks flushing, hoping he didn't overhear Reed's endearment. But it's clear he did. Because the minute my eyes meet Barry's, he looks down at his phone, and *pretends* not to have heard a thing.

"Barry knows about us, doesn't he?" I whisper.

"Barry is my personal bodyguard, whenever I need one," Reed says matter-of-factly, as if that explains everything.

"Now, get yourself some food and do some work before Alessandra gets here. I'll catch up with you soon."

"Okay. See you later." I float happily into the kitchen to grab a bite, and to my surprise, discover Amalia standing at the island with the caterer. "Amalia!" I say, loping toward her, my arms extended. "I didn't think you came in on Saturdays!"

Amalia hugs me. "I always come in on party days to coordinate with the caterer."

After a bit of small talk, I load up a plate, and Amalia joins me at the small kitchen table to keep me company while I eat. She tells me a cute story about one of her grandsons, who just discovered the word "ridiculous." I tell her about Alessandra, and how excited I am she's coming over shortly, and will be staying overnight with me in the blue room.

After about fifteen minutes, in the midst of my conversation with Amalia, the kitchen door swings opens and two young women bound into the room. A woman with long, strawberry blonde hair, and another one with a dark bob with bangs and bright blue eyes.

"Amalia!" the brunette says.

"Hello, sweetie!" Amalia says warmly, leaping up from the table to administer hugs. Amalia introduces the women, and I learn the brunette is Reed's sister and the blonde her best friend.

"And this is Georgina," Amalia says to the women. She opens her mouth, like she wants to elaborate, but closes it. And I don't blame her. In this context, it would be weird to introduce me in relation to *Rock 'n' Roll*. But who am I to Reed? And what am I doing here? It's obviously not for Amalia to put a name to it.

"I'm writing about Reed for *Rock 'n' Roll*," I say, trying to sound casual. "And also staying here with Reed." Ugh. That was awkward.

"Reed mentioned the article," Reed's sister says. "And also that you're staying here. He seemed excited about both."

My heart leaps. "I'm excited about both, as well."

"That's good." She flashes me a warm smile. "We're going out to the pool. Would you like to join us?"

"Oh, thank you for the invitation. But I've got to finish some work before my stepsister, Alessandra, arrives."

"Maybe when Alessandra gets here, then."

"Sounds good. I'll see you then."

Back in my room, I text Alessandra and ask her to pack bathing suits for both of us, so we can join Reed's sister and her friend at the pool later today. And, luckily, my timing is good—I've caught her before she's left her mother's place.

Swimsuits handled, I sit on my bed with my laptop, open the guest list, and pick up where I left off earlier. The next name on the list? *Laila Fitzgerald.* Well, there's no need to look her up. Laila is a superstar, thanks to a sophomore album that's spun off hit after hit this past year.

Aloha Carmichael. No need to look her up, either. After years of watching her Disney show *It's Aloha!* as a kid, and nowadays seeing Aloha's ubiquitous face on viral music videos and shampoo commercials, I'd know that pop star's gorgeous face and famous green eyes anywhere.

Keane Morgan. Okay, that's a name I don't know. But after a search, I quickly realize he's an actor from a show I binge-watched last year. In that show, he was in a small, but pivotal role. But, now, it seems he's moved on to a co-starring role on a hugely popular show I've never seen. Well, good for him. I'm glad to see he's doing so well.

Madelyn Morgan. I'm assuming from the name she's Keane's wife. I google her, and find out I'm right about that. But I also find out she's a kickass woman—a documentary filmmaker who was nominated for an Oscar last year. I'm a bit surprised, actually. In the show I saw, Keane came off like a total "bro." But, obviously, if he's married to a woman like Madelyn Morgan, there must be more to him than meets the eye.

Dax Morgan. Well, that's another easy one. 22 Goats has been one of my favorite bands for the past few years, ever since they broke onto the scene with a music video that went viral. With his gorgeous face and long, blond hair, Dax Morgan, their frontman, is instantly recognizable to me and half the world. But even so, I look him up, just to see if he's related to the actor, Keane Morgan. And, yup. Wikipedia tells me Dax and Keane are the two youngest brothers of five siblings in the Morgan clan.

Colin Beretta. Another easy one. He's the drummer of 22 Goats.

Matthew Fishberger. Hmm. I don't recognize the name, so I google it, and, instantly feel like an idiot. That's *Fish!* The bassist for 22 Goats who's come across as easygoing and likeable in every interview of the band I've read this past week.

Josh Faraday. Another easy one. Reed's "male model" best friend from college, whom I met at the bar.

Kat Faraday. I google her and find out Josh's wife is a gorgeous blonde bombshell who recently published her first romance novel—a romantic comedy entitled *Suck It.*

Well, this I've got to see. I find Kat's book online, and when I behold the smoking hot cover, and read the sassy synopsis, I buy that sucker on the spot.

"Kat Faraday," I murmur. "I think we're going to be two peas in a pod."

Ten minutes later, I'm flying through the names on the list, until I reach one that stops me in my tracks.

Isabel Randolph.

Gah. On the one hand, I'm dying to interview her. She's been one of my favorite actresses since before she became a massive movie star. On the other hand, though, I'm not sure I'll be able to pull off an interview of her, to the best of my abilities, when I have these feelings for Reed. Will I be distracted the entire interview, with feelings of jealousy and insecurity? Will I imagine Reed doing all the things he does to me... to *Isabel*? I don't want to wonder these things, but I can't help it. Did Reed tie Isabel up, the way he did to me? Did he fuck her in a sex swing? Did Reed give Isabel whatever might have been her equivalents of a Peloton, a Pilates reformer... and the most perfect, breathtaking ruby necklace the world has ever seen?

My heart pangs.

Why am I torturing myself? She's engaged now, for God's sake! And Reed explicitly told me he and Isabel have become more like siblings than ex-lovers. But, see, that's the thing. The idea of them being like siblings simply doesn't ring true to me. How could Isabel get fucked by Reed the way I've gotten fucked, and then, somehow, magically, desire nothing more from his hot body than a brotherly peck on the cheek? I don't care how badly Isabel might have gotten hurt by Reed at some point in their relationship—how big an asshole Reed might have been to her in the end. I can't imagine she'd turn down the chance to fuck Reed senseless again, regardless, if the opportunity presented itself...

If Reed cheated on Isabel, then, yes, maybe I could imagine her never wanting him to lay another pinky on her. That's how I feel about Shawn. Physically ill at the thought of him touching me. But that's not what happened between those two, or they sure as hell wouldn't be "like siblings" now. And, anyway, Reed says he's not a cheater, and I believe him. But if things between them really did simply peter out, if things really did just "run their course," as Reed said, then I can't imagine Isabel being completely over Reed. Unless, of course, she's now so madly in love with her new fiancé, she can't imagine wanting anyone else, ever again, even someone as swoon-worthy and smoking hot as Reed.

Which brings me to the next name on the list. *Howard Devlin*. The guy Reed told me is Isabel's fiancé. As I recall, Reed said Howard Devlin is a big shot billionaire movie producer and studio owner. Which made me retort, "Oh, then he's the Reed Rivers of the movie industry?"

I input Howard's name into Google, excited to see how this guy matches up to Reed, and when I see his photo, I gasp. Howard Devlin looks like Isabel's pervy grandpa! Gaping like a fish on a river bank, I read the guy's Wikipedia page and quickly learn he's *sixty-five* years old—thirty-four years older than Isabel!

Holy hell. I know I'm the one who always says "age is just a number." But, damn. I'm having a hard time believing a woman as young and vibrant and successful as Isabel said yes to spending the rest of her life boning *that* guy. Although, I suppose Isabel only said yes to spending the rest of *Howard's* life boning him. Which, when you're talking about your pervy grandpa, maybe isn't all that big a commitment.

Okay, I'm being a total bitch right now, and I need to stop. Looks aren't everything. And age really *is* a number. For all I know, Howard Devlin is a lovely, kind, generous man who's a tiger in bed. A guy who treats Isabel like his queen. Plus, who the hell do I think I am to judge any woman for being in a relationship with a wealthy, powerful, older man? Come on, Georgie. A girl who lives in a glass house—or, in my case, a house with a whole lot of floor-to-ceiling windows overlooking the Hollywood Hills—shouldn't throw stones.

I read a bit more on Howard Devlin and suddenly realize I've seen his face before. But where? I pause. Stare at the wall. And, then... Oh, yes! In that photo spread from CeeCee's fiftieth birthday party!

I pull out my color copy of the article and scan the photos... and sure enough, Howard is standing in a group shot with a slew of music and movie stars. Wow. How crazy is that? Isabel and Howard were *both* at that party ten years ago. Is that where they first met? Or is this a case of future spouses crossing within inches of each other, never realizing it? Isabel wasn't a successful actress back then. Not even close. Plus, Reed was at that party, too. So, it wouldn't surprise me if Isabel and Howard never said two words to each other that night.

On the other hand though, Isabel had to have had acting ambitions back then. Did she spot Howard, a famous movie producer, and try to charm him, or was she too young and inexperienced to recognize him at a party attended by far more recognizable faces?

And what about Howard? Did he spot Isabel that night, from afar, perhaps when she was talking to a young, gorgeous stud in an Armani tux, and think to himself, *One day, that woman will be my wife*?

Okay, my imagination is running wild now. But, regardless, I make a mental note to ask Isabel about that party. I doubt there's any sort of "written in the stars" or "love at first sight" angle there in regards to Isabel and Howard, but, still, I'd be remiss if I didn't at least poke around to find out.

Peter Hennessy. That's the next name on the list. And one I don't recognize. But when I google the guy, and see his photo, I palm my forehead. *He's Henn*! Reed's nerdy-looking best friend from college. When I met him at the bar, he instantly put me at ease with his authenticity and sweetness.

Hannah Hennessy. Henn's wife, I assume. I google and find out she is, indeed, Henn's wife—an adorable brunette with glasses who works in the publicity department of a movie studio... the same studio owned by Howard Devlin, as a matter of fact. Huh. What a small world! Or is it? Did Reed have something to do with Hannah getting that job? Did Reed pick up the phone and use his connections to help Hannah get an interview? Because that's exactly the kind of thing I could see Reed doing: pulling strings behind the scenes to help his best friend's woman get her dream job . . .

Ping.

A murky thought raps gently at the back of my brain. *Ping.* The thought is like a soft cotton ball lobbed at me from ten feet away...

It's only a blurry idea at the moment, tugging at the outer fringes of my consciousness. But before the cotton ball hardens into an actual pebble, my phone buzzes with an incoming text that makes me squeal and forget all about the fuzzy thought gently pinging in the back of my head. It's a message from Alessandra that reads:

I'm at Reed's front gate, baby! LET ME IN! It's time to pre-party like ROCKSTARS before we party with ACTUAL ROCKSTARS! (But first, a sandwich. Please. For the love of all things holy, I'm starving.)

Chapter 27
Georgina

"Oh my *God*," Alessandra says, gaping at the seven gleaming cars lined up before us in Reed's massive garage. We're at the last stop of the house tour I've been giving Alessandra for the last thirty minutes. And Alessandra is clearly as blown away by the spectacle of Reed's glittering car collection as she was the rest of the house.

I lead her down the row of vehicles, expertly rattling off whatever I know about each make and model—all the same factoids Reed told me during my house tour, plus some stuff I think I might have made up—and Alessandra "oohs" and "aahs" and makes snarky comments about Reed's over-the-top "bougie-ness" the whole time.

When we come to a standstill in front of Reed's yellow Ferrari, the second-to-last entry in the collection, I say, "Reed finally got this beauty back from the body shop yesterday. A few weeks ago, he was driving it too fast around a curve and, according to him, a tree 'leaped out into the middle of the road,' right in front of him."

"Oh my gosh. Was Reed hurt?"

"No, thankfully. But the right front of the car wasn't as lucky. Apparently, it was really smashed up... right through *there*."

I crouch down and peer closely at the area in question, and Alessandra bends down and joins me in scrutinizing the body shop's handiwork.

"You can't even tell it was ever busted," Alessandra marvels.

"Yeah, it looks as good as new. Wow."

We straighten up and walk a few steps to our left.

"And last but not least... this is Reed's favorite, by far." I motion to Reed's beloved Bugatti. "It's a Bugatti *Chiron*. Which, believe me, is far superior to the Bugatti *Veyron*. The Bugatti folks *really* upped their 'pickup' game with the Chiron."

Alessandra scoffs and rolls her eyes along with me. "Like I always say, the Veyron is a straight-up piece of shit."

I burst out laughing. "*That's exactly what I said!*"

We laugh and laugh.

"Wow, Georgie," Alessandra says. She pauses to look around the expansive space. "Reed really did make you his Cinderella, didn't he? Just like he said that night at the bar."

I inhale sharply. *Holy crap.* Alessandra is right. *He did.* Indeed, that's exactly how I've been feeling this entire week with him. Like Cinderella at the ball.

Alessandra walks a few steps away to inspect Reed's sporting equipment on the far wall, but I stand frozen and flabbergasted by my epiphany. Have I been a fool to let myself get swept into a fairytale with a man like Reed Rivers—a man who's made it quite clear he's got no desire to be anyone's Prince Charming? There can't possibly be a happily ever after at the end of this fairytale I've been play-acting with Reed. I really need to remind myself of that fact, and prepare myself for the alternate ending. I need to pull back. Stuff these feelings down. Guard my heart so it won't get hurt. I glance at Reed's sparkling yellow Ferrari, and think, *If I give my heart to Reed and he smashes it, I can't imagine I'd come out the other side looking as good as new, the way this Ferrari did.*

"Earth to Georgie," Alessandra says.

I look at her blankly.

"I asked if you're ready to go to the pool now, Cinderella?"

"Oh." I take a deep breath. "Yeah, great. But, please, don't make Cinderella my nickname. It only makes me think I'm one midnight away from everything around me turning into a pumpkin."

***

After changing into our swimsuits, Alessandra and I arrive at the pool to find Reed's sister and her friend enjoying the sunny day, joined by Josh and his pregnant wife, Kat, who's rocking a white string bikini with her baby bump, and Henn, who's here with his adorable, bespectacled wife, Hannah.

Introductions are made, and easy conversation ensues. After some preliminaries, Kat asks me about the special issue and how I got my cool gig, so I tell the group the story of how I ambushed CeeCee at an on-campus event for music students.

"Sounds like she's your spirit animal, Kat," Josh says to his wife. "A woman who knows how to get shit done."

"He's complimenting you," Kat assures me. "Josh loves my devious side."

"Oh, absolutely," Josh says, laughing. "The way Kat cleverly gets what she wants is one of my all-time favorite things about her. Kat's family calls itself the Morgan Mafia. And she's definitely 'The Godmother' in that clan."

"Oh, you're a *Morgan*?" I say to Kat, putting two and two together. "Are you related to Keane and Dax?"

"They're my brothers. My two little brothers. I've also got two big brothers. I like to say I'm the meat in a Morgan brothers sandwich." She giggles at her own joke.

"Are your two older brothers coming to the party tonight, too?"

I don't recall seeing any other Morgans on the guest list.

But, then again, I didn't make it through the entire list before Alessandra showed up.

"No. My oldest brother, Colby, isn't a big partier. And my second-oldest brother, Ryan, loves to party, but not with Reed."

My stomach clenches. "Oh."

Kat looks embarrassed. "Oh, no, it's nothing big. Reed flirted with Ryan's wife, a million years ago, and Ryan's never forgotten about it."

"*Oh*," I say again, at a loss for words. Reed hit on a married woman? And not just any married woman, but his best friend's sister-in-law? I'm well aware Reed's always liked the ladies, but, come on, there's an entire planet of women who'd fall at his feet. There was no need for him to hit on Josh's sister-in-law.

"Oh, Georgie, no, no," Kat says, apparently reacting to the look on my face. "Tessa wasn't even Ryan's wife back when Reed flirted with her! She wasn't even Ryan's *girlfriend*!" Kat cackles with laughter. "My brother, Ryan, is a lunatic when it comes to his wife. A crazy-man with a grudge. Reed did nothing wrong. Tessa was single and fair game when he flirted with her. It was at our destination wedding in Maui, and everybody was hitting on everybody." She laughs uproariously, and I exhale with relief.

More conversation ensues, drink orders are taken by some dude, and more people arrive. First, the three guys of 22 Goats—Dax, Fish, and Colin—waltz in, nearly making both Alessandra and me pee in the pool. Shortly after that, the actor Keane Morgan and his cute documentarian wife, Maddy, arrive, along with their two best friends... who, get this, are none other than former Disney-star-turned-pop-star, Aloha Carmichael, the woman Alessandra and I both watched on *It's Aloha!* throughout our childhoods, plus, Aloha's bodyguard-husband, Zander.

More drink orders are taken. Music begins blaring out of

hidden speakers. And, suddenly, we've got ourselves a legit pool party.

At first, I'm nervous and stiff around so much star power. And Alessandra is a mute. But soon, it's impossible not to loosen up in this easygoing group. We find out Keane's wife, Maddy, is the younger sister of Henn's wife, Hannah. We find out Kat is the one who introduced Henn to Hannah— that Kat used to work with Hannah in Seattle. "The minute I met Henny," Kat declares, "I knew he'd fall ass over tea kettle for Hannah!"

With the group looking on and laughing their asses off, Keane tells Alessandra and me a long, twisted, bizarre story about the day he first met Zander when they got stuck together in an elevator at a porn convention... before finally bursting out laughing at our expressions and telling us, no, actually the pair met in math class in eighth grade.

And on and on it goes, with music blaring and cocktails flowing all the while. And through it all, I find myself feeling more and more relaxed and like myself, despite all the glamour and star power around me. Even Alessandra begins to find her groove after a while. Mostly, thanks to Fish, the lanky, shaggy bass player of 22 Goats, with whom she's now chatting in a corner of the pool.

"So, do you mind if we talk about my interview of 22 Goats for a second?" I ask Dax.

I'm standing in the shallow end of the pool with him and his sweet wife, plus, Colin and his adorable girlfriend. Also, Josh and Kat, and Henn and Hannah. Behind us, Zander, Aloha, Keane, and Maddy are playing an enthusiastic game of chicken.

"Sure," Dax says. "Reed mentioned you're trying to come up with unique angles for all your interviews?"

"That's the idea," I say. "For instance, with Dean Masterson, I'm going to hang out with him at his house in Malibu. I'll watch him surf. He'll make me some stir-fry and show me some personal photos. I'm hoping to be able to write something really different about him than the world has seen before."

"That sounds cool," Dax says.

"You guys could show Georgina around Seattle," Kat suggests. "It could be an 'origin story' type thing. You could show her where you guys used to rehearse in Mom and Dad's garage. And where you used to skateboard. I have a thousand photos I could show you, Georgie."

Dax says he's in favor of the idea, and his drummer, Colin, agrees.

"Should we ask Fish if he's okay with it?" I ask, glancing across the pool at Fish and Alessandra.

"Nah," Dax says. "Fish is always cool with whatever."

And, just that fast, it's settled: In the near future, I'm going to spend the day in Seattle with 22 Goats!

"You should stay with Josh and me when you come," Kat says. "That way, we can hang out and relax while I show you all my photos and tell you all the stories the Goats would never want you to hear."

I laugh with her. "That sounds amazing, Kat. Thank you."

"Let's exchange numbers, so you can use me as your point of contact to schedule everything," Kat says. "It'd take you five times as long to get anything done if you had to go through official channels."

And off we go to the ledge of the pool to grab our phones and exchange information.

"So, hey," Kat says, after she's input my number. "I think I might have put my foot in my mouth earlier, when I said that thing about my brother, Ryan, not liking Reed. Josh overheard that and got pissed at me. He doesn't want you thinking badly of Reed, and neither do I. Reed is actually a good guy, Georgie. A sweetheart, once you get past all that swagger."

I open my mouth to reply, but quickly close it again. Kat knows about Reed and me? Or is she simply concerned she's said the wrong thing about her husband's best friend to the woman assigned to write an article about him?

Kat continues, "Honestly, Georgie, I can't even count all the times I've seen Reed being a fantastic friend or brother. Did you know he paid for all his sister's schooling? He also hosted Henn and Hannah's wedding here at his house. Also..." She looks behind her, apparently making sure nobody is within earshot. "This is off the record, okay? Not for your article."

"Sure."

"Don't tell my brother, Keane, but Reed really helped his career behind the scenes." She looks behind her again. "When Keane first moved to LA to try his hand at modeling and acting, his agent wouldn't send him out to audition for anything serious. Every role he auditioned for was a dumb jock or stripper or frat boy. Keane was grateful for the work, and excited at first, but after a while, he really wanted to throw his hat in the ring for more serious roles. So, he took acting classes, and really worked hard, but, still, his agent wouldn't take him seriously. So, Maddy told me about Keane's predicament. She said Keane was getting discouraged. So, I mentioned it to Josh, just, you know, to catch my husband up on my life. I didn't expect Josh to *do* anything with the information. But Josh, being Josh, he immediately took action and called Reed. Who then called the head of Keane's talent agency—because Reed knows *everybody* in this town—and Reed told the guy it would be a *personal* favor to *him* if Keane's particular agent would start taking a chance on him and send him out to a few serious auditions. And guess what happened? Keane got hired for the first serious role he tried out for! And that led to the next role, and the next. And now he's starring in a hit show!"

Of course, none of this surprises me. Indeed, everything

Kat just said sounds *exactly* like something Reed would do. Like Reed told me that day in the gym, he won't compromise his professional judgment, but he'll do just about anything else for the people on his short list. And since Josh Faraday is one of the people on that list, all he had to do was give Reed a call to send him into action.

"And that's Reed for you," Kat says, her blue eyes twinkling. "And Josh, too. Both of those guys are so generous."

"Why don't they want Keane to know they helped him? Wouldn't Keane want to know, so he could thank both of them for helping him out? If someone helped me with *my* career behind the scenes, I'd want to know about it, so I could thank them profusely."

"Josh and Reed don't want to take anything away from Keane. Especially Reed. He never wants the spotlight for himself. He loves pulling strings behind the scenes."

Ping.

That soft cotton ball from earlier *poofs* softly against the back of my head again. A fuzzy idea is once again trying to sharpen and take root inside my brain. But before the amorphous thought crystallizes, Kat speaks again.

"And Keane is just another example on a long list of them. When Hannah first moved from Seattle to LA to be closer to her then-boyfriend, Henn, do you know what Reed did for her, simply because she was Henn's girlfriend?"

"He helped her get a job?" I throw out.

Kat looks surprised. "Actually... yes. I was going to say Reed gave Hannah a smoking good deal on an apartment in one of his buildings. But, yes, Reed *also* helped Hannah get her current job, too. I guess he knew someone who knew someone, and that got her in the door for an interview. Oh! He also got Zander an interview with Big Barry, when Zander first moved to LA, too. That's how Zander became Aloha's personal bodyguard." Kat grabs her club soda off the ledge and takes a long sip. "Seriously, if you've got Reed Rivers vouching for you, you can't lose."

"The Man with the Midas Touch," I say.

"Exactly. But, see, most people don't realize Reed's golden touch extends to far more things than music. Oh! Maddy is another example. Reed brokered the distribution deal for one of her documentaries—the one she did with Aloha—and he also introduced her to one of his producing partners for her next project. And, *boom,* Maddy's very next film, she wound up getting nominated for an Oscar!"

"Wow."

"The same kind of thing happened with Isabel Randolph. Josh told me Reed brought Isabel to one of Josh's parties, way before she was famous. Josh said Reed introduced her as a 'rising star' and 'one to watch'... and, well, you know how that turned out. I'm telling you, Reed is *never* wrong about spotting talent. He can spot it better than anyone."

I force a smile, but my stomach is tight.

"Oh, crap," Kat says. "I did it again, didn't I? Put my foot in my mouth. Georgina, Reed and Isabel are ancient news. You have nothing to worry about there. I don't know if this is public knowledge yet, so don't post about this, but she's getting married. In fact, Josh said she's bringing her fiancé to the party. And, regardless, Reed has no interest in her. Josh says Isabel is the one who's always carried a torch for Reed. Not the other way around. So, now that she's getting married, I guess that's that, right?"

Jesus Christ. Does *everyone* at this little pre-party know I'm having sex with Reed? Do the three guys of 22 Goats, who I'll be interviewing, know? Do they think I got this job, thanks to Reed pulling strings for me behind the scenes, the same way he did for Keane and Zander and Hannah?

Ping.

That cotton ball knocks me in the back of the head again... Only this time, it's a tiny pebble. But before another pebble hits, and the thought takes shape, a hurtling body cannonballs into the pool, immediately to my left, dousing Kat and me with a virtual tsunami that makes us squeal.

I didn't see the cannonballer, but I'm instantly assuming it had to be Keane Morgan, or maybe his best friend, Zander, since those two have been goofing around like kids in the pool for the past twenty minutes. But, to my shock, it's *Reed* who suddenly breaks the surface of the water next to me, like a great white shark breaching the ocean's surface to nab a frightened seal in its gaping mouth. Laughing at my shocked reaction, Reed swoops me into his arms and plants an enthusiastic kiss on my mouth, right in front of his entire group of friends.

For a split-second, I'm aggravated. I've been adamant with Reed that I don't want anyone knowing we're sleeping together. But then, I remember Kat almost certainly already knows about us, which means Josh and everyone else probably does, too.

And just that fast, I realize I'm feeling electrified, not upset, that Reed wants the people closest to him to know about us. In fact, I couldn't be happier about it. With a swooning sigh, I wrap my legs around Reed's waist and my arms around his neck and kiss the hell out of my gorgeous man, so everyone he cares about can plainly see I'm every bit as attracted to him, as he is to me.

Chapter 28
Georgina

R eed's party has been like a dream. A perfect fantasy. Everything Reed promised it would be, and so much more. The people-watching has been insanity. The impromptu performances and jam sessions have been mind-blowing. And, best of all, at least from a personal standpoint, I've felt like an actual guest tonight, as opposed to an awkward bystander or voyeur. And that's thanks to Reed's friends—the ones who so enthusiastically welcomed Alessandra and me at the pool earlier. They've made me feel like I truly belong here tonight. Not as a reporter for *Rock 'n' Roll,* but as Reed's girlfriend.

Kat, especially, has been the president of my fan club tonight—hell-bent on making me feel like the little sister she never had. At one point, when I said something that made Kat hoot with laughter, she threw her arms around me and said to Hannah, "See, Banana? I told you: Georgie's me, if I were seven years younger and a hot as fuck brunette!"

And I'm not the only one feeling comfortable here tonight. I can tell Alessandra feels relaxed and happy, too, thanks to her amazing connection with Fish. He's been a dream to her. Introducing her around. Pulling her into conversations and games of ping pong and HORSE. Thereby drawing her out of her shell in record time.

And I can't forget the smashing success of the "business" side of this amazing party, as well. Reed said I'd be able to bond with his artists at this party, in a way that would elevate the content of the special issue. And he was exactly right. I've played ping pong with Savage from Fugitive Summer. Corn hole with members of Danger Doctor Jones. For God's sake, Laila Fitzgerald and I now have our own secret handshake—an intricate maneuver we concocted while teaming up to beat Aloha and Zander in beer pong.

And through it all, Reed has been perfect. As requested, he's treated me with nothing but professionalism tonight. Well, to the naked eye, anyway. Covertly, we've flirted like crazy with each other across the crowded party all night long, the same way we secretly flirted with each other throughout the entire panel discussion a lifetime ago.

The panel discussion.

Wow.

It really does feel like a lifetime ago, even though it's only been a few weeks. Since then, I've graduated college. Met my idol. Snagged my dream job. I've moved into Reed's mansion, and befriended famous, glamorous people like it was a totally normal thing to do. I've breathed a sigh of relief to have my father's medicine and condo paid for, and worn a ruby necklace worth *eighty thousand dollars* around my neck. I've experienced a kind of pleasure I didn't know existed, and found a powerful new kind of confidence in the process...

And, of course, last but not least, I've fallen head over heels for an incredible, generous man with a huge heart. A man who makes me feel safe and adored in a way I needed so badly, but didn't even realize. Yes, I've fallen head over heels for Reed. I can't deny it any longer. I belong to him—mind, body, and soul.

Will everything turn into a pumpkin at the stroke of midnight? My brain is telling me the odds are high. But my heart doesn't give a crap. My heart is barreling ahead, with zero ability to swerve. At this point, I'm Reed's yellow Ferrari. And if Reed is the tree that's going to leap out into the middle of the road, then so be it.

The crowd at the party cheers wildly, jerking me from my thoughts. I'm standing at the foot of the stage with some of my new friends, while the current "super-group" of musicians onstage—a group that includes Fish, Aloha, 2Real, Dax, and more—finishes their performance.

The musicians pile offstage to back slaps and high-fives, and the minute Fish sees Alessandra standing next to me, alongside Hannah, Maddy, and Kat, he heads straight for her.

"I could use some fresh air," Fish says to Alessandra. "You want to go outside with me?"

"Absolutely," Alessandra says, looking as happy as I've ever seen her.

He puts his hand out. She grabs it like it's the most natural thing in the world. And off they go.

"Well, that was the cutest thing I've ever seen in my life," Hannah says.

Maddy, Kat, and I agree.

"They're like Bambi and that female doe, when they first meet as babies," Kat says.

"Faline," Hannah supplies.

"Yes!" Kat says, laughing. "They're like Bambi and Faline. Both of them are so sweet and awkward and bashful together."

"I can't believe how quickly Fish has already drawn Ally out of her shell tonight," I say. "She went to an all-girls' high school, where she had literally zero experience with boys. And now, in college, she says half the guys are gay, and the other half have friend-zoned her, so she's still a big-time newbie when it comes to boys."

"Hey, just like you," Hannah jokes to Kat, and Kat pats her big belly and laughs.

"Well, if Alessandra is a newbie, then Fish is a perfect starter kit for her," Maddy pipes in to say. "Just the other night, he and the Goats were over, and Fish said he's sick to death of the kinds of girls he meets on tour. 'Star-fuckers,' is what the Goats call them. Fish said he's done with girls who like him just because he's in 22 Goats."

My heart is fluttering with excitement for Alessandra. "Well, Fish is barking up the right tree with my stepsister. She's—"

"Excuse me," Reed says, appearing at Kat's side. "Sorry to interrupt. Georgina, I want to introduce you to a couple friends of mine." He steps aside and gestures to the two figures to his right. "This is Isabel Randolph and her fiancé, Howard Devlin."

Chapter 29
Georgina

Inwardly, I feel like I'm going to hyperventilate at the sight of Isabel Randolph standing before me. But, outwardly, I manage to keep it together and smile like a normal person.

Reed gestures to me and says, "This is Georgina Ricci, a brilliant writer whom CeeCee has personally tasked with coming up with content for *Dig a Little Deeper,* in addition to the River Records special edition of *Rock 'n' Roll.*"

"Hello!" I say, a bit too enthusiastically, shaking the pair's offered hands, and they laugh and say hello.

"Hey, I work for you!" Hannah blurts next to me. She's speaking to Howard. "I work in your PR department, Mr. Devlin."

Howard chuckles at Hannah's enthusiasm. "What's your name?"

"Hannah Hennessy, sir."

He smiles graciously, but it's clear he's never heard of Hannah in his life. "Come get a drink with me, Hannah Hennessy. While Isabel chats with Georgina, you can tell me all about what it's like to work for me."

Panic flashes across Hannah's adorable face. She grabs Kat's hand and says, "Sounds great. My friend Kat has always wanted to meet you, too." And off the trio goes, as Isabel and I move to a quiet corner to talk.

Of course, I tell Isabel I'm a fan, right off the bat, and she thanks me and tells me a couple behind-the-scenes anecdotes about my two favorite movies of hers that thrill me and make me laugh—and, also, make me feel genuinely comfortable and relaxed in her presence. Or, heck, maybe it's the massive rock on Isabel's left ring finger that's relaxing me and calming my green-eyed monster. Either way, I quickly decide I genuinely like her. And that I'm elated at the prospect of interviewing her. Indeed, as she's been telling me those anecdotes, I've hardly imagined her sucking Reed's dick at all.

"So, Reed tells me CeeCee is contemplating a 'Women in Hollywood' issue of *Dig a Little Deeper*," Isabel says.

Ah, sneaky Reed. He set us both up, did he? He told Isabel that CeeCee is contemplating such an issue while telling *me* I should pitch the idea to CeeCee. But rather than being upset with Reed for his maneuverings, I'm only grateful to him. If this idea could ultimately impress CeeCee, and lure Isabel into giving an in-depth interview to me, all of which might lead to me getting onto the permanent writing staff of *Dig a Little Deeper*, then I don't care who might have concocted the idea first.

Obviously, I have no way of knowing if CeeCee would run with the idea of a "Women in Hollywood" issue. Or, if so, if she'd put Isabel on its cover. But CeeCee *did* say she'll consider "anything" I might submit to her for *Dig a Little Deeper*... So, fuck it. I decide to run with the idea with Isabel and ask for her forgiveness later, as needed.

"CeeCee was very clear she wanted me to submit interviews for *Dig a Little Deeper* that will blow her away," I say carefully. Yes, I'm letting Isabel assume that conversation was in the context of a special issue, but oh well. "And I genuinely think we could come up with something amazing together. Something that shows a new side to you." As an example, I tell her what I'm doing with Dean Masterson and 22 Goats for *Rock 'n' Roll*. "But for *Dig a Little Deeper,* we have to go deeper, obviously."

"Maybe I could give you a tour of my house?" she suggests.

But I've already seen her do that exact thing in one of the articles I read about her last night. "I think we should do something that's never been done before," I say. "With you getting married, maybe I could tag along on a day of wedding planning. We could talk about love, and marriage. Generally and specifically. We could talk about your childhood, and what you saw of marriage growing up . . .?"

Isabel is stone-faced, and I know I'm losing her.

"Or, maybe... is there something you've never done before, but always wanted to do? A hip hop dance class? Knitting? Archery? Or, maybe, is there something that scares the crap out of you, but you could conquer it for the article?" I gasp. "Yes! Isabel! You're about to play a superhero! That could be our angle. 'Isabel Randolph. A Superhero Onscreen. All Too Human in Real Life.'"

She's visibly elated with that last pitch. And suddenly, we're caught up in enthusiastic brainstorming that concludes with our decision to go skydiving together, even though she's terrified of heights and they're most definitely *not* my favorite thing.

"Oh, Isabel," I say. "I bet the conversation we're going to have after you've faced down a gigantic fear will be the best interview of your life."

"Wow, Georgina. Reed told me you're CeeCee's favorite, and I can see why."

"Thank you. That's so nice."

"How did you meet Reed, exactly?" she asks. And, instantly, I can tell she's wondering if there's something going on between Reed and me.

"Through CeeCee," I say smoothly. "CeeCee assigned me to write for the River Records issue, as well as for *Dig a Little Deeper,* so, I met Reed backstage at the Red Card Riot concert. Actually, my boyfriend was super jealous about me hanging out with RCR. He was worried I was going to run off with C-Bomb—their drummer."

Isabel visibly relaxes when she hears the words "my boyfriend" come out of my mouth. Which pisses me off, actually, even though that was my intended effect. She's engaged, for fuck's sake! And isn't Reed nothing but a brother to her now? Why should she be relieved to find out the reporter hanging around River Records for the summer has a jealous boyfriend?

"Well, C-Bomb *is* hot as hell," Isabel says. "I can see why your boyfriend was a bit worried there. I'd certainly do him."

How about you stick to your fiancé, hon? "Naw, my boyfriend is even hotter than C-Bomb. He doesn't have anything to worry about. Not regarding C-Bomb or anyone else."

Isabel looks pleased. Very, very pleased. Which, again, pisses me off.

"How did *you* meet Reed?" I ask. "You know, way back when, for the first time?"

She sips her drink. "Through a mutual friend."

And that's it.

She says nothing more.

The hairs on the back of my neck stand up. That's strange. If the mutual friend who introduced Reed and Isabel was CeeCee, as I'm thinking she means, then why not name CeeCee to me, seeing as how I just now said *I* met Reed through CeeCee? Wouldn't it be a natural thing, given the circumstances, for Isabel to say, "What a coincidence! I *also* met Reed through CeeCee, the same as you!"?

Hmm.

The investigative reporter inside me is suddenly awake and very alert.

"Who was the mutual friend?" I ask casually, trying not to sound like I feel—like a hungry shark smelling blood.

Isabel pauses. Ever so briefly. "Josh Faraday. Have you met him? He's around here somewhere. He's one of Reed's best friends."

Liar. "Yeah, I met him earlier. How did you know Josh?"

She sips her drink again. "From the party circuit. I met Reed at one of Josh's parties."

"And the rest, as they say, is history," I say brightly.

"Yep," she replies.

"Life can be crazy that way. You never know when someone you meet at a party will be in your life for years to come."

"So true."

Okay, seriously now. What the fuck is going on here? Kat didn't seem the least bit confused in the pool when she told me, quite clearly, that *Reed* had brought *Isabel* to one of Josh's parties, as *Reed's* guest, and then told Josh she was a "rising star" and "someone to watch."

My mind is whirling. Clacking. Processing. *Isabel just lied to me.* There's no doubt about that. And, based on what I saw in that photo of Justin Timberlake, I'm almost positive Reed's lied to me, too, about the very same topic. But, *why*? Why, why, why to all of it?

I take a long sip of my drink to hide my scowl, before saying, "I think CeeCee is a person like that for Reed. You know, someone he happened to meet at a party and then she unexpectedly became a deeply important person in his life. Well, correction. He didn't 'happen' to meet her. Reed actually told me he crashed CeeCee's fiftieth birthday party to get her to write about Red Card Riot's debut. But the fact still remains, after that one encounter, they've been genuine, great friends ever since."

"That's a great story," Isabel says.

And that's it again. She doesn't say another word. She doesn't say, "Hey! I was at CeeCee's fiftieth birthday party!" She doesn't say, "Hey! Wait! I just remembered *that's* the

party where I met Reed, not a party thrown by Josh!" And she certainly doesn't say, "You want to hear something crazy? My future husband, Howard, was at that same party!"

Quickly, I decide to press the eject button and get myself out of this crazy-making conversation. Because, holy fuck, I'm not going to be able to keep a poker face for much longer.

"Well, I'll let you enjoy the party," I say, smiling. "I can't wait for our interview, Isabel."

We talk logistics briefly. She gives me the number of her publicist, and we say a warm and hearty goodbye, sealed with a you're-my-new-best-friend hug.

"Sincere congratulations on your engagement," I say, pulling out of our embrace. "I'm so happy for you."

"Thanks," she says. But her smile doesn't reach her eyes.

With a little wave to me, she takes a few steps into the crowded party, and stops. She scours the crowd, presumably looking for Howard. But when her eyes obviously land on him at one of the bars, where he's talking to several high-profile people from the entertainment business, she turns and strides purposefully away, in the exact opposite direction of her future husband.

Chapter 30
Reed

After leaving Georgina with Isabel and Howard, I do a quick lap around the party, looking for Henn. But when I spot Aloha, chatting with the other writer from *Rock 'n' Roll* assigned to the special issue, I decide to intervene.

It's been a bit of a juggling act to gently steer certain artists to Georgie, rather than Zasu, seeing as how I'm not technically supposed to be involved with interview assignments. But, still, I've managed to finesse things to my liking. Specifically, I want Georgina to interview my highest profile artists. People like Aloha. Because, of course, I want Georgina to get the lion's share of the glory and accolades when the special issue comes out.

That said, however, there are a couple high-profile *males* on my roster I don't want coming within ten yards of Georgina. Lady-killers with big swinging dicks. Savage from Fugitive Summer is definitely one of them. Also, Endo from Watch Party.

"Hey, ladies," I say to Aloha and Zasu. "Aloha, Georgina was looking for you. She wants to nail down what you're going to do for your interview with her."

"Oh. Zasu and I were actually—"

"Hey, Zasu. I think Georgina's idea for Aloha's interview sounds great. Would you mind letting her take that one?"

"Of course not. That's fine with me."

"Great. How about you interview Savage and Endo? They're both around here somewhere. Maybe you could touch base with them now."

"Oh. Okay. Sure thing."

"I saw Endo playing corn hole a few minutes ago," Aloha says.

"I'll wander over there now," Zasu says.

"Great idea." When she leaves, I turn to Aloha. "Nail something down with Georgina. I want her to get the best interviews."

She bats her eyelashes. "Aw, Reed. Is someone a smitten kitten?"

"Just do it, Aloha."

I head back to the main room to look for Henn, and spot Georgina talking to Isabel across the room in a corner. Of course, I stop and watch for a moment. It's something I've been doing all night—secretly watching Georgina as she charms my artists and friends. I've loved seeing how seamlessly Georgina fits into my world. How she lights up everyone who encounters her, the same way she lights up my house when she walks through the front door.

But, also, I've been watching Georgina from afar all night because I've been guarding her. Making sure nobody hits on her.

Georgina wants my artists to think my relationship with her is purely professional—so I've respected her wishes and kept my distance tonight. But the downside of me keeping my distance is that none of my artists knows the hot-as-fuck reporter from *Rock 'n' Roll* is taken. Indeed, they think she's fair game. Frankly, it's been a crazy-making situation for me, not being able to kiss her in front of everyone to make it abundantly clear she's all mine.

As I watch Georgina and Isabel talk, it seems to me things are going well. They're smiling and looking friendly. After a bit, the women hug, which tells me Georgina has landed an in-depth interview, and then Isabel heads off into the party.

I take two steps toward Georgina, intending to head over to her, when Savage from Fugitive Summer swoops in on his mark. Motherfucker. The pair high-fives enthusiastically, which tells me this isn't their first meeting of the night. Fuck. They chat enthusiastically, their body language familiar and highly friendly. But I keep my distance, out of respect for Georgina's wishes. I let her do her job. But when Savage puts his hand on Georgina's shoulder—*and then nonchalantly moves a lock of Georgina's hair off her shoulder*—all bets are off.

My heart thundering, I march through the crowd, and straight to the pair.

"I need to speak with you," I bark to Savage.

"Can it wait? Georgina and I—"

"It can't wait. Follow me."

I grab his sleeve and pull him with me, leaving Georgina standing in shocked stillness, her mouth in the shape of a perfect "O."

"Reed, come on, man. You're cock-blocking me."

Damn straight, I am.

I lead him around a corner and into an empty hallway and whirl around.

"Do *not* hit on the *Rock 'n' Roll* reporter."

He shakes me off him. "She's hot as hell."

"She's hands-off."

"Who says?"

I pause. *Fuck.* I promised Georgie. "She's here to do a job. Not to get hit on. I promised her boss nobody would hit on her."

He scoffs. "I think we should let her decide if she wants to get hit on or not."

"Go find the other writer. Her name is Zasu. She's been assigned to do your interview."

"Georgie and I have great chemistry. And we already have the whole thing figured out."

"You're doing an interview with Zasu. It's not a request."

He leans his shoulder against the wall of the hallway. "You want Georgina for yourself, don't you?"

"My motivations don't matter. The only thing you need to know is the owner of your label is telling you she's off-limits. Now, go find Zasu."

He pulls out a cigarette and slips it into his mouth. "Got a light?"

"No."

He pulls the cigarette out of his mouth, winks at me, and saunters out of the room, throwing over his shoulder. "You're too old for her, anyway, man. She's only twenty-one."

Fuck.

I run my palm through my hair and take a deep breath and leave the hallway.

Quickly, I spot Henn at one of the bars with Hannah, Josh, and Kat, so I beeline over there.

"Old Man Rivers!" Josh calls out when he sees me. He's been calling me that nickname since our college days, but, in this particular moment, I'm not amused.

"Don't call me that tonight. And order me a shot of tequila."

Not surprisingly, everyone but preggers Kat enthusiastically joins me in doing a shot. After which, I lean into Henn's shoulder. "Have you gotten access to his devices yet?"

Henn rolls his eyes. "Not since you asked me about it at the pool this afternoon."

"Why hasn't the bastard clicked on any of your phishing emails yet?"

"Sometimes, these things take time. But don't worry. There are other ways to skin this cat. I'll focus on it first thing Monday morning, once Hazel's party is behind me."

"Can you work on it tomorrow before Hazel's party? I'm going to explode if I don't get the ball rolling on this as soon as possible, Henny. I need you to do this for my mental health."

"Who is this guy?"

I pause, weighing how much I can divulge to my best friend without feeling like I'm betraying Georgina's confidence. Henn is one of two people in the world—the other being Josh—I trust completely. One of two people who get me completely. And, besides all that, if I expect Henn, a white hat hacker, to use his superpowers to completely destroy someone, I'm going to have to convince him he's using his superpowers for good.

"This is confidential."

"Of course."

"Not even Hannah, Henn."

"I understand."

I pause. "Gates was Georgie's teacher in high school. Her senior year, he pinned her arms behind her back and kissed her against her will. He tried to rape her, but she ran away screaming."

"Holy shit."

My heart is pounding. My blood simmering. "It fucked her up, Henn. I don't want to go into too much detail, but she's traumatized."

"Understandably. There's so much that's wrong about all that. I don't even know where to begin."

"I want to destroy him, Henny. Well, actually, what I really want to do is strangle the life out of him with my bare hands. But since I don't want to go to prison, I'll settle for ending life as he knows it."

Henn's jaw sets. "I'm on it. I'm pretty drunk right now, and I've got Hazel's party to deal with tomorrow. But I'll get access as soon as possible."

"Thanks, brother. I don't know how much longer I can

keep myself from driving to the Valley and handling him myself."

"Don't do that." He pats my shoulder. "Have a drink. Actually, have several."

"I already have."

"Have some more."

He turns to the bartender and orders a gin and tonic for me, just as the Fantastic Four, as they call themselves—Aloha and her husband, Zander, and Keane Morgan and his wife, Maddy—reach the bar where my group is standing.

"No, I haven't talked to Georgina yet," Aloha says to me, before I've said a word. "We've been dancing."

"Well, chop, chop."

"Okay, okay." But when the DJ starts playing "Sweet but Psycho" by Ava Max, Aloha shrieks and pulls Maddy, Hannah, and Kat to the dance floor.

When the ladies are gone, Henn addresses Zander and Keane. "Hey, do either of you have any weed on you? Reed needs to take the edge off."

"Are there dicks in gay porn?" Keane says, holding up a joint.

"Do me a favor and take Reed onto the patio to smoke that thing. He needs something more than a gin and tonic to keep some homicidal thoughts he's having under wraps."

"Homicidal thoughts?" Keane says. "That's no bueno. Come on, Reed. Z and I will fix you right up."

Chapter 31
Reed

Once outside on the patio, Keane, Zander, and I move toward a dark, isolated corner by a low retaining wall, where we can smoke out and gaze at the amazing view without a hundred people approaching to kiss my ass, or bum a hit off the joint, or gush over Keane. But when our threesome comes to a stop, Fish's voice rises up from the ground only a few feet away.

"Well, hello there, fellas," he says. And when I look down, there he is, camped with Georgina's stepsister on the opposite side of a low retaining wall, their backs against the wall as they gaze out at the sparkling view.

Keane, Zander, and I look at each other, nonverbally acknowledging what we all instantly understand: we're totally cockblocking Fish right now.

"Sorry, brother," Zander says. "Carry on. We came out here to smoke a joint, but we can certainly find another spot."

"Oh, no need to do that," Fish says, hopping up with a laugh. He pulls his girl up with him. "Did everybody meet Alessandra at the pool?"

"Yeah," Keane says. "Hey, Ally Cat."

She waves shyly.

"Hello again, Alessandra," I say. I met her briefly this afternoon, but she was so intimidated, she barely held my gaze. And this time isn't much better. Which, frankly, annoys me. Whether she's intimidated or not, she needs to put on her big girl panties and try to impress me. She's a music student, for fuck's sake! And I'm the head of River fucking Records. If she can't pull her shit together enough to at least *try* to seize this once-in-a-lifetime opportunity, how is she ever going to make it in the music business? Has this girl *never* heard the phrase "seize the day"? How about "fake it till you make it"?

Exhaling with frustration, I take the joint from Keane and inhale extra deeply and then hold it out to Zander, who takes an extra-long hit, too. He offers it to Fish, who does his thing, before offering it to Alessandra, who, not surprisingly, politely declines.

"Give Reed her share," Keane says. "Murder can really fuck up a guy's life."

"Not if they don't catch ya," I say, taking the joint from Fish. Another inhale. Another hand-off. A long gulp of my gin and tonic. And I'm feeling pretty good. I smile at Alessandra. "If you're worried about breaking the law, don't be."

She looks at me blankly.

"Weed. It's legal in California."

"Oh," she says, catching my meaning. "Only if you're twenty-one, right? I'm nineteen."

We all chuckle, thinking she's kidding. But when her face blasts with color, we all have the good sense to respectfully pipe down.

"You want another bottle of water?" Fish asks, looking at his girl. "Something to eat?"

Alessandra looks relieved Fish has just offered her an eject button out of this stressful situation. "Yeah, I could use a water. I'll come with you."

"Why don't you stay here and chat with me for a minute, Alessandra," I say.

She freezes, looking like she's about to crap her pants.

"Just for a couple minutes," I say soothingly.

"Uh oh," Keane says. "What'd you do to get called to the principal's office, Ally Cat? You done fucked up, sis. *Godspeed.*"

"She didn't fuck up anything," I say. "I just want to chat with her for a minute about music. Georgina mentioned you're studying music at Berklee."

"Yes," she manages to say.

"I know a lot of people who graduated from there," I say. "It's a great music school."

She nods.

I address the three men. "Will you boys excuse us for a few minutes?" I look at Alessandra. "That is, if you've got a couple minutes to spare?"

She looks like she's going to throw up, but she says, "Of course. Great."

"I'll come back in a bit," Fish says. He looks excited, like he's thinking this could be a once in a lifetime opportunity for this girl, if only she plays her cards right.

"Okay," she squeaks out.

"If you're not here when I get back for some reason, I'll find you."

"Great," she replies, but her red cheeks make it clear she's inwardly freaking out.

When Fish and the other guys are gone, I lead Alessandra to a nearby bench in a quiet corner. Once we're situated, I take a long swallow of my drink, finishing it off. I put the empty glass on the ground next to me, gaze for a long moment at the view, and then say calmly, "I've heard your demo, Alessandra. All three songs." I look at her. "And you've got some work you need to do, if your dream is to make a living as a professional artist."

She presses her lips together, her eyes wide, but says nothing.

"The good news? I like the quality and tone of your voice. I love your vocal control. Very impressive. I also think you've got a good sense of melody and how to build a song. But if you don't figure out who you are as an artist—as a *person*—then these next two years of time and tuition are going to be wasted, assuming you went to Berklee because you want to make music your career. As things stand now, I could get you work as a demo singer. Maybe even a backup singer. You could write songs for other artists. But if you want to be an artist in your own right, if you want to perform your songs and make a living doing that, then you've got a lot of work to do."

She opens her mouth. But closes it. Her nostrils flare.

"Some of those vocal tics you do? Knock that shit off. That's not *you*, and you know it. You're copying the artists you admire. Being a Laila knockoff. Strip that bullshit off your vocals and tell the truth, whatever it is—good, bad, or ugly. If you get real, you'll get confident, Alessandra. The two things go hand in hand. And then maybe you'll smoke the proverbial joint of life when it's offered to you. Or you'll turn it down, if that's truly what you want to do. But when you turn down the joint of life, don't do it because you're nineteen, and the legal age is twenty-one. For fuck's sake, turn it down because you don't want the fucking joint! Which is a perfectly valid thing, by the way, as long as it's the truth."

She's clearly holding back tears.

"I'm talking about the joint as a metaphor, Alessandra. I'm not the bad guy in an after-school special." I smile, but she's not even close to being able to return the gesture. "Look, I'm trying to do you a favor here. You get that, right? You're hiding behind your music, rather than revealing yourself through it. Fix that, and I think you could have a shot. But, as it is, until you get real, and get the confidence boost that will come from that, I can't imagine you'd be able to command a coffee house full of people as an artist, let alone an entire stadium."

She swallows hard, fighting to keep her emotions from seeping out her eyes. And I momentarily feel bad to see my words make her want to cry. But I've come too far to stop now. I'm helping this girl. Giving her the keys to the kingdom, actually. And I'm not going to stop now, without saying everything that needs to be said. The truth hurts. But it also sets you free. And this girl, most definitely needs to be set free.

"If I'm full of shit, then prove me wrong." I point toward the house. "Go in there, grab one of the acoustic guitars onstage, and sing the shit out of one of your songs the way I'm telling you to do it. Be *you,* not a Laila knockoff. Show me you can *reveal* yourself through your music, rather than hide behind it, and maybe today will turn out to be your lucky day."

"I couldn't possibly do that," she whispers.

"I get that it's an intimidating room. But so what? They're just people. They were in your shoes once. Grab this opportunity I'm giving you. Get up there and knock me out. This is the chance of a lifetime. Grab it."

She looks down at her hands and shakes her head.

"If you're too nervous to play solo, then pull Fish onstage with you. He plays acoustic guitar and sings. You two could sing anything together. 'Hey, Jude' or 'Stand by Me,' for all I care. All that matters to me is you have the balls to get up there and grab this shot I'm giving you. Show me you've got what it takes, Alessandra. Prove me wrong."

I get up from the bench, praying she'll follow suit—hoping she'll rise, literally and figuratively, and square her slender shoulders and march her shy little ass straight inside and onto that stage and knock it out of the park with a performance she didn't even know she had inside her.

But, no.

She's crumbling before my eyes.

Her chin trembling and her eyes pricking with tears, she stammers, "Thank you for taking the time to explain all this to me." Before lurching off the bench and sprinting away into the night.

"Alessandra," I call out after her. But only half-heartedly.

Shouting at her isn't going to make her stop running away. And I'm certainly not going to physically chase her. If she's intimidated by me, then hunting her down is the last thing I should do. Plus, fuck it. I'm not here to hand out participation trophies. I tried to help her, but some people can't be helped. Yes, I was honest with her. But if she can't handle honesty, then she can't handle the music industry. And that's a fucking fact. My heart pounding, I sit back down on the bench, grab my empty glass, and take an ice cube into my mouth. Fuck.

"Where's Alessandra?" Fish says, appearing before me with two water bottles. He looks around. "Did she go inside?"

"Yeah, I think so," I reply. "I'm not sure."

"She didn't say where she was going?"

"No. But I can tell you where she hopes *I'm* going. To hell."

Fish's face falls. "What happened? What does that mean?"

"It means I said something that upset her, apparently. She ran off, on the verge of tears."

Anger flashes across Fish's usually congenial face. "What'd you say to her?"

"I told her the truth, without sugarcoating it. I told her I listened to her demo and, basically, that she's got to get past the bullshit if she wants any shot—"

"Goddammit, Reed!" Fish booms, shocking the hell out of me. "Why are you always such a prick, man? Before you came out here, Alessandra and I were having the most amazing conversation! She was telling me how she got into music after her dad died when she was a kid. She was telling me about her stage fright. Asking me for tricks to overcome it. And then you had to come out here and tell her she sucks and her music is bullshit? Goddammit, Reed! Fuck you, you fucking prick."

With an angry wave of his hand, he turns on his heel and sprints away, presumably to find Alessandra, his lanky body moving faster than I've ever seen it move it before.

"Well, that was unexpected," I mutter to myself.

Shaking my head, I gaze at the sparkling view for a long moment. Fuck. That sucked. I must say, though, I'm thoroughly impressed with the way Fish just told me off. Not because he's right, of course. I wasn't a prick to Alessandra. I was actually being *kind* to her. Cruel to be kind, as they say. But kind, nonetheless. I'd swear to that under oath.

But, still, it was cool to see Fish climb aboard his white horse. That dude hasn't raised his voice to me once in the entire time I've known him, let alone called me a prick. Well, not to my face, anyway. I think it's now obvious he's called me that, and worse, plenty of times behind my back. But that's fine. He's not the first person to think I'm a prick. He won't be the last. If, somehow, me being the bad guy lets him be the good guy with this girl, then I'm happy to oblige.

Although... Shit. I suddenly realize... *Georgina.*

When she hears Alessandra's version of this story, will she assume I treated Alessandra the way I treated that blonde at the bar? Because I didn't. Yes, I was honest with Alessandra, but I took special care to be gentle with her. I flashed her several reassuring smiles, which is something I never do. I was careful to use a calm and soothing tone of voice. Also, not my typical MO. But will Georgina understand any of that, or will she hear some disjointed, emotional version of the story from her stepsister and immediately assume I'm the devil incarnate?

My heart pounding, I rise from the bench, intending to head back into the party to find Georgina. But I've no sooner taken two steps than Isabel appears from around a corner.

"There you are!" she says.

"Not now, Isabel."

"Yes, *now*. It's important. A matter of life or death."

"I've got something important I've got to do," I say.

"It's an emergency," she says. "I need five minutes."

I exhale in frustration. "Five minutes. Not a second more."

The sound of people laughing nearby wafts toward us, emanating from the other side of a hedge.

"Not here," Isabel says. She grabs my hand. "Come on, love. Let's go somewhere we can talk in private."

Chapter 32
Georgina

Where the heck is Reed? I've been looking for him for the past ten minutes, but I can't find him anywhere. And I can't find Alessandra, either. I'm guessing she's off in a quiet corner, chatting with Fish. Or maybe even *smooching* Fish. Which, of course, would tickle me pink. And would also provide a damned good reason not to be answering my texts. But Reed is a different story. This is his party, so, why has he disappeared?

I'm bursting at the seams to talk to Reed—to tell him the news that I landed the interview of Isabel. And, also, yes, to try to get to the bottom of the lies I think he and Isabel have both been telling me. Does it matter to me how they met? No! But it sure as heck matters to me they both seem to be lying about it.

Thus far, I've done two laps around the ground floor areas, including the patio and pool, in my pursuit of Reed. And now I'm doing a lap of the entire upstairs, too—even though I can't fathom Reed would have come up here while his party raged on below. But, again, I'm coming up empty. Crap.

I descend the staircase, feeling more and more frustrated with every step I take. At the bottom of the stairs, I run into Aloha Carmichael. She's with Barry, Reed's head of security. Getting a piggyback ride from him, actually. And when she sees me, she calls my name warmly.

"Reed told me to talk to you," she says.

"Have you seen him recently?"

"Not recently. I saw him at the bar a while ago."

"Which one?"

"The one by the French doors." She points. "That one."

I feel deflated. I passed that bar, not too long ago on one of my laps, and Reed was nowhere to be found. "Did Reed say where he was going, from there?"

Aloha purses her lips. "No, but while I was dancing after that, I saw him head out those French doors over there with Keane and Zander. Which can only mean one thing."

She puts her index finger and thumb to her lips, like she's smoking a joint. But I don't think she's right about that—because when I did a loop outside, not too long ago, I didn't see Reed out there. Not with Keane and Zander or anyone else.

"So, about my interview," Aloha says, laying her cheek on Barry's broad shoulder from behind. "Daxy told me he and the Goats are going to give you a tour of Seattle. And Laila told me she's going to make pottery with you. And Savage told me he's taking you ATVing... "

I force myself to look into Aloha's emerald green eyes, rather than looking around the party maniacally for Reed. "Yeah, the idea is for the interviews to be fun and different and really personal. I'm hoping getting a glimpse of you guys doing something that's meaningful to you, that's outside of music, will inspire a different kind of conversation than the typical interview."

"I love that idea." She pauses. "I go to children's hospitals quite a bit, to cheer up sick kids. Would you maybe want to tag along on a day like that?"

"Sounds great. Let's also make sure we talk about the success of your documentary. And I don't mean the financial success. The impact it has had on mental health awareness."

"Oh, absolutely."

"Someone told me Reed helped get distribution for that film?"

"He sure did. Some people have said Reed only threw his weight behind the documentary for business reasons—you know, because a hit film would lead to more music sales, which, in turn, would line his pockets. And a few years ago, I probably would have believed that narrative. But the last few years, I've started to think there might be an actual beating heart inside Reed's chest. I think he genuinely believed in the movie's message and cause."

"Of course, he did," Barry says.

"I know Reed comes off as all business sometimes," Aloha says. "But, behind the scenes, he's pretty generous with a bunch of charitable causes."

Ping.

That cotton ball from earlier today turns into a stone.

Behind the scenes, Reed is pretty generous with a bunch of charitable causes.

"Do you know if Reed donates to a charity that helps families affected by cancer?" I ask, my heart racing.

"I'm not sure," Aloha says. "But I wouldn't be surprised. I know for sure Reed donates to several cancer charities. Of course, he's extremely involved with The Superhero Project. And then there's also..."

But I've stopped listening. Because, all of a sudden, that cotton ball that turned into a stone has now turned into a motherfucking brick.

Crash.

In rapid-fire succession, my brain connects the dots between several comments made by Kat, Aloha, and Reed himself.

Reed likes pulling strings.

Reed likes playing star-maker behind the scenes.

Reed secretly pulled strings to help Keane get the auditions he wanted.

Reed pulled strings to get Zander a job interview with Big Barry.

Reed pulled strings to help Hannah get a job interview at a movie studio.

Everybody's got a price.

I clutch the banister on the staircase, feeling faint. Reed had something to do with that cancer charity paying for my salary! *If there's a cancer charity at all.* Did he pull strings to get me my internship... because he wanted to fuck me?

But how could that be? CeeCee hired me, because she believes in me. She told me so herself, and she wouldn't lie to me.

I'm so confused. Why would CeeCee hire me... but Reed secretly pay my salary? Why the secrecy? Am I crazy? Paranoid? Oh, fuck. *Did Reed find CeeCee's price?* Did Reed offer CeeCee unparalleled access to his entire roster for the special issue, plus, an in-depth interview of himself, if only she'd hire the fuck buddy of his choice?

No. I can't believe CeeCee would have gone along with that! I simply won't believe it. But my mind is reeling. My insecurity is raising its ugly head. Did I get this internship solely because some asshole—in this instance, Reed—wanted to get into my pants?

"Excuse me," I say to Aloha, cutting her off mid-sentence. "I'm sorry. I just remembered I have to talk to Reed about something important."

"No problemo. Just get my number from Reed or Owen." She pinches Barry's ear. "Come on, Big Barry! This cowgirl wants to *dance!*"

Practically hyperventilating, I sprint toward a set of French doors leading outside. But when I get outside and race around like a chicken with my head cut off, I still don't see Reed anywhere. Not on the patio. Not by the pool. Not in the area just outside the garage where some of the members of Fugitive Summer and Watch Party are playing a rowdy game of corn hole. Frustrated, I turn around, intending to march back toward the house... but freeze on a dime.

The garage.

It's the only place I haven't looked for Reed.

But what the hell would he be doing in there, with the party raging on out here? Oh! Maybe he's showing someone his car collection! Yes, that must be it. Reed is giving some buddy or VIP a tour of his beloved cars.

My heart exploding, I turn around again and head down the path, telling myself the whole time I'm being paranoid— that there's no way Reed had anything to do with my salary or CeeCee's decision to hire me. CeeCee would never betray me like that. *And neither would Reed*. He's a liar, for sure. But only about highly personal things. Also, small things, sometimes, as well, for reasons that elude me. But he would never lie to me about something so important. But if he *did*, he certainly wouldn't continue lying to me, after I told him about Mr.—

The side door to the garage opens, and to my shock—and *heartbreak*—Reed and Isabel step through the doorframe, exiting the garage.

I'm standing, frozen, about ten feet away from them. And the minute Reed and Isabel see me, they freeze, too. And, instantly, from Reed's stiff body language and the guilty expression on his face, I know he's just been caught red-handed. Remorse washes over his guilty face. Followed immediately by barely contained *panic*.

I shift my gaze to Isabel, hoping whatever I see there will make everything okay. But, no, Isabel's face only makes matters worse. Her lipstick is smeared. Her hair disheveled. In short, she's a hot mess—a woman who just got fucked. She wipes her mouth—apparently trying to remove the evidence of Reed's mouth on hers—and a cavalcade of emotions flood me. Rage. Hurt. Rejection. *Heartbreak*. And then nothing but rage, rage, rage, rage, rage. But, somehow, I manage to disassociate from my white-hot emotions, long enough to get through this mortifying moment.

"Hello, Isabel," I say calmly, like a sniper looking through a scope. I shift my gaze to Reed, my eyes like lasers. "*Reed.*"

"Hello again!" Isabel says, sounding nervous. Is she worried I'll run straight to her billionaire fiancé and tell him what I've just seen?

"Reed was just showing me his cars," Isabel blurts.

"Oh, yeah?" I say. "I've heard about them, but haven't seen them for myself. Are they pretty?"

"Very pretty."

I return to Reed, my nostrils flaring. "Would you be willing to show me your pretty cars, Mr. Rivers? I'd love to see them. Maybe I could feature them in my article about you."

Reed's Adam's apple bobs. "Sure."

"I should probably find Howard," Isabel says, walking briskly past me. "I'm sure he's looking for me."

When Isabel is gone, Reed steps toward me, his palms raised. He whispers, "Georgina, I know how this looks."

I point toward the garage. "Turn your lying, cheating ass around and get into that fucking garage. I'm not going to do this out here."

Chapter 33
Reed

M y heart crashing, I close the garage door behind me and turn around to face Georgie's wrath. "I know how this looks, baby, but—"

"Don't you dare call me baby!" she seethes, her eyes like meteors. "When your dick is still wet from another woman's pussy!"

Oh, Jesus. "I didn't fuck her, Georgie."

"*Liar.* I saw her flushed face, Reed. Her smudged lipstick. Her tousled hair. That look in her eye like she just got fucked. You not only fucked her, you fucked the living shit out of her!"

"No. Calm down and listen to me."

"Why? So you can tell me I'm crazy and paranoid? So you can look me in the eye and lie through your teeth?"

"I'm not lying to you, Georgie. I didn't fuck Isabel."

She crosses her arms over her chest. "You expect me to believe you and Isabel came into your garage, while *your* party was raging in *your* house, for who knows how long... because you suddenly felt the need to show her—a woman you've known for ten years—your car collection?"

My stomach twists. Shit. Fuck. Shit. *Fuck.* I run my hand through my hair. *Fuck!*

Georgina's eyes are wild. "If I hadn't stumbled upon you two at exactly the right moment to catch you red-handed, would you have come clean about what you did? Or would you have taken me to your bed after the party, and fucked me right after fucking her? Would you have at least done me the courtesy of showering before you fucked me, to get her off your dick and lips?"

"You need to listen to me. Isabel asked me to talk in private, about something important, and the garage was the only place I knew nobody would barge in on us."

"Do you think I'm stupid?" she screams. "I saw her smudged lipstick, Reed!"

Oh, God. I feel the ground giving way underneath my feet. Panic streaks through me. Regret. Remorse. But there's no way around it. If she saw Isabel's smudged lipstick, then I have to come clean. I have no choice. "Yes, I kissed her," I admit, my stomach twisting and churning. "But, I swear, I didn't fuck her."

"Liar!" she shrieks.

She pushes on my chest and whizzes past me, racing past the hoods of my cars, and I follow her, my panic spiraling.

"She asked me to give her a goodbye kiss, for old time's sake, and I did it," I blurt, keeping step with her. "How could I say no to that? But it meant nothing to me."

She whirls around in front of my Porsche, her eyes aflame. "I don't believe you only kissed her as far as I can throw you. But let's pretend you're telling the truth, for a minute. *How could you say no?*" she asks, echoing me. "How could you *not* say no, Reed?" Tears fill her eyes. "You said it made you crazy to think of me kissing anyone else. You promised exclusivity was a two-way street, and I believed you. You said you're not a cheater! You said that to me, and I trusted you!"

Anguish grips me. Why did I do this? Why did I fuck up the best thing that's ever happened to me? I want to rewind the clock. Take it all back. *I have to fix this.* "I'm so sorry, Georgie. I admit I fucked up. But you have to believe me, I only kissed her, and it meant absolutely nothing to me. In fact, I told her—"

217

"Even if you 'only' kissed her, which I don't believe, does that really make it okay in your book? If I secretly disappeared with someone... Let's say Savage. He's hot as hell. Let's say I disappeared with Savage into your garage, in the middle of the party tonight, without telling you, and I made out with him in here until my lips were swollen and my lipstick smeared and my face bright red and my hair tousled— *but it meant nothing to me!*—that would be perfectly fine with you? That wouldn't break your heart, after everything that's happened between us this week?"

"Georgie," I choke out, the enormity of what I've done slamming me. "Please, put yourself in my shoes. The example of Savage isn't the same thing. I've known Isabel ten years. She's getting married and wanted one last kiss. It was a goodbye kiss, Georgie. It's unreasonable for you to expect me *not* to give her that, after ten years of knowing her, when I've only known you a matter of weeks."

She looks crushed. Furious. *Heartbroken.* "Obviously, this past week meant a whole lot more to me than it meant to you." She throws her hands over her face. "God, I was so stupid to let my guard down with you. I was so stupid to think this week could have meant anything to you."

I feel like my heart is physically cracking in two. "Georgie, don't say that. Please don't doubt how much this past week with you has meant to me. It's been the best week of my life. Every minute with you, Georgie—"

"Save it!" She marches away, whizzing past my cars, all the way to the back wall filled with sports equipment, which is where she whirls around to face me. "How'd you meet her, Reed?"

"Who?"

"Isabel!"

"I told you how I met her. At CeeCee's birthday party."

"Josh didn't introduce you to Isabel?"

I pull a face of confusion. "No. Why are you asking—"

"Josh didn't introduce you to Isabel at one of his parties?"

"No. *I* introduced *Josh* to Isabel at one of Josh's parties. Why are you asking me this?"

"Because Isabel told me she met you through a mutual friend. And when I asked the name of the friend, she said *Josh Faraday.* She said she went to one of Josh's parties, and *he* introduced her to *you* that night."

My stomach is twisted into knots. My breathing is shallow. Fuck. "Isabel is mistaken," I say. "Which is understandable, since it was ten years ago."

Georgina throws up her hands. "Why are you both lying to me about this? It's something so meaningless and insignificant! I don't get it!"

"We're not both lying. I'm telling the truth, and Isabel is simply mistaken. Why are we even talking about this?"

"Because it's just further proof that every word out of your mouth is a fucking lie. You didn't take Isabel into your garage, in the middle of your party, to kiss her goodbye. You fucked her goodbye. And you didn't meet Isabel at CeeCee's birthday party, either. I saw the photo spread in *Rock 'n' Roll* from CeeCee's party, and in one of the shots, behind Justin Timberlake, you and Isabel were arriving *together* to the party. Reed, you were getting out of the limo *with* Isabel. Ergo, you did not 'meet' her at that party, as you've told me. You cannot meet someone you've arrived with. Ergo, you *lied* to me about that. And you're lying to me about this."

I feel like I'm going to throw up. "Isabel and I were on a blind date that night," I blurt, desperation seizing me. "We hadn't met before that night, but I'd seen her photo. She didn't want me to pick her up at her house. So, she asked me to pick her up in the limo a mile away from the party. I think I picked her up in front of a McDonald's. And that's why that photo showed us arriving together. But, in my mind, when I told you I'd 'met' Isabel at CeeCee's party, I was telling the truth. I mean, technically, we met a few blocks away, yes, but I wasn't intentionally *lying* to you. It was just too complicated to explain the logistics. Yes, she was my date that night. Yes, we arrived together. But I swear to God, I also met her that night. I was telling you the truth about that night, Georgie. And I'm telling you the truth about tonight. I'm sorry I kissed her. I shouldn't have done that. But, trust me, if you'd seen the way it went down, you'd understand it didn't take anything away from the amazing week we've had—and the amazing summer—"

"I told you about Mr. Gates!" she screams, a sob lurching out of her. "I told you about Shawn, and you said you're not a cheater! You said nobody is allowed to hurt me, ever again, and then you came in here and threw me away like I never mattered!"

My heart feels like it's physically shattering. I take a step toward her, determined to convince her. To fix this mess I've created. "I'm sorry. I think maybe, in part, I was sabotaging myself. I think a piece of me maybe got scared of how much I'm feeling for you, Georgie. Because, I swear, I've never felt the way I do with you before."

She stares at me with disdain for a very long moment, before saying, calmly, "I have one question. And I want you to answer it with complete honesty."

My heart leaps. Is she throwing me a lifeline? If I answer this question right, will she forgive and forget that stupid kiss ever happened?

"Whatever you want to know, I'll tell you."

Her nostrils flare. "Did you have anything to do with me getting my internship, including but not limited to donating the money that ultimately went to me as my salary?"

Oh, fuck. "Yes. But let me explain..."

But she's done listening to me. As quick as lightning, she grabs a golf club out of my bag and marches straight for my Bugatti, the club raised high above her head.

"Not the Bugatti!" I shout at the top of my voice. "Georgie, please! *Not the Bugatti!*"

To my surprise, Georgina stops mid-swing, barely missing the hood of my Bugatti, and marches to the next car in line. My yellow Ferrari. The first expensive car I bought when I started making some real money. Up Georgina's golf club goes... and then down it comes, smashing into the Ferrari's newly repaired right front fender.

"You told me to go Left Eye Lopes on the next guy who hurts me?" she shrieks. "Well, guess what, asshole? You're that guy!"

As I stand to the side, watching in shocked silence, Georgina raises her club and smashes my Ferrari's windshield. "This one's for you, Reed!" Panting, she heads to the car's passenger door. "And this one is for Shawn!" She brings the club down again. Next up, the passenger window. "Another one for Reed!" She walks around to the back of the car and whacks both taillights and the bumper with her club. But this time, the name she yells breaks my fucking heart. "Mr. Gates! Mr. Gates! Mr. Gates!" From there, she marches to the driver's door and whacks it with all her might, yet again in Mr. Gates' name. The same thing with the driver's side window and left front bumper. "Mr. Gates! Mr. Gates!"

And through it all, I say nothing. Do nothing. I stand back and watch, and take my punishment. It kills me to hear her scream my name along with Mr. Gates'. And worse, it shatters me to know I deserve it. Indeed, I deserve every single dent in that car. Every drop of her rage. She trusted me completely. I asked her to surrender to me, without holding back. And she did. In body, heart, and soul. And I knew it. And then, I turned around and betrayed her. What's wrong with me? Women have been asking me that my whole life. And now I'm wondering the same thing. *What's wrong with me?*

As I watch Georgie turning my three-hundred-thousand-dollar car into a pile of scrap metal and shattered glass, I feel pain and remorse and regret like nothing I've felt before. But I also feel two unexpected emotions, too.

One, I feel pride. I'm damned proud of Georgie for going Left Eye Lopes on me, and on all the men who've hurt her. As she should. Smash that Ferrari, baby. Smash it and never let anyone hurt you again.

And, two, as strange as it sounds, even as I watch Georgina decimate my Ferrari, I feel a twinge of hope. Because, even in the midst of her justifiable rage and confusion, *Georgina didn't bring her club down on my beloved Bugatti.*

Yes, Georgina is heartbroken and angry and deeply confused. She doesn't know what happened between Isabel and me in this garage tonight. She doesn't understand how or why the money for her salary came from me. All of which isn't good for me. Obviously. But, thanks to my Bugatti, and the fact that there's not a scratch on it, I have reason to believe it's not hopeless for me. Indeed, thanks to my pristine Bugatti, I have reason to believe Georgina is holding out hope I'll eventually be able to win her back.

Chapter 34
Reed

I'm panting as I follow Georgina out of the garage and toward the house.

"Hey, Georgie!" Savage calls to her as she passes.

He's at the ping pong table with Davey from Watch Party. And I swear to God, I'm this close to wringing his fucking neck.

"Hey there, handsome!" Georgina calls back to Savage. "I can't wait for you to take me ATVing!"

Savage looks at me, and I shake my head, letting him know whatever they've planned is never going to happen.

"Let's do dinner and drinks afterwards!" Georgie calls to Savage as she continues marching toward the house.

"Stop it, Georgie," I whisper-shout to her. "You're not going anywhere with Savage. Zasu is doing his interview."

"I'm done taking orders from you, asshole. *Ciao, stronzo.* I'm not only going to interview Savage, I'm going to fuck him, too, and then lie to you and say I only 'kissed him goodbye.' But it won't matter, right? As long as it meant nothing to me?"

She barrels into the house and, immediately, gets greeted by Kat and Hannah, who happen to be standing just inside the French doors. And the minute Kat sees Georgie's tear-stained cheeks and puffy eyes, she morphs into a grizzly bear protecting her cub.

"You've been crying," Kat says, her face etched with concern. "What happened?"

"I haven't been crying. I'm just drunk."

"You don't look drunk. You look *devastated.*" Kat's blazing blue eyes dart to mine. "Why has she been crying?" Her eyes narrow to murderous slits. "*What did you do?*"

Georgina looks frantically around. "Have you seen Alessandra?"

"Not for a while." Kat shoots me another death stare. "What happened, Reed?"

"We've had a disagreement."

"A *disagreement.*" Georgina scoffs. She returns to Kat. "Have you seen Fish?"

As if on cue, Fish walks up, looking distraught. He shoots me a death stare that rivals Kat's, before addressing Georgie. "Alessandra needs you. Reed told her she sucks, and that her music is bullshit, so she ran upstairs to your room to cry."

Oh, for the love of fuck. "That's not how it went down *at all,*" I blurt.

But nobody is listening to me, least of all Georgina. Indeed, suddenly, it feels like everyone around me is gathering up their pitchforks, and I'm the guy with a rather conspicuous hump on my back.

"I tried to comfort her," Fish says, "but she said she preferred being alone, until you could come."

"I was trying to *help* Alessandra," I say lamely. "I was *encouraging* her."

Fish flashes me a look that plainly says, *Prick.* Kat shoots me one that says, *I've seen your version of encouragement many times, Reed. And it ain't pretty.* And Georgie doesn't even look at me. Indeed, her skin flushed and jaw tight, Georgina marches away from me, without so much as a glance at me, through the packed party, straight to the staircase, and up the entire flight of stairs, like a woman possessed.

Of course, I clamber after her, desperate to clear my name on this one thing, at least. "I told Alessandra she's talented!" I shout from behind Georgie, matching her every bounding step. "I told her she has great vocal control. All I said was she's trying to be someone she's not and—"

"I told you not to say anything to Alessandra about her demo!"

Oh, shit. That's right. She did.

"Are you capable of keeping *one* promise to me?" she shouts. "Why do you even bother pretending to make promises, if you're literally *never* going to keep any of them?"

"I forgot you said that. I think I was stoned? I'm sorry. I was just trying to help her, and I guess I just... forgot what you said about that. I don't know." I run my hand through my hair. "Georgina, if you'd just let me tell you *exactly* what I said to her, you'd know I was actually doing her a favor."

But she doesn't stop. She keeps bounding down the hallway toward her room.

"All I said was she needed to tell the truth in her art. That she shouldn't try to mimic—"

She stops in front of her closed door and whirls around on a dime, making me nearly run into her. "You told Alessandra to 'tell the truth' in her art? Oh, that's rich, seeing as how you don't even know the meaning of the fucking word." She turns and swings open the door to her room, and gasps at what she finds inside: her stepsister lying on the bed in tears. "Ally!" she shouts as she runs into the room, leaving me in the doorway, like a vampire who hasn't been invited inside.

Georgina takes her beloved stepsister into her arms, while I stand watching helplessly from the doorway. After a moment, though, when she notices me, she gets up, marches to me, and slams the door in my face. And that's when I know: all hope is lost. If Georgie were standing over my Bugatti now, holding a golf club raised above her head, she'd smash it to Kingdom Come, even more so than she did to my Ferrari. And no command or plea from me would stop her.

I place my palms flush against the closed door, my heart feeling like it's physically bleeding onto the wood. *Let me in, Georgie. Please, please, let me in.*

After what feels like forever, the door swings open, making me lurch back into the hallway, and Georgie and Alessandra barge out of the room.

Georgie's wheeling her suitcase behind her, her regal head held even higher than when she wore that ruby necklace. Alessandra's wearing a backpack on her back, and holding the cardboard box Georgie doesn't know I know about. The one containing the documents from Stephanie Moreland's lawsuit, plus, God knows what else.

"Where are you going?" I choke out.

"None of your business," Georgie tosses over her shoulder.

I follow the girls down the hallway. "Alessandra, you misunderstood me. I'm sorry if my words seemed harsh, but—"

"Don't speak to her," Georgie hisses. "And don't speak to me, either. Ever again."

Down the stairs they go, with me following behind like a stray dog.

A new "super-group" is performing onstage now, which means, thankfully, everyone at the party is crowded in the main area, blissfully dancing and cheering with their backs to us. It's the perfect time for the girls to make a getaway, completely unnoticed. Which is exactly what they do. Indeed, they walk straight out my front door, past security, and into the cool night, without anyone noticing a damned thing.

I follow the girls, of course, talking the entire time. Explaining. Apologizing. Defending. Rationalizing. Fixing, convincing, *begging*. Yes, fuck it. I'm *begging* Georgina to stay. To listen. To forgive. It's something I swore I'd never do with Georgina again. But now isn't the time to be proud. Now is the time to make her understand. To fix this mess I've gotten myself into. To make her forgive me.

But Georgina isn't having any of it. And Alessandra follows her lead, looking straight ahead like she can't hear my pathetic pleas.

The girls march down my circular drive toward my iron gate, where four security guards greet us.

"Hello, Mr. Rivers," one of the guards says. "Ladies."

"Hello," Georgina says brightly, her tone oozing with sex appeal. "My, you look handsome tonight, sir."

"Thank you."

"We're here to wait for our Uber," Georgina explains.

"That's fine."

"Are you wearing cologne? You smell amazing."

"It's just soap."

"Well, whatever it is, it smells good enough to *eat*."

"Georgie, that's enough," I say calmly. "Come inside, so I can explain—"

"No, thank you, Mr. Rivers. I think you've explained more than enough."

Fuck. Begrudgingly, I shut up. If I don't, it's quite possible she'll offer to suck a security guard's dick, just to watch me commit murder and go to prison for it.

Headlights.

They're shining on the guards' faces. And then on the girls'. And then on mine. They're shining in my eyes. Illuminating the blackness of my fucking soul.

The car stops. The girls pile into its backseat and slam their doors, without looking back or saying a word to me. And off they go, just like that, into the night. Leaving me standing at my gate in the cool night with stinging eyes and a lump in my throat.

I stand frozen as Georgina's car drives away, watching its retreating taillights and holding my breath. *Turn around, Georgina. Flip me off through the back window, so I know you still care. Flip me off, baby. Please. Hate me, if you must. Just care enough to flip me off.*

It's my last hope—that Georgina will grace me with the tiniest flicker from her glorious flame.

But, no.

The car is gone now.

And Georgina never turned around.

She never met my eyes, so they could tell her how sorry I am. She never met my eyes, so they could beg her to come back to me. She never met my eyes so I could tell her I'm fucked up in ways I don't understand. Ways I can't help. Ways I can't fix. She never turned around so my eyes could tell her I've never felt the way I do with her. She never turned around so my eyes could explain I don't know how to do this. I don't know how to *feel* this. I simply don't know.

"Is everything okay, Mr. Rivers?" one of the guards asks.

I look down at the ground for a long beat.

If any other girl had left me standing here, I'd look directly at the guard, smile, and say, "Yes, everything is great. Everything is perfect. I'm on top of the world, motherfucker. The Man with the Midas Touch."

But I can't say any of it now. Not when the girl who's left me is Georgina. Not when the girl I betrayed, the girl I hurt, is the same girl I'd move heaven and earth to protect. I can't say it now, when it's Georgina who thinks I'm a liar. Even though, I swear, a solid three quarters of what I said to her was the God's truth.

I look up and meet the guard's eyes. "No. Everything's not okay." I drag my palm across my jaw and take a deep breath. "In fact, Jeremy. To be honest with you, everything just turned to total fucking shit."

Chapter 35
Georgina

The moment the Uber is out of sight from Reed's house, I crumple into the backseat. *Everybody's got a price.* Reed warned me that was his life philosophy. Why didn't I listen to him when he told me exactly what kind of monster he is? Why did I trust him with the most vulnerable, sacred parts of myself? *Why, why, why?*

Everybody's got a price.

What was CeeCee's price, I wonder? Did she ever truly believe in me, as she and Reed both claimed, or was she all too happy to help her good friend, Reed, get the tits and ass he desired, if it meant she could get a River Records special issue, including a Reed Rivers interview, for herself? I thought CeeCee was my friend, my hero, my inspiration—and it turns out she was my pimp.

"I can't believe you lied to me," Alessandra says, looking out her window.

I swivel my head to look at her, at a loss.

"About my demo. Why didn't you tell me Reed had already listened to it? Why did you lie to me? You thought I couldn't take it? You think I'm so weak and pathetic I can't handle the truth? I was totally blindsided, Georgie. I couldn't speak."

I wipe my eyes. "I'm sorry. I didn't tell you because I didn't want you to feel awkward at the party around Reed."

"That's not why."

"What do you mean?"

"You were a coward. You didn't want to have to break the news to me."

"Well, of course. But, mostly, I didn't want you to lose faith in yourself. Reed's opinion isn't the gospel."

Alessandra shakes her head and looks out the window. "I missed out on a great chance to have an honest discussion with him. To ask him questions. Maybe even try to impress him. But I was too blindsided to say or do anything. I just sat there, like an idiot. And now, thanks to you, he thinks I'm mentally deficient, in addition to being a 'Laila knock-off.'"

"He called you that? Asshole! He swore he wouldn't say anything to you tonight."

"So, the answer to this problem is for Reed to have lied to me, too? Guess again, Georgina. Frankly, I'm glad Reed told me the truth. I only wish you had, too, so I could have been ready for him. He told me to get up on that stage and knock his socks off. If I'd known he'd listened already, maybe I would have... I don't know. Maybe I would have *done* something."

I wipe my eyes. "I'm so sorry."

She scowls at me. "I said from the start he'd never want to sign me. Remember? I never once thought I'm good enough."

"You are. He's stupid."

"He's *right.*"

"No, Ally."

She looks out the window for a long moment. "Just, please, don't lie to me again. Not about anything. I know you think you need to protect me, but you don't. I don't want your protection. I want your respect."

I choke back a sob. "I'm sorry."

She looks at me and melts when she sees the emotion ripping through me. "Aw, sweetie. What happened to you tonight? What did Reed do?"

I shake my head, too mortified to say it out loud, even to Alessandra: *he broke my heart.* "I don't want to talk about it." I rub my eyes. "Tell me about Fish. Did you kiss him?"

She sighs wistfully. "No. I was positive he was *finally* about to kiss me, when stupid Reed showed up with Keane and Zander to smoke a joint, and the moment was lost."

"Oh my God. Reed was freaking Godzilla tonight. Smashing everything in his path."

"Even if we'd kissed, nothing could have come of it, anyway, with me going back to Boston on Monday." She exhales. "But, dang it, I just wanted to kiss him so much, even if I never saw him again. I just wanted to cap off the perfect night, with the perfect boy, with the perfect kiss..."

"Fucking Reed! In addition to everything else, he fucked up a lifelong memory for you? God, I *hate* him."

"Okay, Georgie. Come on. You have to tell me what the hell he did to you." She grabs my hand. "Because the way he was following us out of the house, babbling and begging, he seemed so desperate and pathetic. So *sincere.*"

A dam breaks inside me. "He fucked Isabel Randolph!"

Alessandra gasps. "When?"

"Tonight. During the party. In his garage!"

"No."

"*Yes.* He said he only kissed her, but I don't believe him. But even if he *did* only kiss her, it doesn't matter. Either way, he's a liar and a cheater and I can't trust him." I wipe my eyes. "I gave him my whole heart, Ally. I trusted him like I've never trusted anyone. But none of that mattered to him. He took my heart and stuffed it into his pocket like a pack of gum." I shake my head at my stupidity. "I bet it drove him *crazy* when he found out Isabel was engaged. I bet he dragged her into that garage, the first chance he got, to remind her what she'll be missing out on when she marries her pervy grandpa."

"Did you actually walk in on them in the garage?"

"No, I saw them as they were coming out. Her lipstick was smudged. Her hair all messed up. She was a hot mess, and he looked like a dog who'd just shit the bed."

"What did they say when you saw them?"

"Well, Isabel ran off to find her fiancé. I'm sure she was freaking out I might tell him what I saw. And then I dragged Reed into the garage and read him the Riot Act. Which is when he swore he only kissed her and it 'meant nothing.'" I pause. "And then I went 'Left Eye' Lopes on his ass."

Alessandra's jaw drops. "You burned down his garage?"

"You know 'Left Eye' Lopes?"

"TLC. Georgie, what did you do?"

I smile. "I totaled his Ferrari with a golf club."

She gasps. "The yellow one that just got back from the shop?"

"That's the one. I'm thinking maybe Reed should take it back to the shop. Although I don't think they'll be able to fix it this time."

"You seriously *totaled* it? Or you just gave it a couple dents?"

"I smashed the crap out of it. I literally broke a sweat, I was swinging that damned club so hard and so many times."

She laughs. "Holy shit. And what did Reed do while you were murdering his Ferrari?"

"Nothing at all. He just stood there watching me, not saying a word."

"Not a word? Not even 'no!'?"

I shake my head. "Nope. He didn't tell me to stop. He stood there with his arms crossed, silently watching me."

"Now that's a guy with money to burn."

"No, that's a guilty man. He didn't say anything because he knew he deserved every swing of that club. Because he knew he was lucky I wasn't swinging the club at his head. Or his Bugatti." I look out the car window at the passing cars on the freeway. "His non-reaction reaction was an admission of his guilt, Alessandra. I mean, what man, I don't care how rich he is, lets a woman total his Ferrari over a freaking *kiss*?"

"Good point." She winces. "On the flipside, though. If he *did* only kiss Isabel—not that I'm okay with that at all—but, if he did only kiss her, then, holy fuck, Georgina, you totaled a Ferrari over a freaking kiss. If that's not going 'Left Eye' Lopes on a guy, then I don't know what is."

She giggles, but I stare at a car passing us in the adjacent lane.

There's more to this story, of course. Namely, that Reed is the one who paid my salary. And, quite possibly, pulled strings behind the scenes to get me this job, in the first place. What strings, exactly? I'm not entirely sure. What I do know is that Reed wanted to fuck me, and he arranged things to make that possible, unbeknownst to me. Was it unbeknownst to CeeCee, as well? Again, I'm not entirely sure. The only thing I'm sure about is Reed wanted me, so he paid whatever price, and pulled whatever strings, to get me. And once he got me, he got bored of the game, as he warned me he always does, and moved on.

But I have no desire to tell Alessandra the truth about any of that. It's far too mortifying to say out loud. Even more so than the idea of Reed having sex with Isabel in that garage.

Is the fact that Reed cheated on me painful? Yes. Embarrassing, too. But it's a betrayal I can wrap my head around, thanks to Shawn. But admitting I was some sort of purchase to Reed, every bit as much as his Ferrari or Bugatti? Admitting I might not have earned my dream job, like I thought, but, instead, got hired because Reed wanted to sleep with me... and, also, that, *maybe*, CeeCee was perfectly willing to go along with that plan? Well, shit, all of that is downright soul-crushing.

Alessandra sighs and grabs my hand. "I'm so sorry, Georgie. I know you really liked him."

No, I loved him, I think. But what I say is, "I really did.

233

And I stupidly thought he was feeling the same way." Another sob lurches out of me. And then another. Until, suddenly, I'm a weeping mess and the Uber driver is handing me a box of tissues.

"Aw, sweetie, come here," Alessandra says. She opens her arms and I dive into them, and then proceed to sob from the depths of my soul the rest of the drive to my father's condo—the tiny two-bedroom in the Valley that, thanks to Reed, is now bought and paid for... every bit as much as me.

TO BE CONTINUED...

Reed and Georgina's heartbreaking, scorching-hot love story continues with the third book of The Reed Rivers Trilogy: BELOVED LIAR. You don't want to miss what happens next with this passionate duo in this epic, all-consuming romance!

Want to read about Reed's best friend, Josh Faraday? Read Josh and Kat's explosive and sexy trilogy, beginning with INFATUATION.

If you want to read about Keane Morgan and Maddy Milliken, or Aloha Carmichael and Zander Shaw, or Dax Morgan of 22 Goats and his mysterious lady love, then read: BALL PEEN HAMMER, MISTER BODYGUARD, or ROCKSTAR, respectively.

Be sure to sign up to receive news of releases or giveaways, by email or text:

NEWSLETTER - WEBSITE

US ONLY: Text the word "ROWE" to 474747

UK ONLY: Text the word "LAURENROWE" to 82228
Find Lauren on social media by clicking the links below!

FACEBOOK - INSTAGRAM - TWITTER

FACEBOOK GROUP - BOOK+MAIN
A brief list of books by Lauren Rowe is located at the front of this book. Further details below.

Books by Lauren Rowe

The Reed Rivers Trilogy

Reed Rivers has met his match in the most unlikely of women—aspiring journalist and spitfire, Georgina Ricci. She's much younger than the women Reed normally pursues, but he can't resist her fiery personality and drop-dead gorgeous looks. But in this game of cat and mouse, who's chasing whom? With each passing day of this wild ride, Reed's not so sure. The books of this trilogy are to be read in order:

Bad Liar
Beautiful Liar
Beloved Liar

The Club Trilogy

Romantic. Scorching hot. Suspenseful. Witty. The Club is your new addiction—a sexy and suspenseful thriller about two wealthy brothers and the sassy women who bring them to their knees... all while the foursome bands together to protect one of their own. *The Club Trilogy* is to be read in order, as follows:

The Club: Obsession
The Club: Reclamation
The Club: Redemption

The Club: Culmination

The fourth book for Jonas and Sarah is a full-length epilogue with incredible heart-stopping twists and turns and feels. Read *The Club: Culmination (A Full-Length Epilogue Novel)* after finishing *The Club Trilogy* or, if you prefer, after reading *The Josh and Kat Trilogy*.

The Josh and Kat Trilogy

It's a war of wills between stubborn and sexy Josh Faraday and Kat Morgan. A fight to the bed. Arrogant, wealthy playboy Josh is used to getting what he wants. *And what he wants is Kat Morgan*. The books are to be read in order:

Infatuation
Revelation
Consummation

The Morgan Brothers

Read these **standalones** in any order about the brothers of Kat Morgan. Chronological reading order is below, but they are all complete stories. Note: you do *not* need to read any other books or series before jumping straight into reading about the Morgan boys.

Hero. The story of heroic firefighter, **Colby Morgan**. When catastrophe strikes Colby Morgan, will physical therapist Lydia save him... or will he save her?

Captain. The insta-love-to-enemies-to-lovers story of tattooed sex god, **Ryan Morgan**, and the woman he'd move heaven and earth to claim.

Ball Peen Hammer. A steamy, hilarious, friends-to-lovers romantic comedy about cocky-as-hell male stripper, **Keane Morgan**, and the sassy, smart young woman who brings him to his knees during a road trip.

Mister Bodyguard. The Morgans' beloved honorary brother, **Zander Shaw**, meets his match in the feisty pop star he's assigned to protect on tour.

ROCKSTAR. When the youngest Morgan brother, **Dax Morgan,** meets a mysterious woman who rocks his world, he must decide if pursuing her is worth risking it all. Be sure to check out four of Dax's original songs from *ROCKSTAR*, written and produced by Lauren, along with full music videos for the songs, on her website (www.laurenrowebooks.com) under the tap MUSIC FROM ROCKSTAR.

Misadventures

Lauren's *Misadventures* titles are page-turning, steamy, swoony standalones, to be read in any order.

-*Misadventures on the Night Shift*—A hotel night shift clerk encounters her teenage fantasy: rock star Lucas Ford. And combustion ensues.

-*Misadventures of a College Girl*—A spunky, virginal theater major meets a cocky football player at her first college party... and absolutely nothing goes according to plan for either of them.

-*Misadventures on the Rebound*—A spunky woman on the rebound meets a hot, mysterious stranger in a bar on her way to her five-year high school reunion in Las Vegas and what follows is a misadventure neither of them ever imagined.

Standalone Psychological Thriller/Dark Comedy

Countdown to Killing Kurtis—A young woman with big dreams and skeletons in her closet decides her porno-king husband must die in exactly a year. This is *not* a traditional romance, but it *will* most definitely keep you turning the pages and saying "WTF?"

All books by Lauren Rowe are available in ebook, paperback, and audiobook formats. Be sure to sign up for Lauren's newsletter to find out about upcoming releases!

Author Biography

USA Today and internationally bestselling author Lauren Rowe lives in San Diego, California, where, in addition to writing books, she performs with her dance/party band at events all over Southern California, writes songs, takes embarrassing snapshots of her ever- patient Boston terrier, Buster, spends time with her family, and narrates audiobooks. Much to Lauren's thrill, her books have been translated all over the world in multiple languages and hit multiple domestic and international bestseller lists. To find out about Lauren's upcoming releases and giveaways, sign up for Lauren's emails at www.LaurenRoweBooks.com. Lauren loves to hear from readers! Send Lauren an email from her website, say hi on Twitter, Instagram, or Facebook.

Made in the USA
Middletown, DE
15 January 2021

31709069R00146